Waltham Forest Libraries

Please return this item by the
renewed unless re~~quested~~ by

KT-381-691

16.10.2019.		

Need to renew your books?
http://www.walthamforest.gov.uk/libraries or
Dial 0333 370 4700 for Callpoint – our 24/7 automated telephone renewal
line. You will need your library card number and your PIN. If you do not
know your PIN, contact your local library.

INVISIBLE
in a
BRIGHT LIGHT

INVISIBLE
in a
BRIGHT LIGHT

SALLY GARDNER

ZEPHYR
An imprint of Head of Zeus

First published in the UK by Zephyr,
an imprint of Head of Zeus, in 2019

9 7 5 3 1 2 4 6 8

A catalogue record for this book is available
from the British Library.

ISBN (HB): 9781786695222
ISBN (E): 9781786695215

Jacket design © Helen Crawford-White
Theatre illustration © Getty Images
Endpapers: Map of Copenhagen Harbour, circa 1611

Typeset by Ed Pickford

Printed and bound in Great Britain
by CPI Group (UK) Ltd, Croydon CR0 4YY

MIX
Paper from
responsible sources
FSC® C020471

Head of Zeus Ltd
First Floor East
5–8 Hardwick Street
London EC1R 4RG

WWW.HEADOFZEUS.COM

This book is dedicated to Freya and Lydia
with all my love.

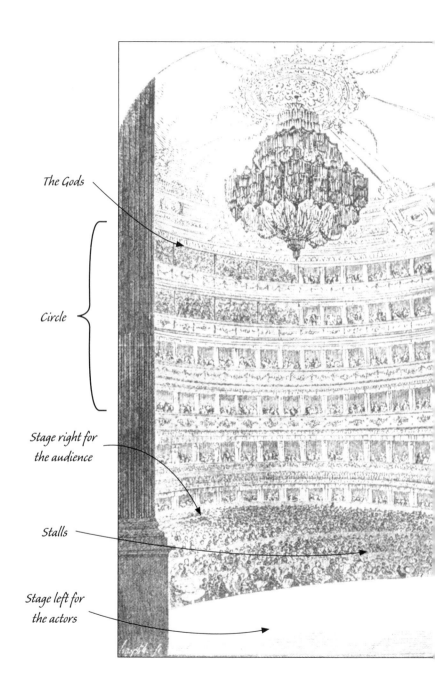

The Gods

Circle

Stage right for
the audience

Stalls

Stage left for
the actors

↓ *Auditorium*

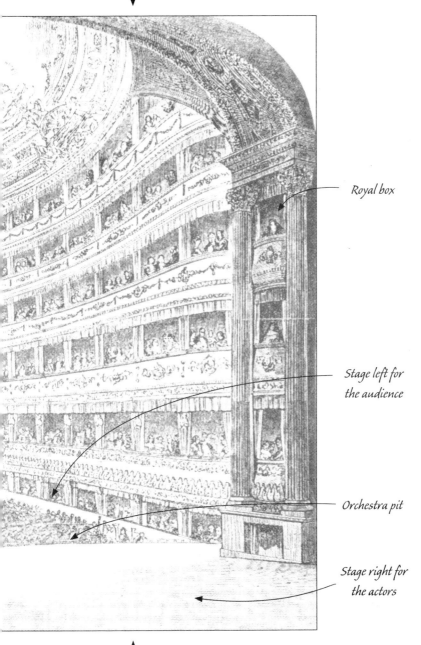

Royal box

*Stage left for
the audience*

Orchestra pit

*Stage right for
the actors*

↑ *Stage*

FOREWORD

This story, in various shapes and guises, has lived with me a long time. It took me ages to work out how a theatre, a ghost ship and a crystal chandelier might be connected. As often is the way with my writing, I found the answer in fairy tales.

I was a child when I first stumbled into the dark forest of the Grimm Brothers. I scared myself with their stories of heartless stepmothers, cruel sisters, wicked witches and silent women. I stayed on the edge of the woods, hungry for more stories. The older I became, the braver I became and by then the magic of the fairy tale had me spellbound. When finally I started writing, I set up home in the sorceress's hut, deep in the ancient world of enchantment. I still live there today, hoping the wolves won't get me.

But before I knew that was where I wanted to be, before I knew I could write, when I was twenty-four years old and still tangled in my dyslexia, I designed the costumes for Gilbert and Sullivan's

Mikado at the Royal Opera House in Copenhagen. It was one of the most magical experiences of my professional life. What fascinated me was the chandelier that hung in the auditorium and, between performances, rose into the dome of the opera house. I had never seen a light that shone as bright. Most become dulled by dust.

I asked if I might see it more closely. And so it was, on a wintry day, the designer and I climbed a wooden staircases to the very top of the opera house and found a door that looked as if it might open onto a broom cupboard. Instead, we found ourselves in the dome. All round this huge circular space were windows that looked out onto the copper roofs of Copenhagen. In the centre was the chandelier – a vast, brooding presence. We also discovered an old lady with a sewing machine, her chamois leather cloths hung up to dry, looking like birds on a wire. Her job, so she told us, was to keep the chandelier shining. No one knew she was there. I felt I had walked into a fairy tale.

It was this time in Copenhagen that inspired my story, *Invisible in a Bright Light.* I sincerely hope it weaves magic into your hearts.

Sally Gardner

Hastings

July 2019

CHAPTER 1

'Do you want to finish the game?' says the man in the emerald green suit.

'What game?' asks the girl.

'One thing is certain,' he says, ignoring her question, 'when you have finished the game, everything will have changed.'

Deep under the sea in the cave of dreamers hang the sleepers, suspended from boat hooks. Passengers and sailors alike, eyes closed, heads held high, their skin fish-flesh white. On and on, in neat rows they go until all that is left hanging from the hooks is empty clothes. Through these, fish swim and eels wriggle, causing trousers and petticoats to dance with the memory of their ghostly wearers.

At the entrance of the cave sits a man in a barnacle-encrusted chair. Before him is a desk. It is his three-piece suit of emerald green that has caught the girl's attention, not his face as one might suppose, for it is a strange face. Behind him, neatly stacked, are hundreds of gleaming white candles.

'You are stronger than I thought,' says the man. 'I wasn't expecting to light another set of my candles. My candles are precious to me and I hate to waste them. Are you sure you want to carry on playing?'

Celeste is spellbound by the emerald green fabric. In it she sees her past all whirled together until it is a thing of threads and stitches.

'Before we go any further, tell me your age again,' says the man.

Only now does Celeste notice his face. She thinks he must be wearing a mask for she can't see his eyes. Perhaps they've been washed away. Fish occasionally nibble at his shiny, bald head.

On the desk rests a ledger. It is like the one she remembers the clerk in the hat shop had when she and Anna went to pick up a parcel for Mother.

'I asked you a question,' he says.

Celeste doesn't answer. She is studying the ring on his little finger. The stone is a bright emerald, the same colour as his suit. He dips a quill in the inkstand and tendrils of ink float away.

'In other words, how old are you?'

'You are asking the questions in the wrong order,' says Celeste. 'The first question should be, "what is your name?"'

The man is taken aback.

'I ask the questions, not you.'

He is unsettled by this girl. Seldom has he met a child with strength enough to move on to the final part of the game. Perhaps for once it will be played out to the bitter end. The thought delights him although he has no doubt who the winner will be. He persists with his questions.

'Tell me your age.'

Again the girl answers with more energy than he would have thought possible. By this point in the game the player should be no more than a shadow.

'My age?' says Celeste. 'I am eleven.'

'I can smell a lie in the water,' says the man. 'I play you, girl, you don't play me.'

The truth is Celeste can't remember if she is about to be eleven or has just turned eleven or perhaps she is twelve. She is pondering this when the man in the emerald green suit turns over the page in the ledger. With his quill he points upwards. Celeste follows the tip of the feather. Above the heads of the sleepers hangs a glass chandelier in the shape of a galleon.

'Seven hundred and fifty candles,' says the man, 'and not one of them is defeated by the seawater.'

For the first time Celeste can see clearly. The beams of light illuminate the faces of the sleepers whose names are on the tip of her tongue.

'Look at me,' says the man. 'Look at me.'

The moment she does the names are gone and somewhere in the cave a ship's bell sounds mournfully. Perhaps it's a warning, she thinks. He begins to laugh, his laughter a wave that causes the sleepers to sway as one.

'What if I don't want to play your game?' she says.

'A brave question, if I may say so. It would be a pity after you have come so far. But I would understand, for the game only gets harder from now on.' He leans back in his chair. 'Do you want to know what happens if you retire from the game?'

'Yes,' says Celeste.

'It's simple. You join the first row of sleepers. It's your decision. This part of the game is called the Reckoning and only I know the rules.'

'Then it isn't fair.'

'I never said it was. I always win. I will help you this much – and I am being too generous. I have already been too generous in letting you have one of the sleepers. Not that she is of any use. I did tell you that at the beginning, before I lit the first set of candles. But that is by the by. Where was I? Yes. The player – that is you, Maria – was abandoned as a baby on the steps of the great opera house in the city of C—. There you were raised by the woman whose job it is to clean the crystal chandelier. When you were eight years old you were found to have a natural gift for dance and you were enrolled in the ballet school. To pay for your lessons you work – when you are not required to rehearse – for the famous singer, Madame Sabina Petrova.'

Maria? She is about to say, 'I'm Celeste,' when she senses rather than hears a voice, a voice in her head, '*No – don't tell him your name.*'

She looks again at the sleepers with a sickening realisation that she knows the name of every one of them. They shouldn't be there.

'If you win the game,' he says, 'they will go home. If you lose, they lose. Forever.'

The man in the emerald green suit moves towards her with unnatural speed. He puts his hand to her face and closes her eyes.

'Just to make sure, double sure,' he says. 'As I have done this once, let me do it again.'

And before she can say another word, all is forgotten.

'Good,' says the man, as he blows out the candles. 'Very good. Let the Reckoning begin.'

Down she falls and down she falls, deep down to the bottom of the sea into the inky black. The darkness becomes a line between the words and the paper, where sea meets sky and still she falls until below her the city with its many domed roofs spreads out before her. She sees the horse-drawn trams, the carriages, the park and the harbour with its tall ships. Down she falls through the dome of the opera house, down she falls, past the crystal galleon and as she passes it she hears the sound of something coming adrift. Down, down she falls...

CHAPTER 2

'Wake up.' Celeste felt the flick across her face. 'I've been looking for you everywhere you lazy, useless girl.'

She wiped the dream from her eyes and climbed sleepily out of the costume basket with its comforting smell of old tinsel and greasepaint. Before her stood a ferocious-looking lady who Celeste knew must be a wardrobe mistress for she wore a grey dust-coat over her clothes, had a tape measure hanging round her neck and pins in her lapels. But it didn't explain why she had seen fit to attack Celeste with a glove.

'What did you do that for?' said Celeste. 'You have no right to hit me.'

'No right?' said the wardrobe mistress. She was twisted with rage and sourer than a lemon that had never seen the sun. 'And who are you, a little rat, to talk to me in such a manner? Don't you dare start giving yourself airs and graces.'

'I'm not,' said Celeste. 'Mother would be furious if she knew you had struck me with a glove and talked to me so rudely.'

'Mother? Mother – oh my word, what dream have you been in? You're an orphan as well you know. Your mother – whoever she was – left you in a basket and forgot all about you.'

'Miss Olsen,' called a stagehand, 'Madame Sabina wants you.'

Celeste was about to tell Miss Olsen that she was wrong, very wrong, when she looked down at the dress she was wearing. It was a thin, worn thing.

'I wasn't wearing this,' she said. 'I didn't put this on this morning. No – these clothes are so old-fashioned. I was wearing a brand-new sailor dress and playing with my toy theatre.'

'When you have quite finished making up fairy tales,' said Miss Olsen, 'Madame Sabina wants her glove and wants it now – in her dressing-room.'

'Madame Sabina,' repeated Celeste. In her dream the man in the emerald green suit had spoken of her. But that was a dream, it wasn't real. It couldn't be real. 'Why do I have to take it to her? Madame Sabina is Mother's understudy.'

Even as she said this she was aware that her

memories were beginning to fall into forgetfulness and there was only this strange, disjointed now. The more she thought of the past, the more it disappeared. Down she falls and down she falls…

'Did you hear me?' said Miss Olsen. 'How dare you talk of the great Madame Sabina Petrova like that.'

Celeste closed her eyes in hope that she might wake up, that everything would be as it should be. When she opened them she knew that something very strange had happened, was happening. The words of the man in the emerald green suit echoed in her head. *'To pay for your lessons you work – when you are not required to rehearse – for the great singer.'*

The only thing Celeste could remember for certain was her toy theatre.

'Which city is this?' she asked.

'The city of C—, as you perfectly well know.'

'There is no city of C—,' said Celeste. 'Where is Anna?'

'Ridiculous girl, I know your game,' said the wardrobe mistress.

'Do you?' said Celeste.

'Yes, oh yes – you think I don't know that you both live up there, in the dome.'

'Do we?' said Celeste.

'I know everything,' said Miss Olsen, ignoring her question. 'I know what goes on behind the scenes and if you act the fool it won't work with me. You are nothing more than a little rat.'

Celeste wanted to be gone from there. She needed time to think. It was easier to run the errand than argue with Miss Olsen. She took the glove and set off in what Miss Olsen considered the wrong direction and the wardrobe mistress stamped her foot.

'Where are you going? You're not to use that door. If I find that you've used that door I will tell Madame, so I will, and you...' Her words were lost in the busyness of the theatre.

Celeste knew this theatre. Or perhaps she knew one similar for it felt familiar, yet it wasn't. Somehow it was different and she thought it had to do with the light; it shone too brightly, illuminating her growing sense of panic. Where was she? She knew one thing to be a truth: that she had spent most of her life backstage in theatres, she had as good as grown up in the rabbit warrens of draughty passages with myriad doors to workshops, to the wardrobe department, the prop shop, the green room. Winding wooden staircases led up to the domes and the fly towers. She knew backstage and front of house better than the lines on the palm of her hand. The theatre was home to her. And, as if to prove to herself that she was right, she had relied on her instinct and taken what she hoped was the fastest route, even if it was strictly forbidden. The other way went down veiny corridors, took too long and was always full of people. Near the wig department, she stopped by a narrow door that you wouldn't notice unless you knew it was there. It was only to be used by the directors and important people and it divided the back of the theatre from the front. As far as Celeste was concerned, they were two different worlds. She looked around to make sure she wouldn't be seen. A blind man was coming towards her, his stick tapping each side of the corridor.

'Out of the way,' he shouted. 'Out of the way.'

With a turn of the handle, she slipped through the forbidden door into the realm of thick, red carpets where the walls were decorated with murals of fairy tales. This was the part of the theatre that belonged to the audience. To Celeste's relief it looked familiar. It was a place she was sure she knew. It would be inhabited by grand ladies in luxurious dresses with bustles, and trains that swished when they moved, and dainty shoes that a princess might wear, their hair sparkling with gems. They would be accompanied by gentlemen in evening dress with starched white waistcoats and collapsible top hats. In the intervals they would hover in this corridor in hope of glimpsing the king.

All Celeste had to do was let herself into the anteroom behind the Royal Box and run down the spiral staircase that led to the prompt side of the stage, then it was only a matter of a twist and a turn to the diva's dressing-room. She smiled to herself, knowing she would arrive well before Miss Olsen who she imagined would have wheezed and plodded down two floors to the stage level, passing the wardrobe department where she would have been unable to resist checking on her seamstresses.

Knowing where she was quietened Celeste's worried mind. More important still, all was as it should be. Perhaps it was Miss Olsen who was losing her memory. She had heard it said that happened to grown-ups. A bit like losing your gloves, she supposed, or your hat. You keep on losing parts of your life until you forget who you are. Celeste told herself that would never happen to her. She remembered, yes, she did remember. It was just the dream that had confused her. She stood in front of the grand, gold-embossed doors that opened onto the Royal Box. Silently, she entered the anteroom and congratulated herself. She knew this theatre. She could see into the Royal Box and beyond to the auditorium with its white and gold walls and red plush seats. High above in the ornate ceiling, surrounded by painted fairies, was a large, circular space through which the glass chandelier would descend, as it always had done, twenty minutes before the audience was admitted.

She stopped for a moment to take in the magic of the auditorium. It had been silly to let a dream upset her.

Celeste had her hand on the banister of the spiral staircase when she became aware that someone was watching her. She spun round. In the shadows she could see only a pair of buttoned boots and two elegant hands resting on a gold-topped cane.

'Do you often come this way?' said a gentle voice.

'I'm sorry,' said Celeste, 'but it's the quickest way to Madame Sabina's dressing-room.'

The owner of the boots and gold-topped cane laughed.

'You shouldn't be here either,' said Celeste.

The gentleman stood and stepped into the light.

'I won't tell if you don't.'

He didn't look anything like the head on the coins, she thought, or the marble bust at the top of the stairs in the auditorium. All urgency left and curiosity took its place.

'Why are you here alone?' she asked. 'Shouldn't there be soldiers to protect you?'

'Protect me from what? Dragon divas? I came to watch the dress rehearsal. I was told that Madame's voice is transformed but I could hear no difference.'

Her large eyes took in the gentleman before her. She was standing upright, hands behind her back.

'You were the little dancer in the first act. You were the best thing about the dress rehearsal.'

'No, sir,' she said. 'I can't dance.'

He laughed. 'Now you are being modest. Were those real wings on your back?' he asked.

Celeste said again, 'I can't dance, sir. Perhaps you have mistaken me for someone else.'

'There is no mistake. It was you and you flew – it was enchanting. And now you are dressed in the costume of a street urchin.'

Shyness overcame her.

'No, sir. May I go, sir?'

'Yes,' he said. He put his long finger to his lips. 'Not a word.'

'Not a word,' said Celeste. 'And anyway, no one would believe me if I told them I'd met the king.'

CHAPTER 3

Mr Gautier was a small man whose role as the director of the Royal Opera House made him appear bigger than he was. But today, as he sat down to eat his lunch, he felt the lack of every inch. For the first time he had to admit that if this morning's dress rehearsal was anything to go by, the production of Frederick Massini's new opera, *The Saviour*, was doomed to failure.

This time two years ago he had been full of excitement at the prospect of staging the opera. What had happened then had been a tragedy. Ellen Winther had been one of the greatest opera singers the city had ever produced but she, along with her husband and children, had been lost at sea. Not for the first time did Mr Gautier wonder if something in his fortunes had suffered a sea-change. Tonight's Grand Opening should have been the jewel in the crown of the Royal Opera House's autumn season. Instead, Madame Sabina Petrova was making everyone's lives miserable. Sitting with Massini in the empty auditorium, the director had felt his age.

The dress rehearsal had started at ten o'clock. Immediately, the gauze that hung in front of the scenery had been badly torn by the batten of one of the main painted cloths. Mr Gautier had waved it aside as unimportant and the rehearsal continued. Madame Sabina refused to go on stage without it in place.

He had made a mistake when he'd told her the gauze was unnecessary and, if anything, distracted from the glorious sets. Madame had retorted that it made all the difference in the world to her, and that no one was there to see the scenery.

'They are here to see me,' she'd said. 'The scenery doesn't sing – I sing.'

Madame Sabina took to her dressing-room and refused to come out until Mr Gautier had apologised and assured her that the gauze would be in place when the curtain rose that evening.

'Now, please,' he'd begged, 'we must finish the dress rehearsal. Imagine what tonight's performance will be like if we don't.'

To his complete surprise, she had said, 'I don't care. All I have to do is sing.'

When she had reappeared, she had just walked through her part. Then to the consternation of the conductor and the orchestra she had started to sing an aria from another opera altogether.

'Stop, stop!' shouted Mr Gautier. 'Madame, what are you doing?'

'I am singing an aria that I am famous for. This opera of Massini's has no memorable tunes at all.'

Frederick Massini had stormed out of the theatre.

Mr Gautier knew that if Sabina Petrova insisted on singing that particular aria, Massini's opera would be a disaster. It was a song that had been made famous by Ellen Winther. It also happened to be the last song she'd sung on this stage.

He had asked to speak to Madame Sabina alone. He had waited in his office, pacing back and forth, wondering who had been responsible for making this woman into an unbearable monster.

'It would be most inappropriate...' he had said when she eventually arrived, but Madame Sabina wasn't listening.

She demanded coffee and 'some of those little pastries'. Mr Gautier, conscious of every wasted second, watched them tick-tock away, defeated by a flurry of china coffee cups and pastries, forks and napkins.

'Don't you want a pastry?' she'd asked with the innocence of a lamb.

'No.' He took a deep breath. 'The aria you sang…'

'Beautiful, wasn't it?'

'That aria would remind His Majesty of the loss of his son. It was a tragedy, you will remember, that also took the life of Ellen Winther, one of the opera house's most beloved singers. That was the last song she ever sang on this stage.'

'Most beloved?' repeated Madame Sabina. 'I don't think so. I am far more highly regarded than ever Ellen Winther was. Her voice was rather thin, I recall.'

'Madame, I'm sure, like us all, you want to impress the king,' said Mr Gautier, speaking slowly as if he was dealing with a toddler on the cusp of a tantrum.

'Of course.'

Mr Gautier swallowed before saying, 'Then I suggest you sing the role Massini has written for you. I believe the opera stands a chance of being a success but not if you refuse to sing the correct score or act the part.'

Madame Sabina had stood up, knocking what was left of the pastries onto the floor. She'd flounced out of his office.

But to his surprise his words worked for she returned to the stage and finished the first act, singing the right words to the right score. But this time, instead of wearing the costume designed for the part, she was dressed in a gown sprinkled with diamonds.

'No, no, no!' Mr Gautier had shouted. 'You are supposed to be a poor, homeless woman in this scene.'

Madame Sabina replied that she would wear what she pleased and it was so very unpleasant to be dressed in a nasty, shabby costume.

Raising his arms to the domed ceiling of the opera house, Mr Gautier had given in. And so the dress rehearsal continued only to be interrupted again when one of the footlights spluttered and set fire to a piece of painted scenery. The flames were doused but the damage meant that the scene painters would be working until the curtain rose. The gas-lighter, whose job it was to light the production, had strode on stage, announcing the place was no better than kindling. It wasn't safe, and he wasn't going to be held responsible if a fire broke out.

Mr Gautier had thanked him for his concern and suggested the rehearsal continue as they were running out of time.

It was at the end of Act One, when he was hoping things might improve, that Camille, the ballet school's second-best ballerina, had tripped as she made her entrance. She sprained her ankle. There was a pause while a replacement, the best dancer from the *corps de ballet*, was found. By then, the stage had been transformed into a forest and in a pool of light a young girl, no older than twelve, tiptoed onto the stage. There was a hush, then the orchestra soared and for a few minutes Mr Gautier was transported by the clever little dancer. He could have happily watched her all day. How much better to work with children than with monstrous adults.

'If she can sing,' said a voice from the row behind him, 'you should give her the role of Columbine in the pantomime.'

Mr Gautier had turned, pleased to see his old friend, Quigley, the clown. He was dressed, as always, in his chequered Harlequin costume.

The director had made a note to find out about the little dancer.

At the end of the dress rehearsal he'd said, 'Well done,' to the rest of the company, though none of them were happy with how it had gone, and all complained bitterly about Madame Sabina. She had sent Miss Olsen to tell the director that she wouldn't see him until she'd rested.

Lunch was brought to his office. He ate slowly. Better, he thought, to go into battle on a full stomach than an empty one. But he wasn't hungry, and he got up from his desk, which was covered with papers and manuscripts, and went to the window. He looked out over the copper domes of the city and he knew that he had four hours before the critics came, the curtain rose and his opera was destroyed by the eager scratching of their fountain pens. Four hours. He felt not unlike a man about to go to his execution. Not even the enchanting little dancer at the end of Act One would be able to save *The Saviour*.

CHAPTER 4

Celeste stood in a corner of the diva's dressing-room, once more foxed by the strangeness of everything. What she saw was nearly right and at the same time all wrong. Her confidence was beginning to fade. Perhaps it was possible that children, like grown-ups, could lose their memories. She seemed to have lost hers. She knew she had it before she went to sleep, before she woke up in the costume basket. But where could it be? The trouble was that if she thought back further than waking up, there was nothing, a long corridor of nothing, with only a vague sense of those she loved. What they looked like she had no notion – even thinking of them made them into ghosts. What didn't leave her was a sense of emptiness, as if a part of her was missing. It was no good telling herself that this was a dream. Dreams weren't solid, they didn't have furniture you could touch, they didn't have a wardrobe mistress and a glove in them. All the dreams she could remember had been wishy-washy and lacking reason.

The one thing she was sure of was the theatre. She remembered its corridors and staircases and where they led. There it was, a silver fish of something, someone half-remembered and instantly forgotten. She closed her eyes in hope of catching it. No use, it vanished, a vital piece of information swimming away from her. If only she could reel it in then this dressing-room, the diva and everything else might begin to make sense.

The dressing-room was the largest and the grandest in the Royal Opera House. Its furnishings were lavish: a piano, a day-bed, a huge dressing-table covered with paint and brushes and expensive bottles from a famous perfumery. An elaborate gilded mirror doubled the size of the room. One of the button-back armchairs was occupied by an overfed and under-loved girl with mouse-coloured hair who made the art of sitting look clumsy. This, apparently, was Hildegard, the diva's daughter. Celeste had no memory of her mother's understudy ever mentioning a child. Then again she had little memory of anything before the dream.

The soprano, resplendent in a kimono, was taking no notice of her daughter. She was more interested in who had sent flowers and the many gifts that had arrived. One of these was a box of chocolates tied with an extravagant bow. Her daughter asked if she could have them and her mother waved an unconcerned hand.

The girl took the box and sat down again. She removed the lid and let out a sigh of pleasure – there were so many chocolates to choose from. She started to eat them one by one, throwing papers onto the floor.

There was a timid knock on the door and the wardrobe mistress crept in.

Madame Sabina said, 'Where have you been, Olsen? I need my corset loosening.' Then to Celeste, 'You, girl, pick up those wrappers.'

Miss Olsen gave Celeste a push and she did as she was told. At that moment the director strode in. He had decided over lunch to tell the diva exactly what he thought. Nothing else had managed to pierce her armour-plated skin.

'I hope, Madame,' he said, barely containing his anger, 'that tonight you will grace us with your voice. The dress rehearsal was a farce – you made no effort. How is the conductor to know when to bring the orchestra up if you will not sing?'

'Do not be so petty, so small-minded,' said Madame Sabina. 'No one cares about your directions. There was no point in exhausting myself with them. I know how my voice sounds, but your production...' She shrugged. 'The audience have paid a lot of money to hear me sing. And no, Gautier, I am not going to move about the stage. I am the great Sabina Petrova – I stand, I sing, I look wonderful. That is what I do.'

Mr Gautier was shaking with rage.

'If you would only do what is asked of you, we would have an opera of startling originality.'

'Rubbish. Absolute rubbish. Don't you agree, Miss Olsen?'

Miss Olsen said nothing.

'At least,' said Mr Gautier, 'you will wear the costumes that have been designed for your role.'

'No,' said Madame Sabina. 'No and no again. My costumes have been created for me in Paris and are embroidered with diamonds – real diamonds.'

Celeste was picking up wrappers as, chocolate by chocolate, Hildegard discarded them. She looked up to find the girl staring at her.

'How old are you?' Hildegard asked, quietly enough not to be heard in the argument between the adults.

Again Celeste's dream came back to her. Wasn't that the question the man in the emerald green suit had asked? This time she didn't hesitate.

'Twelve,' she said.

'I'm thirteen,' said the girl. 'Eeurgh!' She dropped a half-eaten chocolate to the floor. 'I don't like orange creams.'

For a moment, Celeste had a great desire to put the half-eaten chocolate in her mouth. She was so hungry. A glance from Miss Olsen made her reconsider and along with the crumpled wrappers, it went in the wastepaper basket. Perhaps, she thought, the empty feeling was nothing more than hunger. But in her heart she knew it wasn't.

The argument had now lost any politeness. Mr Gautier's patience had already been overstretched that day and his voice became louder and angrier.

Celeste watched Hildegard stick out her tongue and put another chocolate on it, closing her mouth around it and licking her lips. What Celeste would give for just one of those chocolates.

Suddenly the girl's mouth stopped moving, her hands went instinctively to her throat, her face turned the colour of a beetroot.

'She's choking!' Celeste shouted to make herself heard.

'Quiet!' said Madame Sabina, turning on Celeste. 'Quiet. It is not your place to speak.'

She was about to turn back to the director when he cried, 'My God – Hildegard!'

Knocking over a vase of red roses he swiftly lifted her by her ankles so that all her petticoats and bloomers could be seen, transforming her, Celeste thought, into a white rose. Miss Olsen slapped her hard on her back. Hildegard's arms flopped in front of her blue-tinged face and now it was her mother who was shouting.

'Call for help!'

Miss Olsen gave Hildegard another slap and something flew from her mouth. She took a great gasp of air and Mr Gautier laid her down on the day-bed. The poor girl couldn't stop coughing and Miss Olsen poured her a glass of water.

'Oh, Hildegard, darling,' said Madame Sabina, wiping the hair from her daughter's face. 'My little mouse, this is too terrible. What did you eat? Was it a nut, my love?'

'No, Mama,' said Hildegard between bouts of coughing and sips of water. 'It was something hard, very hard.' Celeste picked up the offending item. Covered in chocolate, a ring lay in the palm of her hand. An emerald ring, just like the one in her dream.

'Bring it here,' ordered Madame Sabina, once more in control. 'No, stupid girl, it looks disgusting – wash it first.'

Celeste washed it, hoping that what she was

holding might really be nothing more than a nut, that it was her imagination that had turned it into something else. But it was clearly a gold ring, set with an emerald. She took it to Madame Sabina.

'Let me see, Mama,' said Hildegard, weakly.

Madame Sabina held the ring up to the light.

'It's an emerald, darling,' she said, 'set in gold.' A smile crossed her thin lips. 'I would say it's rather valuable.' The fact that it had nearly choked her daughter became of little consequence. 'You,' she said to Celeste, 'you – whatever your name is – smash all the chocolates and see if there are more gems.'

Miss Olsen oversaw the process and when Celeste had broken and discarded every chocolate in the box, said, 'No, Madame, they are just chocolates.'

'Bring me that box,' said Madame Sabina. 'Is there no card? Nothing to say who it is from?'

Hildegard pointed to the inside of the lid where a ribbon held an envelope in place. With very little grace, Madame Sabina tore it open and pulled out the card. There was a moment's silence in which the soprano's face clouded with fury. The box dropped to the floor. She glared again at the card then tore it into four pieces and let them fall on top of the box.

'Out,' she shouted. 'Out, all of you. I don't want to see any of you.'

'But Mama, you can't mean me,' said Hildegard as Madame took her daughter's hand and threw her out along with everyone else. They heard the key being turned in the lock.

Hildegard started to cry and Miss Olsen took her to a nearby dressing-room.

Celeste had picked up the empty box and the pieces of torn card as she left the room and was waiting for instructions.

'Give me those,' said Mr Gautier. He took the fragments of card and pieced them together. '*To Hildegard from Papa*,' he read aloud. 'I always thought the father was dead.' He seemed to notice Celeste then for he said, 'You danced beautifully this morning. And now I have to somehow worm my way back into that room and calm the dragon.' He smiled at her.

Miss Olsen returned and, taking Celeste by the arm, pulled her aside.

'You are wanted by the dancing master in the rehearsal room,' she said.

'Why?' asked Celeste.

'Try not to be more stupid than you already are. You know perfectly well why.'

'But I don't.'

'Just because you have been picked to dance in tonight's performance don't think you will be given any more privileges,' said Miss Olsen. 'You'll still be working for me and Madame.'

Celeste felt panic rise in her. It was one thing for the king to mistake her for a dancer, quite another for Miss Olsen.

'I can't dance,' she said.

'I would agree with that,' said Miss Olsen. 'But Mr Gautier doesn't, so go. And don't be late for your costume fitting. It must be perfect for tonight's performance.'

CHAPTER 5

Celeste had just come from the costume fitting. Miss Olsen had told her she'd checked her measurements earlier but the leotard the seamstress had been making was for someone bigger.

'You can't have lost weight so soon,' Miss Olsen had said.

Celeste didn't know what to say. What she knew was that Miss Olsen hadn't measured her that morning.

'And you are slightly shorter. Don't tell me you have shrunk between breakfast and teatime?'

The costume was being taken in.

Where have I shrunk to, thought Celeste, and why does everyone think I can dance? She counted her fingers, checked her limbs, to make sure they were all there. She'd had to ask Miss Olsen where

Anna was and the wardrobe mistress had snapped at her and pointed to a wooden staircase.

Celeste stopped by a meagre door that could well have opened a broom cupboard. Then a flash of light in her mind's eye, no more than a stone skimming the waves, brought her a hard-won memory. She knew she had been to the dome before, but she couldn't say when. There had been an old lady with a sewing-machine, and the chamois leathers she cleaned the chandelier with hung on a washing-line. There were birds actually inside the dome, gulls, gannets and pigeons, lots of them. Someone had even said they'd seen an albatross there, that's why they'd come up here. But who were they? Who was it she had been with? An image drifted away from the edge of her memory. By the time Celeste wearily climbed the stairs, she was completely lost.

That afternoon she had gone to the rehearsal room as instructed. The dancing master had sat facing the long mirror where the floor sloped to replicate the floor of the stage. He had tapped out the rhythm while the piano played and she had stood, bewildered and motionless.

'What's wrong with you?' he asked. He looked at her closely. 'Have you lost weight? You seem – smaller. Are you feeling ill?' Then seeing her confusion, he said, 'Let's break.'

Celeste had held onto the barre as if it were a life raft until Mr Gautier appeared.

'I've just come to say that you were the best thing about the dress rehearsal,' he said. 'In fact the only good thing about it.'

The dancing master took him aside and spoke quietly to him. Celeste caught the odd word.

'Are you sure?'

'... exhaustion... perhaps with rest...'

Mr Gautier had turned to her and said, 'You are a very talented dancer. I'm sure once you are rested you will be ready for this evening's performance.'

Her only hope now was that Anna would untie the knots in her woolly mind. At least she remembered her governess. No, she thought, she's *our* governess. She felt muddle-headed. *Our* governess – what did that mean? What else had she forgotten, apart from knowing how to dance? But she had never been able to dance – she had two left feet. Who was it who used to say that to her?

It was dark in the city; it had been dark since midday. Outside snow was falling and the copper rooftops shimmered with a blue light. Inside, on a table laid for two, a candle flickered while the only other light came from the well in the floor. It was an eerie kind of light that lit from below a brooding monster that was the chandelier, draped in its covers, waiting to be illuminated. It was so dark that she couldn't see Anna. All she could make out in the gloom was an ancient, crochety stove that looked more like a stage prop than anything useful. It glowed grumpily in the bitter cold of the place. By the stove was a neat pile of logs and the smell of vegetable soup bubbled from a pan on the stove itself.

The moment Celeste saw Anna she felt safe and her head stopped hurting. Here was someone she trusted, who looked after her and – more importantly – knew she wasn't a dancer. Anna was thin, but not boney, with a kind face and eyes that laughed at life. Her words were always wise. Celeste had no idea how old Anna was; quite a bit younger than Mother and surely Mother wasn't old. Anna would know where her mother was. And then all knowledge was gone again and only an ache remained.

Anna held out her arms and Celeste was wrapped in the comforting smell of roses.

'My clever little treasure,' she said. 'I heard that you'll dance tonight and that Camille's costume is being altered to fit you.'

Celeste's heart missed a beat.

'I can't dance, Anna. You should know that.'

'Are you being funny? This is such good news. I'm so proud of you.'

'Did you see the dress rehearsal?' asked Celeste.

'Of course I did – you were magnificent. Is everything all right?'

'No,' said Celeste. 'It's all wrong.'

'Come, sit down,' said Anna. 'You are in a pickle over nothing. Don't worry. There will be more money – you will be paid and with what I earn we might even find rooms near the theatre.'

'I can't dance and I'm not—'

Anna interrupted her. 'It's because you are a perfectionist that you think that you're no good. But you are so talented, my little treasure.'

Celeste saw there was no point in telling Anna what had happened that afternoon. No point at all.

'Is it the logs that are worrying you?' said Anna. 'Of course, that's what's the matter. I should have said something straight away.'

'Why should the logs worry me?' she said.

'Because you are always so anxious that we'll be discovered, and I knew you would notice them.'

Surely she should know what it was Anna was talking about? But her mind was blank.

'A young man came up here,' said Anna. 'He's been employed to work in the fly tower and he wanted to look out over the rooftops to the harbour. He discovered me making soup. He told me that he used to be a sailor and was good at rigging but he wanted a job on dry land for the winter. His skills are much needed in the theatre. Of course, I told him we didn't live up here, I even went so far as giving him a false address. But I'm not a good actress. He didn't believe me, but he was kind. His name is Stephan Larsen. He came later with the logs and swore he would not tell anyone that we're here.'

'It's not Stephan Larsen that's worrying me,' said Celeste.

She wanted to say that what was worrying her was she had no memory of any of this.

'It's Miss Olsen. She knows we're living here.'

'Leave Miss Olsen to me. Don't let her upset you.'

'Everything is upsetting,' said Celeste.

But the soup tasted delicious. Celeste tore a piece of bread from the loaf.

'The bread – Stephan gave us that as well. And you should eat more slowly,' said Anna. 'You usually eat slowly. You don't want to be too full when you dance. You are very fussy about that. And why are you holding your spoon in your left hand?'

The words of the man in the emerald green suit came back to Celeste. *I have already been too generous in letting you have one of the sleepers. Not that she is of any use.*

Celeste had thought that the strangeness of the

afternoon would be over when she was with Anna, but it wasn't. There was no one she could turn to.

'Don't forget, my little treasure, that Madame Sabina will still want you in her dressing-room before you change.'

As Celeste was leaving Anna said, 'Is that another hole in your stocking?'

Celeste looked at the hole. 'Another hole? I don't think so. Why?'

'Well, this morning I painted it in with black ink as there was no time to do any mending. Don't you remember?'

Celeste looked again at the hole. Her white skin shone through it.

There was silence and then Anna said in a tight, cheerful voice, 'It must have rubbed off.'

What neither of them said, and what both of them knew, was that ink is hard to get off skin and even if washed with soap and water it leaves a bluish mark. There was no mark.

'Never mind, Maria,' said Anna, 'I'll mend it tonight.'

'Maria,' whispered Celeste to herself and knew in that name, that other name that wasn't hers, there lay the answer to all that was missing.

CHAPTER 6

Celeste stopped on her way down from the dome and looked over the fly tower onto the stage below. For a moment she rested her head on her arms. Somewhere between falling asleep in the costume basket and waking, something had happened that had changed everything and convinced all those about her that she was someone else, that she was a dancer.

She felt a hand touch her shoulder and heard a familiar voice. *'Think – if this is a game, the Reckoning, then could it be that you are not the first player?'*

She spun, staring into the shadows, refusing to be frightened.

'Who's there?'

No one answered. Her heart racing, she ran to the stairs and collided with a boy.

'I heard you're going to dance the solo tonight,' he said to her. 'I said you would be a star.'

'You did?' said Celeste.

She had no idea who he was but felt her answer should have been 'Yes, you did,' and not a question.

He was looking at her now as if he knew her well. She was looking at him as if he was a stranger. He had dark brown eyes and dark skin. He looked a little older than her. Who was he?

As if reading her mind, he said, 'It's Viggo, Maria. Are you feeling all right?'

'Viggo,' she repeated. 'I'm not…'

She stopped. Could it be she had woken up and forgotten a part of her life? Had she left her other self in the costume basket? Both of them looked away, embarrassed.

'There's trouble with the scenery,' he said.

'Oh,' said Celeste and quickly started down the stairs.

Viggo called after her, 'I hope it goes well tonight. I'll be watching.'

Celeste felt like weeping. What was going to happen when the music started and the little dancer didn't dance?

The door to Madame Sabina Petrova's dressing-room was wide open and Celeste slipped in unnoticed. There is an art to being invisible and at least, she thought, I think I have mastered that. Hildegard looked miserable. She was seated in the same chair as she had been earlier.

Madame Sabina glanced up from putting the finishing touches to her face. To Celeste it was a grotesque mask.

'Do you know, Hildegard,' said Madame Sabina, 'there's a potential star in this very room?'

'No, Mama,' said Hildegard. 'Where?'

Madame Sabina beckoned Celeste. 'This pretty little creature can dance, according to my idiot director,' she said as Celeste nervously moved closer to her. 'He says she's enchanting. Oh dear mouse, I don't think "enchanting" is a word that could ever be used to describe you. It makes me wonder if you have any talent – except for eating chocolates so fast that you nearly choked yourself on an emerald ring.'

'She's only a theatre rat,' said Hildegard. 'And it's not fair to say that about me.'

Her mother ignored her and, putting a hand to Celeste's face, said to her, 'You see, a talentless child such as mine can be a terrible burden, one that I will have to carry with me to the end of my days.'

'I can sing,' Hildegard piped up.

'Sing, little mouse? Oh no,' and she started to laugh.

The stage manager was calling half an hour to curtain up.

'What have I done wrong?' said Hildegard, fighting back tears.

'Quiet,' said the great diva. 'I need to prepare myself for my audience. I don't want to listen to your nonsense.'

Hildegard looked crushed and Celeste tried not to catch her eye as a tear rolled down her cheek, a crystal drop that hung until it plopped to the floor. Hildegard sniffed.

'Don't sniff,' said her mother. 'What have I told you about sniffing? Stop it immediately.'

Celeste felt in her pocket and handed Hildegard a handkerchief she found there. Hildegard said nothing but blew her nose too loudly for Madame Sabina's liking.

'That's it,' she said. 'Out you go. Outside – now.'

The door shut behind the weeping Hildegard and the dressing-room was filled with a brittle silence, broken by the entrance of Mr Gautier. Celeste thought he looked like a man who had been rehearsing a speech, but before he could begin, Madame Sabina said in a voice that a Persian cat might use if a Persian cat could talk, 'I promise to sing the opera that has been written for me and that the company has spent three months rehearsing.

I will not sing arias from other productions. And I will do my best to remember the stage directions. There,' she added with a smile, 'you see there's no need for you to tell me that you find actors unbearable, singers little better and divas… oh dear me, I forget how you ended that little ditty of yours. Miss Olsen did tell me – was it something about "monstrous"?'

Mr Gautier replied with a tremble in his voice, 'They grow monstrous through flattery, but they don't start out that way.'

'That's it,' said Madame Sabina. 'You are so witty.'

Neither of them was laughing. If anything the director looked genuinely alarmed at what Madame Sabina might do next.

She sighed. 'Children, all of you,' she said, and lay down on the day-bed closing her eyes.

'I'm glad to hear you've been thinking about your performance,' said Mr Gautier. 'And the costume?'

'I will wear the one designed for my role. And you will have the gauze in place?'

'Yes,' said Mr Gautier. 'We are working on it now. You won't forget your gloves in the first act? You have your gloves?'

Madame Sabina opened one eye. 'Girl,' she said gesturing to Celeste, 'are my gloves on the dressing-table?'

'There's only one glove,' said Celeste. It was the one she had brought to her earlier.

'How careless of me. I must have left the other on stage.'

'Go and find Madame's other glove,' said Mr Gautier to Celeste as he left the dressing-room, 'and bring it back here before the curtain goes up.'

CHAPTER 7

Celeste was grateful for an excuse to get away from Madame Sabina. She found Hildegard shivering in the corridor.

'Do you think I can go back in?' she asked with a sniff.

'I don't know,' said Celeste.

'Perhaps I'll come with you,' said Hildegard. 'Where are you going?'

'To find a glove that your mama left on stage.'

'I'm good at finding things,' said Hildegard. 'That's what Mama always says. You're Maria, aren't you?'

'No, I'm Celeste.'

'Then why do they call you Maria?'

Celeste was about to say there had been a

mistake, that it wasn't her name, when Madame Sabina called for Hildegard.

For a moment Hildegard hesitated and later she wondered what would have happened if she had ignored her mother and gone with Celeste. Perhaps everything would have been different. But instead she went back into the dressing-room while Celeste walked out onto the stage.

In the wings she'd noticed a group of stagehands and scene painters standing round Mr Gautier. They were in a deep discussion about the gauze.

The stage manager walked past Celeste and said, 'Good luck for tonight,' then she heard him tell the director that it would be best to announce to the audience that there would be a fifteen minute delay before the curtain went up.

Celeste easily found the missing glove. She put it in her pocket and instead of going back to the dressing-room as she should have, she walked to the front of the stage and looked up.

Mr Gautier came over to her. 'Are you feeling better?' he asked.

Celeste nodded. 'I've found the glove,' she said.

'Good, good.'

He too glanced up at the dome. Any minute now the chandelier would slowly make its entrance into the auditorium.

'I always marvel at the fact that this chandelier is lit with candles,' he said. 'Gaslight would surely be much easier. I read somewhere that it weighs over six thousand kilos and is nearly as tall as three men. Seven hundred and fifty candles illuminate its bronze and crystal. Here it comes.'

Celeste held her breath as a bright ball of light beamed through the hole in the dome. Very slowly the chandelier began to appear, for it was believed to be unlucky if a candle was blown out on its short journey. Celeste couldn't take her eyes off it.

'I've worked in many opera houses,' said Mr Gautier, 'and I can't remember any chandelier that shone as brightly as this one. You know, it was commissioned by the king as a memorial to all those passengers who vanished from the *Empress*. His son was among them.'

'Vanished?' repeated Celeste. 'What do you mean – vanished?'

But Mr Gautier seemed not to hear her. 'One day,' he continued, 'I'll go up to the dome and see who's responsible for cleaning it, for lighting all those candles. Yes, one day.'

Celeste, spellbound by the sight of the chandelier, took a step closer to the edge of the stage.

'Be careful you don't fall into the orchestra pit – we don't want any more injuries,' said Mr Gautier.

As if in a trance she stared up at the chandelier, at its blazing candles. She now saw that it was a vast crystal galleon. This was the chandelier from her dream, the one that the man in the emerald green suit had pointed to with his quill.

Once nightly the majestic vessel, fully rigged, leaves the harbour of the dome and descends with its weighty cargo of candles that illuminates the glass and bronze rigging, the shimmer giving wind to the stiff crystal sails. Gracefully it comes to rest on the sea of stagnant air, suspended between a fairy tale sky and the rocks of the red plush seats below.

'This isn't right,' Celeste cried. 'This is all wrong.'

Some things are never meant to fall. One is the grand galleon chandelier that hangs in the Royal Opera House. As Celeste watched, the tide changed, the galleon broke free from its moorings and for a moment it hung lopsided. Mr Gautier pulled at her but she didn't move. She heard screams and behind her the thudding of feet, but she couldn't look away. Anchored to the spot, all she could see was the great glass galleon set sail. It took all time, no time, for it to be wrecked by gravity on the red rocks where it exploded in the empty auditorium. A storm of glass rained down on her.

⁓

Down she falls. And down she falls.

⁓

'Here you are again,' says the man in the emerald green suit. 'And too soon, if I may say so.'

'I don't know how to play the game,' says Celeste.

'What game?'

'The Reckoning.'

'Why should you know? I never told you,' says the man.

'Does that mean I've lost?' says Celeste.

'Entirely to the contrary. I think it means that you are very much in the game. If you survive. Which, at the moment, I think is doubtful. You have a very high fever and hundreds of fragments of glass in your skin. It would be a pity if you were to die.'

He leans back in his chair and gazes up.

Celeste thinks she must study this picture, remember it well. What is different from the first time I saw the man in the emerald green suit? she asks herself. Yes, of course, there is no crystal galleon. Everything else is the same – the suit, the... where's the emerald ring?

'Are you drifting off?' asks the man in the emerald green suit.

'No, no. I don't understand the rules of that game, that's all.'

'I wouldn't call them rules. I hate rules. You heard me wrong. You have to bring me three things. You see, I said it was easy.'

'What are they?' asks Celeste.

'Oh, you've asked me that before.'

Celeste hesitates. I haven't, she thinks. But I'm not the first player.

'What makes me unique,' says the man in the emerald green suit, 'is that I don't answer questions. You believe in rules that don't exist. Or perhaps I confused you. Tut, tut, tut.'

'Three things?' asks Celeste.

'Easy, bright and breezy. Three is a good number.'

How best, thinks Celeste, to find out what the things are without asking a direct question?

'It doesn't matter,' she says. 'I seem to be doing all right without knowing. I'll just carry on. The three things can't be of any importance, or you would have said.'

Celeste turns her back on him.

'One is the song of a bird who can't sing,' says the man in the emerald green suit. 'Two is a play too small for actors. Three is a light that blinds the seeing.'

Celeste feels more lost knowing the three things than she did before. She sighs and says, 'Then it is no harder than carving an elephant from a grain of rice.'

'You said that to me before,' says the man in the emerald green suit.

'Is this a fairy tale?' asks Celeste.

'No, and that is a question. But I will be generous. I am generous to a fault. You are in the gutter of time. A world full of endless possibilities.'

'That's nonsense,' says Celeste.

'On the contrary, it is quite straight forward. I put your lack of understanding down to your fever. One possibility is that you die, which given your present state is probable. Another is that you live. Another is that the chandelier never fell. And another possibility is that I'm lying. You decide. Are you following? Yes? No?'

'I think so.'

'Good. These endless possibilities disappear into infinity, taking with them all the might-have-beens, the could-have-beens, the should-have-beens, the would-have-beens.'

Celeste sighs. 'I'm still lost. There seem to be a lot of beens. It must be like the seven times table and I have never understood the seven times table.'

'It's nothing like it. Really, I thought you were cleverer than that. I must have been mistaken. Wake up – you're drifting off again.'

'Two sevens are fourteen.'

'Are you listening?'

'I think so.'

Celeste looks up and catches a glimpse of herself hanging from a boat hook. How, she thinks, am I here and not here?

She realises she must have said it aloud for the man in the emerald green suit says, 'Don't be ridiculous. Of course you can be in two places at the same time.'

'Can I?' says Celeste.

'This is why I hate passenger ships because there are always innocents on board and one innocent means I have to play the Reckoning. Go, and don't come back unless you have won the game.'

Down she falls. Oh, how the world has tumbled.

CHAPTER 8

The noise of the chandelier exploding resounded in every corner of the opera house. It mingled with the screams of onlookers, with the metallic groans of the bare, bronze bones of the galleon as it broke in two. Most of the candles were extinguished by the fall but some of the red plush seats caught fire and men with buckets of sand rushed to put out the flames. The auditorium was filled with dust and smoke and the front of the stage was lost in a fog of destruction.

Unseen and powerless, Maria watched as Celeste drowned in a deluge of glass. She saw that one other person, like her, stood motionless. It was the blind piano tuner, listening intently to the sounds of chaos.

When at last the smoke cleared, Mr Gautier, holding a handkerchief to his mouth, found the little dancer crumpled, a broken doll, nearly buried in a shower of tiny crystal shards.

The sight of her brought an unearthly silence to the theatre, everyone too shocked to speak. Mr Gautier bent down.

'She's alive,' he said, gently picking her up. 'She's breathing. She must be taken to hospital – immediately.'

At the hospital Celeste was taken to the operating theatre. Maria could only hope that she was conscious of her voice whispering in her head.

'Celeste, if you die, the sleepers will never wake. The game will be over, and we will all be lost forever.'

Maria was no more solid than a shadow, her strength gone. It had been foolish for her to believe that she could win the game. Only now did she realise how she had misjudged the man in the emerald green suit. She had thought him ridiculous until he'd cast a spell of forgetfulness over her, which made everything harder as the memories she held dear had floated away.

It was this watery loss of days and dates that had made her most angry, for Maria had to use so much of her strength to keep Celeste in her mind. To begin with she had told herself it wouldn't be difficult to play the game. If only she could remember the rules, she was sure she would win and free the sleepers. But she had concentrated on becoming the best dancer in the *corps de ballet* and now she'd forgotten what the rules were.

'Oh dear, dear,' said the man in the emerald green suit when he'd first seen her, 'I do so hate it when I find a child on board a ship. Are you alone? Are you the only one?'

Maria had been so startled to find herself standing before him, without Celeste by her side, that she was momentarily lost for words. She didn't understand why he asked the question but instinctively she felt protective of Celeste.

'Yes, I'm the only child,' she'd said, keeping her fingers crossed behind her back and hoping that he couldn't see Celeste.

'Sure?' he'd asked. 'Certain? No trace of doubt? Not a weeny-teeny bit of a lie?'

Maria felt her heart racing. 'I'm sure,' she said.

He sighed. 'Then I will have to light a set of my candles,' he said. 'They are precious to me, my candles. But a child is a child and the game is the game and there is naught that can be done about either. But once all my sets of candles are gone then the game is well and truly over. Time's up, ladies and gentlemen, a new page. With a flourish I will start again.'

'You have hundreds of candles,' said Maria.

'No – there you are wrong. Doubly wrong, terribly wrong. I only light each set once. If one candle gutters or goes out, I light another set. I never use the same set of candles twice.'

'That's a terrible waste,' said Maria. 'There was a queen who did that and they chopped off her head.'

'My head is not for chopping. It is firmly attached to my neck.' He dipped his pen in the ink. 'Name? Age?'

He had written down her answers in his ledger and then seemed to look at her again though she couldn't see his eyes.

'Are you quite sure you are the only child aboard?' he'd said. 'Positive? Not a flicker of doubt? No mistake?'

She was sure, she'd said again. He had lit a set of candles with a long white taper, and now she could clearly see the sleepers and the shadows they cast on the cave wall. Although she knew she was there, she couldn't see Celeste, who was hidden behind the gowns and coats. To her great relief it did indeed appear that she was the only child.

The man in the emerald green suit told her a story; that she had been found in a basket on the steps of the opera house.

'When you were eight years old,' he continued, 'it was discovered that you had a natural gift for dance and you were enrolled in the ballet school. To pay for your lessons you work – when you are not required to rehearse – for the famous singer, Madame Sabina Petrova.'

'That's not my life,' she'd said as the candles flickered.

The man in the emerald green suit put his middle finger to his lips.

'Speak in a whisper that has no breath,' he said, 'otherwise you will blow out the candles. Wax can be very moody. But wait. I don't want you to think I can't be generous. I am generous to a fault. I will make you a gift of one of the sleepers. You choose. Not that anyone will be of any use.'

Maria had hesitated. She had wanted to choose her mother. But she knew that straight away her mother would have asked, 'Where is Celeste?' Then, she thought, all might be lost.

'I am waiting,' said the man in the emerald green suit.

Maria had chosen her governess, Anna. She hoped Anna might remember what had happened to them, how they had come to be hanging from boat hooks in this watery cave. But Anna, although a comfort, had been no more help than a puppet; as empty as a whistle. Maria began to find it hard to know what was true, what was a game.

Just when she felt that she might be winning she had woken one night to find herself before the man in the emerald green suit again.

To her surprise, he'd said, 'Perhaps we could shorten the game – go past the beginning to the end.'

'How could we do that?' she asked.

'It's simple. You can guess my name. If you're right then they,' he waved an indifferent hand in the direction of the sleepers, 'can all go home.'

Surely he couldn't just change the rules of the game, she thought. It must be a trap. She decided to stay quiet.

'You're not going to give it a try? That's a pity. You can have three goes, no more, then I win.' When she said nothing, he continued. 'It looks as if I'll have to light more of my precious candles.'

For a moment Maria wondered if she should at least try to play the game.

'Go on,' he said. 'Make one guess.'

But being a cautious girl, she said, 'No thank you.'

'Wise, wise. I wouldn't have imagined such a wise head on young shoulders. Age?'

'You've asked that before. Twelve.'

'You will never never guess my name,' said the man in the emerald green suit. 'No one ever does. It's what you call a silver herring.'

That morning, when she had danced, she'd thought that when the man in the emerald green suit saw her on stage, dancing the lead against the odds, he would say that of course the sleepers should all go home. Instead she'd found her strength had vanished and she was once more in the cave of dreamers. When he had called her, she'd realised her only hope was Celeste. Her fear was that Celeste would unwittingly give the game away. She hadn't. The first hurdle passed and Maria's memory was slowly returning as her body became a thing of shadows. The only chance of survival for the sleepers, she knew, lay in her and Celeste outwitting the man in the emerald green suit.

Maria was waiting outside the operating theatre in the white tiled corridor when Viggo arrived with his uncle, Peter Tias, the head scene painter. Peter went to find out what he could from a nurse and Viggo sat down on a green wooden bench. Maria sat next to him and rested her hand on his. He looked up for a moment and stared right through her. She wanted to tell him, 'I'm still your friend.'

Peter Tias returned, shaking his head, and sat the other side of his nephew. Nurses and doctors bustled past as night turned into dawn.

Viggo said, 'When I saw Maria this afternoon, she was a bit strange with me. I thought she looked different too.'

'In what way?' said Peter.

'She was smaller.'

They both stood as a doctor, accompanied by a nurse, walked towards them.

The doctor looked surprised when Viggo said, 'Is Maria going to be all right? Can I see her?'

'Why are you still here?' said the doctor and turned to the nurse. 'Didn't you tell them?'

'Well… er… no, sir, I forgot.'

Viggo's heart almost stopped beating. 'She's – she's not dead?'

'No,' said the doctor. 'Madame Petrova insisted that Maria should be cared for at her house. The surgeon who operated on her last night and one of our nurses took her there early this morning.

There's no word on her condition. Good day.'

'Wait,' said Peter, 'who is paying for the operation? And for the doctors, the nurses?'

'Madame Petrova,' replied the nurse.

'I wonder why,' said Peter as the nurse went on her way.

Even Maria hadn't realised that Celeste was no longer there. Usually I would know that, she thought, I always know where she is, what she is thinking, even when I can't be with her, I see her, I feel her presence. And it struck Maria hard to think that Celeste might have died without her being aware she was gone. If she was dead, then everything was lost. Everything. How dare the man in the emerald green suit call this a game. He was playing with their lives.

CHAPTER 9

Rich in time are the sick and injured, near drowning in long days of boredom, swimming in and out of sleep. Celeste tried to use these unchained hours to make sense of where she was: in an iron bed with linen sheets and ironed pillowcases.

For the first few days after the accident she felt that she was drifting on clouds, hanging on a thread between sky and sea. Her whole body was bandaged, white upon white. There was snow and only a short breath of day that was all too soon swallowed in the darkness of curtains drawn tight against the cold. Candlelight danced across wallpaper making strange shapes that wandered into her dreams.

Celeste couldn't remember the order of things that had brought her to this soft bed. Time passed, people came, she heard what they had to say. Among them was Madame Sabina Petrova, talking to the doctor.

'Will she live?'

'I cannot say,' he answered. 'Her injuries are extensive.'

'How long then before she dies?'

Celeste thought that was a good question. She imagined she would float away from here.

'It is in the lap of the gods,' the doctor said. 'If the fever passes, she might survive but I have no idea if she will ever see again from her right eye. She will be severely scarred and, of course, the chances of her dancing are remote.'

These visits were punctuated by sleep and the ticking of clocks, changes of bandages and silence. Celeste woke once with a start to see an angel sitting at the end of her bed. Celeste couldn't think why she was wearing such flimsy clothes on such a cold night. Her dress was pure white without any decoration except for a pair of gauze wings. Celeste recognised it as one of the costumes from *The Saviour.* How strange, thought Celeste, that the Angel of Death should be wearing a ballet costume. Miss Olsen would be furious if she found out. Celeste tried and failed to make the angel's face come into focus. Her hair was the same colour as her own. Celeste smiled.

'It is good to see you smile,' said the angel. *'I have been so worried about you. I have tried to give you all my strength so that you might get better.'*

'Why?' said Celeste.

'Because I thought you were going to die.'

'Am I imagining you?' asked Celeste. 'You are not my reflection?'

'No, I am not. I have been with you all the time, you just haven't seen me until now.'

'I can't believe it,' said Celeste. She laughed.

'What's so funny?' asked the angel.

'Miss Olsen would be cross if she knew you had stolen one of her costumes,' said Celeste. She turned her head, expecting either or both of them to vanish.

The angel came closer.

'Are you an angel? Or are you a ghost?' Celeste asked.

'Don't you remember me?'

'No, but I think I know you,' said Celeste. 'Have you come to take me home?'

The angel, who might be a ghost, shook her head. *'We can't go home unless you win the Reckoning. Do you remember the game you were playing before the accident?'*

'How do you know about the game?'

'Because I played it first.'

'Who are you then? Do you have a name?' she said.

'I'm called Maria.'

'You're not here,' said Celeste. 'I can see through you.'

The door opened and as the nurse came in, Maria disappeared.

'Are you warm enough?' asked the nurse.

'Yes, thank you,' said Celeste. 'Did you see anyone here just now?'

'No, of course not.'

A clock chimed twelve somewhere deep in the silent house. Celeste didn't know if it was midnight of that night, or if more nights had come and gone.

She heard Madame Sabina say, 'I can't have her taking up this room forever.'

It wasn't to the doctor or the nurse that she spoke but to Mr Gautier who was standing by the bed.

'She is a child,' he said.

Madame Sabina's voice was harsh. 'All I mean is that I will be very pleased when this is over – one way or the other.'

'The papers are full of your great benevolence,' said Mr Gautier drily. 'They say you are the spirit of this city.'

Madame Sabina sighed. 'I suppose as long as they keep writing those articles she can stay. However, I tell you it costs me money – and I'm no charity.'

'Have you any idea what would have happened if the audience had been admitted to the auditorium and the curtain had gone up? An accident like that would have been the ruin of the opera house.'

'At least,' said Madame Sabina as she left the room, 'it's given Massini time to write some decent tunes for me to sing.'

Mr Gautier looked down at Celeste and said softly, 'I wonder what game she's playing.'

Game. The word made Celeste remember the cave with the sleepers. She must wake up, she told herself, she must wake up to win the Reckoning.

The fever had passed. Celeste lay propped on a small mountain of pillows and the curtain was drawn back to let in winter's watery sunshine. The room seemed smaller now she could see it better. She realised it was in the attic.

The doctor took the bandages from her arms and face.

'How much do you see with your right eye?' he asked.

'There are two of you and one is floating,' said Celeste.

'It may improve with time,' he said. 'You are young.'

He nodded to the nurse, who handed her a silver-backed mirror. Celeste saw her face and arms were pitted with scars. Her right eye was bloodshot and there was a line across the pupil.

'It's a shock, I know,' said the doctor.

He bowed and left her, taking the nurse with him.

Celeste held up the mirror to her face and was astonished to see two faces staring back at her – one scarred, the other not. The ghostly angel had appeared from nowhere, dressed just as she had been before.

'I'm here to help you remember.'

'How can you help me?' asked Celeste.

'I was helping you. I was trying to, but you didn't hear me. You kept saying you weren't a dancer, and you didn't let me in.'

Celeste was certain she was dreaming and closed her eyes.

'Wake up! You must wake up. You can't sleep any more. If you do, I'll never find you again.'

'I am awake,' said Celeste.

'Tell me what happened.'

'You mean when the chandelier fell?'

'No, when you met the man in the emerald green suit,' said Maria.

Celeste suddenly felt that she had walked out of the forest of forgetfulness into a clearing and for the first time in a long while she could see sunlight. She leaned forward, as close as she could to the angel.

'I know who you are,' said Celeste. 'You're my twin.'

'At last!' said Maria.

'I can't believe I'd forgotten you,' said Celeste. 'The other half of me. I should have known you. Why didn't I?'

'*The man in the emerald green suit casts a spell of forgetfulness over the player. My memory is coming back to me. I played the first part of the game. I didn't have the strength to go on, but I am not a ghost.*' Celeste held out her hand and watched Maria's fingers disappear in hers. '*I can help you as long as he doesn't find out we're not the same person. Did the man in the emerald green suit ask you to guess his name?*'

'No,' said Celeste. 'I'm not dreaming, am I? You are here?'

'*You know I am,*' said Maria. '*Try to concentrate. What story did the man in the emerald green suit tell you?*'

'That I had been found on the steps of the opera house.'

'*Did he tell you you could dance?*'

'Yes.'

'*That's good, that's very good. Because he believes there was only one child on the ship.*'

'It's as well that I didn't have to dance, otherwise I would have given the game away,' said Celeste.

'*I always used to tease you that you had two left feet,*' said Maria.

'I saw the man in the emerald green suit again,' said Celeste. 'After the chandelier fell.'

'*He's very contrary,*' said Maria, '*and not to be trusted. He told me first he wanted me to dance. But he didn't.*'

'What else?'

'*To guess his name. I believed that was a trick, so I concentrated instead on my ballet.*'

'You are the answer to all that's been missing,' said Celeste. She lay back on the pillows. 'Do you remember that fairy tale? It was to do with midnight.'

'*Yes. I thought it was just a story to frighten children,*' said Maria, moving onto the bed.

'I used to think that too,' said Celeste. 'I remember one part – if you were to wake on the dot of twelve minutes to midnight then... then you...'

'*Then you would vanish into the gutter of time,*' said Maria. '*A kingdom ruled by...*' She paused, trying to recall the story.

'A man in an emerald green suit?' suggested Celeste.

'*I can't say who or what it was. I know we were both terrified of the idea of there being...*' She stopped. '*I remember. The man in the emerald green suit told me, what will be hasn't yet happened and what has been is being played again and it was*

up to me to stop the inevitable, to uncover where the
past meets the present and...'

'Find the future?' said Celeste.

'*I think that's right,*' said Maria.

CHAPTER 10

Maria didn't come again. Celeste waited for her, called her name under her breath. Please, please don't be nothing but a dream, I couldn't bear that. The idea was so upsetting that she thought instead about Anna. She wanted to tell Anna about Maria, and perhaps if she knew they were twins it would jog her memory. She couldn't understand why Anna hadn't visited her at Madame Sabina's house. Had she come and been turned away? Yes, that she could believe.

The nurse, a twig of a woman, answered all Celeste's many questions with, 'You need to rest, dear, and concentrate on getting better.'

Every day Celeste asked if Anna had come and her question was always brushed aside. Only Hildegard had an answer. She'd slipped into Celeste's bedroom in the maids' quarters unnoticed by the nurse.

'Mama said that woman shouldn't have been living in the dome and it was her fault that the chandelier fell.'

'That's stupid, it isn't true. Anna had nothing to do with it,' said Celeste.

'When you speak to me,' said Hildegard, 'I would like you to address me as Miss. Miss Petrova. Anyway, your beloved Anna will stand trial and will be put in prison forever. So there.'

When the nurse found Hildegard in the bedroom, she shooed her away. 'Loud voices are not good for my patient,' she said firmly.

After that, for a reason she didn't understand, Celeste had been moved from the attic room into a guest bedroom with a wooden sleigh bed and a white china stove. The room was decorated with a wallpaper of overblown lilies. Occasionally, she would wake in the night to find Madame Sabina and strangers staring down at her.

'What would have happened to her,' one whispered, 'if you hadn't taken her in?'

'I can't see the scars,' said another. 'Are they visible only in daylight?'

'Yes, poor creature,' said Madame Sabina.

'You are kindness itself, Madame.'

And chattering still they would disappear in a rustle of silk.

The stove gave out a smothering warmth that made Celeste's head heavy and she longed for the window to be open, to smell fresh air. She felt she would never get better there. One morning, a Saturday, a parcel arrived for her.

She heard the butler, outside the bedroom, say to the nurse, 'You can give her this. Madame wishes to know what it says on the card.'

Celeste opened the long box to find inside a doll so beautifully dressed that it nearly made her burst into tears to think that someone should send her something as lovely as this.

'Is this for me?' she asked.

'Yes, dear,' said the nurse.

She didn't say that presents had arrived for Celeste every day since the terrible accident and that she was quite a celebrity in the city of C—. None of the many gifts had found their way upstairs; all had been opened by Hildegard and kept by Hildegard.

There was a card. Eager to see who it was from, the nurse said, 'Shall I read it to you?'

'No, thank you,' said Celeste. 'I can read.'

The nurse hovered, trying to catch a glimpse. Celeste saw a golden crest and quickly put the card under her pillow.

Saturday was a day that had a purpose to it, unlike the other days of the week that ran into each other and had nothing to make any of them stand apart. Saturday was the nurse's day off; since the fever had broken, Celeste had had this day to herself.

She was sitting in the armchair near the window where she could see the street below and the park opposite.

'I will be back at four,' said the nurse, tucking a blanket tight round Celeste's legs. 'Here's a bell, ring it if you need anything. The doctor has given strict instructions that you are only to sit up – no trying to walk.'

Celeste nodded and held tight to the doll.

'Shall I put the card on the side for you?' said the nurse.

'No, thank you,' said Celeste again.

The door closed with a sharp click and the nurse's shoes could be heard descending the stairs. Celeste examined the doll. Its hair was the same colour as her own, but the doll's hair was in neat ringlets. It had a hat with a pink rose, a royal blue coat embroidered with gold, and shiny black button boots.

Celeste took the card from under the pillow and studied the crest that had caught her attention. It was a bird inside a crown. On the card was written:

Dear Maria,

I had her specially made to look like you. I hope you approve. I would like you to join me at the palace for tea when you are well enough.

It was signed by the king himself.

Below, the front door closed and, looking out, Celeste saw Madame Sabina being helped into her carriage. Bells could be heard ringing in the broad, tree-lined street as the horse clip-clopped away. A moment later the nurse, too, had left. Celeste watched her adjusting her hat and gloves and crossing the road to the park opposite where she was greeted by a gentleman. The park was full of children tobogganing, their parents wrapped up tight against the weather. A tram came rattling along and stopped to let out more children, warm with excitement, and to take on board those who were defeated by the cold. When she looked again the nurse and the gentleman were gone. There was a sound outside the bedroom door.

'Maria? Is that you?' said Celeste, quietly.

The door opened and Hildegard came in.

'Who are you talking to? The doll?'

Celeste stayed quiet.

Hildegard said, 'Let me see that doll.' And with one tug she snatched it from her.

Celeste slipped the card under her blanket.

'"Maria" doesn't suit her,' said Hildegard. 'Anyway, I can see she was meant for me.'

Celeste was shocked that Hildegard had so rudely snatched the doll from her. But as Hildegard left with the doll and the bell, Celeste realised that more than the doll, more than anything else, she wanted to see Anna.

'If you help me,' she called after Hildegard, 'you can keep the doll. I wouldn't mind.'

'I don't have to do anything for you,' said Hildegard. She was about to close the door when a thought came to her. Mama was always saying what a burden the girl was. If she left of her own free will, Mama would surely be very pleased. 'How exactly would I help you?' she said, coming back into the room.

'I want to go home. If you help me do that then I won't make a fuss and the doll is yours.'

'It's true Mama doesn't want you here,' said Hildegard. 'She's told me many, many times that she's not a charity. All right. But first you write on a piece of paper that I can have the doll.'

Hildegard found a pencil and Celeste retrieved the card from under the blanket. She wrote on the back: 'I give this doll to Miss Petrova in return for her helping me to go home.' She signed it 'Maria'.

Hildegard didn't bother to look at the front of the card. She put it in her pocket.

'You must hurry. Before Mama comes back.'

'What am I to wear?' Celeste asked.

That nearly tripped up Hildegard. She disappeared, taking the doll, and returned a few minutes later with her maid and some clothes.

'Dress her,' commanded Hildegard.

'But Miss Hildegard...' said the maid.

'If I ask you to do something, you do it,' said Hildegard. 'I will be waiting in the hall and you,' she pointed to the maid, 'are to stay up here and send her down when she's dressed. You are not to go to the servants' hall.'

'I will be in terrible trouble for this,' said the maid as she helped Celeste into the clothes.

'I doubt that,' said Celeste.

'You're not well enough to go out,' said the maid.

'I want to go home,' said Celeste. 'I can't stay here. I will never get well if I do.'

The maid sighed. The girl had a point. The house was hung with a damp sadness that no amount of fires could warm.

'Are you sure?' said the maid as Celeste, swaying slightly, stood at the top of the stairs.

'Yes,' said Celeste.

Celeste looked over the banister to see a spiral shell leading down to the marble floor in the hall below. There was something about the house – a shimmer – that was familiar. A shiver went down her spine. *Déjà vu*, that's what it's called, she thought.

Once – when it was, she didn't know – she had run down these stairs, chasing Maria. In her mind's eye she saw pink bows dancing ahead of her as the owner of the ringlets laughed and twisted round and round the stairs, towards a voice that sang.

'Girls, girls...'

There were four floors to the house, not counting the servants' quarters. Celeste held tight to the banister. By the time she had reached the hall, she thought her legs would buckle under her.

Hildegard was waiting. As the clock chimed eleven o'clock she opened the front door, and a blast of icy wind rushed in bringing with it a flurry of snow.

'Go now, before any of the servants come up,' said Hildegard. 'What are you waiting for?'

'I need a coat,' said Celeste. 'I need a scarf. I need a hat.'

Hildegard was in no mood for any delays.

'Just go!'

Celeste didn't move. Hildegard took her by her

thin arms and tried and failed to push her out of the front door. Celeste stood her ground. It was one thing to decide of her own free will to go, quite another to be pushed out. She was furious to be treated so. She was no one's little rat. Her rage was warming, it gave her a burst of energy. Quite suddenly, Hildegard backed away, a look of fear crossing her face.

Celeste became aware of flickers of light sparking across the hall but thought nothing of them. Hildegard ran up the first steps of the staircase and clung to the banister.

Good, thought Celeste, and without waiting to be told she opened a door to a cloakroom and put on the warmest things she found there. Only then did she step outside, closing the front door quietly behind her.

She took a deep breath of fresh air and set off in the direction that Madame's carriage had gone. One step, two steps. She stopped and held onto some railings. One step, two steps and she reached the end of the road and knew she couldn't go any further. She sat down on a step, not a good idea, but all her energy had left her. The day was already falling into darkness.

'What now, Maria?' she said softly.

There was no answer.

CHAPTER 11

Viggo was determined to see his friend, Maria. Since the accident he had given a lot of thought to their last meeting. The more he thought, the more he was sure that whoever it was he had met on the stairs the day of the accident hadn't been Maria.

The only way to be certain was to see her again, but he had visited the house of Madame Sabina Petrova four times and each time he had been turned away.

Viggo lived with his uncle, the head scene painter, Peter Tias, in an apartment not far from the opera house. That Saturday, his uncle had asked him to run some errands. As the first would take Viggo in the same direction as the house, he thought there would be no harm trying once more. He was impatient to be gone.

'Wait, wait,' said his uncle. 'If you are by chance going to knock on Madame Sabina's door, may I suggest you take your toboggan.'

'It will slow me down, Uncle,' said Viggo.

'You knucklehead, take the tram, and it won't. And it will give you the perfect excuse as you will be going to the park opposite.'

'Good idea,' said Viggo.

His toboggan was his favourite possession. He and his uncle had made it together and Viggo had tested it and made changes until it was the fastest toboggan he had ever ridden.

'It's the perfect day for such a sport, wouldn't you say?' said his uncle.

Peter's apartment was jumbled in a magical way. Model ships, flying machines and strange paper dragons hung from the ceiling. The living room was occupied by a large table on which were piles of boxes, tins, and jars of coloured pencils. Miniature furniture from model sets decorated shelves that sagged under the weight of books. Peter refused to have a maid and insisted on looking after Viggo himself.

'What's the use of dusting?' he would say to any tut-tutting visitor. 'It's a fruitless battle. Dust will always win.'

It mattered not a jot what people said. To Peter and Viggo, the apartment was as orderly as a library.

On the table Peter placed two neat packages; one containing enough money for the tram ride, a hot chocolate and a bun, the other the money for the paint supplier.

'Put them somewhere safe,' he said, 'and Viggo, try not to get into trouble.'

'I promise.'

'Here's your scarf,' said Peter. 'And your hat. And you would lose your fingers without your gloves.' He sighed. 'And you would lose your head if it wasn't attached to your neck. Go on – and don't be back too late. Or get too cold.'

Viggo picked up his toboggan and rushed down the stairs, two at a time and in the hall ran straight into Stephan Larsen who worked in the fly tower and was stamping snow off his boots onto the mat.

'What's the hurry?' he said.

'I'm going tobogganing,' said Viggo.

The tram dropped him outside the diva's house. Glancing up at the windows he saw Hildegard looking down at him. He straightened his coat and knocked. The butler opened the door and told him for the fifth time that, on doctor's orders, the patient was not allowed visitors, and closed the door politely.

Viggo crossed the road to the park where he turned and took another look at the house. Then he climbed the slope and, along with many laughing children, hurtled to the bottom faster than any of them. He sat there for a moment and sighed. Just as he'd decided he would set off on his uncle's errands, he saw her. Maria dressed in the same nymph costume that she'd worn when he'd seen her dance at the dress rehearsal.

'Maria, what are you doing here? You'll freeze to death.'

As he started to take off his coat to put round her, a child on a toboggan careered down the slope.

'I'm the fastest of all,' he cried.

He and his toboggan ran straight into Maria. Viggo had the scream in his throat – he could almost taste it – and then he saw that the child had not hit her. It was as if he'd gone straight through her. Snow rose in a mist and settled again. There was Maria, unharmed, holding out her hand to him.

Viggo looked around. Everything was as it should be. No one else seemed to have noticed her despite her costume. Was he imagining her? But she was there, looking at him – waiting for him, of that he was certain. He followed her out of the park and watched in horror as she walked across the road in front of a tram.

This is stupid, thought Viggo. I'm seeing things. I need to eat something. He started to walk away but, on the other side of the road, Maria beckoned him.

He crossed the road when it was safe to go. Maria moved further along the street and stopped, pointing at a bundle of clothes covered in snow.

It suddenly occurred to Viggo that Maria had died after all and this apparition was her ghost.

'Are you dead, Maria?' he asked sadly. 'Are you a ghost?'

The ghost didn't reply but continued to point at the bundle of clothes. Viggo went closer. The bundle moved and panic overcame him. He bent down, brushing snow away, and found a girl looking up at him, her face, though blue with cold, was Maria's face.

He picked her up. She weighed next to nothing.

'Maria...' he said, uncertainly.

'I'm Celeste,' the girl murmured. 'I'm trying to find Anna but I can't walk any more.'

Viggo looked from her to where the ghost still stood.

'Don't take me back to Madame's house,' said Celeste, weakly. 'Please, not there.'

For a moment Viggo had no idea what to do. But then the ghost girl walked into the path of a cab and it seemed as if the horse saw her. It halted and Viggo carried the girl, this stranger who looked like Maria but wasn't Maria, to the cab and called out his address to the driver. The driver ignored him.

'Come on, you stubborn animal,' he shouted at the horse. 'Move!'

The horse stood still while the ghost girl stroked its nose.

Viggo said again where he wanted to go.

'Oh yes, and I'm Father Christmas,' said the driver.

With difficulty, Viggo fumbled in his pocket and took out one of the envelopes that his uncle had given him.

'Here,' he said, 'and there will be more if you go fast.'

Only when Viggo was safe inside the cab did he look for the ghost girl. She was nowhere to be seen. He rubbed Celeste's frozen hands, trying to warm her. 'Can't you go faster?' he shouted to the driver.

Never had a journey felt longer.

'You mustn't fall asleep,' he said to Celeste. 'Talk to me.'

'I... I was given a doll today... by the king. She was so...'

'Yes, Mar... yes, Celeste – she was so... what?'

'Beautiful.'

'What was she like?' he asked, staring out of the window.

It was not far now. Just round the next corner and they would be home.

'Is she your sister?' asked the driver, who had softened.

'Yes, and she's ill.'

'I can see that.' The cab pulled up. 'Hold on,' said the driver and he jumped down from his seat and gathered up Celeste. Viggo held open the door to the building then ducked in front of him and ran up the stairs, shouting as he went.

'Uncle – Uncle Peter, come quickly.'

The doors to all the apartments opened. To Viggo's relief, his uncle's face appeared at the top floor. Stephan Larsen reached Viggo first.

'Viggo, what's happened – is that Maria?' called Peter as Stephan took Celeste from the driver.

'No, it's... I mean, yes, it's Maria,' said Viggo.

'Here,' said the driver, handing Viggo some money. 'You paid me far too much. And you've left your toboggan – I'll get it for you.'

'What have you done?' asked Peter. 'Did you kidnap her?'

'No – I found her in the street.'

'Never,' said Peter.

'She needs a doctor,' said Stephan, lying Celeste on the sofa.

'Dr Marks in Flat Three,' said Peter as he fetched some blankets. 'He'll help. Viggo, you go.'

The doctor came slowly from his meal.

When he saw Celeste, he pulled his napkin from his shirt and said, 'Bring me my bag, Viggo, it's in the hall.'

Viggo ran to do as he was asked.

The three of them waited as the doctor examined Celeste.

At last the doctor said, 'She is fortunate that you found her. Any longer and, well, I don't know. Indeed I don't.'

'She said she was looking for Anna,' said Viggo.

'What do we tell her?' said Peter.

'The truth,' said Stephan.

There was no need to tell her that afternoon for the doctor had given her a sleeping draught.

Viggo went to sit with her. He looked closely at her face and thought the scars were not unlike stars. As he looked, something half-forgotten came to him. Maria, he remembered, had freckles on her skin. Now she had no freckles, only the scars from the glass.

So who was she, this girl who called herself Celeste? And what had happened to Maria?

CHAPTER 12

Hildegard had ordered the maid not to say a word.

'You will lose your job if you do,' she'd said, and had locked her in her room in the attic as soon as Celeste was out of the door.

She hadn't expected her to keep quiet for as long as she had. More surprising was that no one had gone looking for her.

At lunchtime, Cook took a tray of broth up to the patient's room. The sight of the empty chair was almost too much for the poor woman, who dropped the tray, spilling the soup and breaking the bowl.

Hildegard heard the sounds from her own bedroom and smiled. Lunch was served as usual in the dining room and she said nothing except that she wanted seconds of pudding. She ignored the turmoil caused by Celeste's disappearance.

Back in her room, which was full of the gifts that had been meant for Celeste, it was the doll that troubled Hildegard's conscience. Its blue eyes seemed to be watching her. It was then that the bravado of the morning left her along with the daylight. In the gloom of the afternoon she was no longer sure that she had done the right thing. But she remembered all the times she had heard her mama declare she was not running a hospital and ask the doctor when the girl would leave.

Surely, she thought, Mama will be pleased. 'My little mouse,' she would say, 'you've done just what I wanted you to do.'

Hildegard caught sight of her reflection in the mirror. Her face was flushed red with guilt. It was too late, miles too late now to find her. Anyway, she would have caught a tram and gone... gone where? Gone home, thought Hildegard. Her home. That's where she belongs.

She heard the carriage draw up and the front door open to let in her mother. All conversations in the hall floated upwards and quietly Hildegard crept to the top of the stairs.

'Madame Petrova, I am sorry to report that Maria has vanished,' said the butler. 'I was on the verge of calling the police.'

'This is terrible – where would she have gone?'

Hildegard heard her mother say. 'And where is the nurse?'

The nurse had returned from her day off and had found the maid locked in her room, sobbing. Hildegard pressed herself into a doorway as the two went downstairs together.

'Nothing will happen to you,' said the nurse to the maid, 'if you tell the truth.'

The maid told Madame Petrova that she would have told the butler what had happened, but Miss Hildegard had locked her in her room. Hildegard, who had heard every word, was wondering where she could hide when the butler appeared beside her.

'Miss Hildegard, Madame Petrova wishes to see you in the drawing room.'

With every step Hildegard wished more and more that she had not been so foolish. She had a sick feeling in the pit of her stomach. It hadn't occurred to her that perhaps the girl might not reach her home. The only comforting thought was the card that Celeste had written. After all, it made it clear that she had wanted to go home. Hildegard had only been helping her, hadn't she? The drawing room door was open and there was her mama, on the verge of exploding. Hildegard handed her the card, but she didn't look at Celeste's note. She read what was written on the front and whatever it was made her scream with rage. Hildegard knew she was in trouble.

Hildegard couldn't know that Mama's rage had been kindled by lunch with the director of the Paris Opera. He had seen *The Saviour* as soon as the opera house had re-opened and been so impressed that he had commissioned Massini to write an opera based on *The Beauty and the Beast*. But he had dared to tell Madame Sabina Petrova that he was casting a younger soprano in the role of Beauty as he believed her a little too old to sing the part.

That, and now this was more than enough. Her temper, once lost, proved near impossible to retrieve. Madame Sabina felt that her anger was justified. If the girl was not found – or found dead – how would she explain that to His Majesty? The sight of her daughter had the same effect on her as paper heaped on a small fire. For a moment Madame Sabina was calm, and then – how she burned. She slammed the drawing room door and Hildegard didn't manage to say a word, not even 'Sorry', before her mama grabbed her by her ringlets and slapped her this way and that. Hildegard was well used to the occasional slap. Never, though, had she been subjected to such an attack. She started to weep but stopped when she saw it had no effect on her mother. Every word of abuse her mother hurled at her was razor-sharp.

'I never wanted a daughter, a useless, boring child. I should have given you to an orphanage when I had the chance. You will go away, to boarding school… and don't you ever dare call me Mama again.'

Hildegard was numb with the beating, but she didn't know what hurt more – the blows to her body or her mother's cruel words.

Madame Sabina Petrova went to stand by the fireplace with her back to her daughter.

'If the girl is dead, I will hold you responsible for her murder,' she spat, and called for the butler, saying, 'Take her to her room and lock her in.'

In her room, Hildegard examined her bruises. They would heal, but her mother's words had already wormed their way deep into her soul.

For three days Hildegard stayed there, was given bread and water and taken out only to use the bathroom. There were bruises on her face and on her arms but none of them mattered as much as the pain in her heart. Her mother had never wanted her. And if it was discovered that the girl was dead, she wouldn't hesitate to hand Hildegard to the police. Every time the door was opened, Hildegard had one question: had the girl been found? Not once in the four days was the question answered.

On the third day, a maid who Hildegard hadn't seen before came into the room and wordlessly washed and dressed her with none of the care that she was used to. Hildegard asked nervously where she was going. The maid didn't reply.

Mama was waiting for her in the hall.

'She can't come looking like that,' said Madame Sabina. 'Put some greasepaint on her face to hide those marks.'

At last the two of them set off in the carriage. Hildegard still had no idea where they were going, though she had a fearful feeling that she was being sent away.

CHAPTER 13

Celeste stayed in bed three days. She slept. When not asleep she watched a wintry sun that could hardly be bothered to rise. It felt to Celeste that the world was frozen, time was frozen, winter had kidnapped the light. Perhaps this is what it's like in the gutter of time she thought, for it was without doubt a different world from the one she was meant to be in. Here the sun had lost all its power and everyone she loved and cared for was lost in dreams, waiting for spring to come. If it ever happened, they would wake and this world of ice and glass, of forgotten memories and unknown events, would melt away.

She pulled the covers up to her chin so that the cold couldn't get in and let her mind wander back to the cave. The man in the emerald green suit had pointed upwards with his quill and she had looked past the sleepers, past the crystal galleon chandelier to a black ceiling of glacial sea. She tried to remember more and couldn't, though something came to her: a memory of being on a ship. There had been no wind, no sun and outside she could hear the moans of the sea freezing. But it was gone, nothing more than a pinprick of light in the darkness of so much forgotten.

Every morning, before Peter and Viggo went to work, Peter would make sure the stove was well stoked and would leave Celeste with breakfast; a thick slice of black bread spread with home-made jam. She lay on the soft pillows listening as they got ready to leave. She would hear the front door closing, sleepily aware that it was still dark outside and the pale snow looked pink against the morning grey sky. The sun hardly had the strength to shine before it was snuffed out completely.

Dr Marks came regularly to check on her and tell her she was improving and Mrs Marks swore by the healing powers of mittens and her chicken soup, which she brought in a bowl at midday. What Celeste liked best was time on her own, the comfort of the ticking clock in the other room, its cuckoo chirping on the hour; the sounds of carriages and people wafting up from the street below. She made the patchwork quilt into a landscape of houses and fields. Viggo had left her his tin soldiers, which she marched up its hills and down its dales. There were books to read and, when she was tired, she stared out of the window at the snow and waited for Maria. This was when they could be together, talking and trying to remember.

'What did you see in the cave?' asked Celeste.

Maria thought for a moment, '*It was mostly too dark to see anything but once, when the man in the emerald green suit called me back, he lit some of his precious candles so I could see him count his ledgers. And then I saw a blue eye and part of the head of a great white bird – its wings cloaked the cave.*'

'What kind of bird was it?'

'*I think it was an albatross.*'

'Of course,' said Celeste, 'just like the fairy tale. I don't know how I forgot that. Can the great bird speak?'

'*No,*' said Maria.

'How do you know?'

'*That's a good question. I don't know, but I never heard it make any sound. I don't know why it was there or where it went when it wasn't. The man in the emerald green suit muttered to himself while he counted. He said the great white bird is a soul-hunter. He said that when he has written the last word on the last day that's when he will turn over a new leaf and start again. He didn't say when the day is, and I don't know how to find out.'*

'Our parents are there, aren't they?'

'Yes, they're asleep and so is the prince and everyone else who was on board. None of the sleepers knows what's happening. We're the only players. That's what's so frightening.'

'It is, but we have each other,' said Celeste.

On her own one day, Celeste gingerly got out of bed and tried to walk. It was harder than she thought, and her legs were weak. The cold air nibbled at her ankles, for the stove, the fiery beast, had lost its heat. She soon found she couldn't stand unaided and held tight to the back of a chair. From there she set off, a step at a time across the room, only to collapse in a heap. She was trying to get up when she saw Maria's reflection in the mirror.

As she crawled back to her bed, Celeste said, 'I have remembered the three things the man in the emerald green suit asked for. Even though he said that he didn't answer questions he did. He said, "One is the song of a bird who can't sing, two is a play too small for actors, three is a light that blinds the seeing."'

'A song,' said Maria, *'that might be easy. The rest is as hard as carving an elephant from a grain of sand.'*

'I thought it was rice, not sand,' said Celeste. 'Wasn't it a family saying?'

'Anna says it,' said Maria.

'Do you remember anything more about what happened before?' asked Celeste.

'I don't think so,' said Maria. *'But we both seem to know the theatre well. I could dance, that much is true. I loved the lessons, I felt full of energy. It was as if my legs were made of rubber – there was bounce in me. I could jump higher than Camille. That all seems real, unlike the rest – the attic room, the dome. I don't remember them, they feel untrue.'*

'Yes, but I mean before – what do you remember?'

'A ship and the sound of the sea freezing,' said Maria. *'The crew were worried about the weather. It was... I don't know when. I see the edge of it, it glimmers and still I can't pinpoint the time. I see you and you are dressed up. We are...'* She stopped.

'Yes?' said Celeste. 'Go on.'

Maria shook her head.

'This must be the place where the past meets the present,' she said.

'It's impossible – we will never find it if we can't

even remember where we were or what we were doing,' said Celeste.

Maria said suddenly, *'It's important that Hildegard isn't sent away.'*

'Why?'

'Because I heard her sing when I was working for her mother. She has a voice that once you hear you can't forget. More important still is that you stay here in C—, near the opera house. You mustn't leave. I think if you do the game is over.'

And she disappeared. This had been happening more often. She would leave without finishing what she was saying. It was as if someone was pulling her back. Back to where?

'Wait,' said Celeste, 'don't go, please. What do you mean?'

'Celeste, we're home. Are you all right?' came Peter's voice from the hall. Coats and hats were removed and snowy boots stamped.

Viggo came into the room bringing winter with him. He opened the stove door and piled in firewood.

'It's freezing in here,' he said. 'Who were you talking to?'

CHAPTER 14

Madame Sabina hired a private detective to find the girl. He visited every hospital and morgue in the city of C—, and while she was relieved to learn that the girl wasn't in any of them, Madame Sabina was haunted by an image of her buried in the snow and the fear that her frozen body would only be discovered come the spring. She had decided it would be best to send her daughter away now – before any body was discovered.

After making many more enquiries, the detective reported that the girl was alive and staying in the apartment of the opera house's head scene painter, Peter Tias. It was unclear how she had found her way there or why Peter Tias had kept quiet about taking her in. Madame Sabina supposed this scene painter would have to be paid off as an incident like that couldn't be allowed to get into the papers.

And so it was that on a cold November morning, five days after the girl had disappeared, Madame Sabina's carriage pulled up outside Peter's apartment building. She was confident that Mr Tias would be easy to deal with and had sent him a letter that she thought looked official enough to frighten him. It was just a matter of making the arrangements, then she would organise a well-publicised tea with the king. The girl would, of course, be accompanied to the palace by Madame. A week or two later, all being well, she could send her to an orphanage. As for Anna, the young woman suspected of causing the accident in the first place, today she was being examined by two doctors. Madame Sabina had bribed them to agree that a madhouse was the best place for Anna. If she was released, it would, she knew, be difficult to bring her to trial as the evidence against her was weak. And it would be impossible to send the girl to an orphanage until the trial was over and a decent amount of time had passed.

This city, she thought, was built on the bones of the poor and the homeless. It was a pity that the ballet school wouldn't take the girl back but there was no hope of her dancing again.

Madame Sabina told her driver to wait. This wouldn't take long. She stood in the street for a moment and stared up at the tall apartment building. A shiver went through her and she remembered when she had lived in a place like this, with no money and no hope, until... She rearranged her fur muffler, adjusted her hat, brushed off the dust of unwanted memories and rang the bell. In the lobby a baby was crying and in another apartment a dog barked without stopping. Somewhere a door slammed. Madame Sabina Petrova, head held high, climbed four flights of stairs and knocked on Peter's door.

Peter greeted her. The flat was warm and smelled of gingerbread. On a long table in the main room a clean linen cloth had been laid, and a candle lit in honour of the guest. There was a plate of freshly cooked pastries and a jug of steaming coffee. She couldn't help but notice the difference between this cosy apartment and her own cold house. She was about to ask where the girl was when a young man carried her into the room and seated her at the head of the table.

She looked much better than she had done before she'd disappeared, Madame Sabina thought.

'Good,' she said, as if inspecting an animal. 'Take her back to her room. If you don't mind. I prefer to talk to Mr Tias alone.'

She smiled at Celeste.

'No, Stephan, sit down,' said Peter. 'Whatever you have to say, Madame, we would like to hear. Speak, we are all ears.'

The great singer cleared her throat.

'It was a most unfortunate incident,' she said. 'Hildegard has been severely punished.' As she spoke she wished that the girl wasn't sitting there. She noticed the injury to her eye. A fragment of glass had cut the pupil and it reminded her of a child's marble.

'Can you see out of that eye?' she asked.

Celeste nodded and looked at her in a way that Madame Sabina found most unsettling.

To her surprise, the girl said, 'You are here because you want me to return with you so we might have tea with the king.'

Madame Sabina laughed. 'No, no. I want to look after you. I'm very anxious that you see an eye specialist.'

'What would you do with me then? After the eye specialist and tea with the king, I mean?'

If only she was able to speak to Peter alone, thought Madame Sabina, she was sure this matter could be quickly resolved. Tripping on her words, she spoke about educating her, but Celeste had stopped listening. Maria was standing in the doorway and Celeste could hear what she was saying to her.

She became aware of the silence around the table. Peter, Stephan and Madame Sabina were looking at her.

'You agree?' asked Madame Sabina.

Celeste didn't know what she was being asked to agree to.

'I want Anna,' she said. 'The minute she is released, I will go back to your house.'

'No, no!' Viggo suddenly appeared from the kitchen. 'You said you didn't want go back there. You said—'

'I've changed my mind,' said Celeste.

It was not quite what Madame Sabina had planned but it would have to do.

'You need not be concerned about Hildegard,' she said. 'I took her to see an excellent boarding school and she is starting there on Monday.'

'No,' said Celeste. 'She will not be sent to boarding school.'

Peter said, 'My dear child, I don't think you can dictate what happens to Hildegard. She is nothing to do with us.'

'Anna is going to look after us both,' said Celeste. 'Anna will make sure that Hildegard doesn't annoy Madame in any way.'

'The imagination of children,' said Madame Sabina, laughing.

'When you say you'll look after me, you lie. You've found an orphanage that will take me, once you think everyone has forgotten me.'

Madame Sabina looked at this determined young girl, surprised that in all the time she had worked for her she never noticed her until just before the accident.

Stephan stood up and said, 'Celeste is not going to an orphanage, and she isn't going to return to your house unless Anna is released to look after her there.'

Madame Sabina was rarely defeated. Usually she was many steps ahead of her opponents; this time she felt she had missed something vital. Flattery, she thought, wouldn't work in the circumstances, but brutal honesty might.

'It's not for any of you to tell me what to do.'

'Madame, you are wrong,' said Celeste. 'If you want me back, you will do as I ask.'

'How dare you tell me what I will or won't do,' said Madame Sabina. 'After all I've done for you, this is the way you thank me. You should be grateful—'

'I think it's best that you leave, Madame Sabina,' said Peter. 'She has told you what her conditions are.'

He held the door open.

'I have never before been spoken to like this,' said Madame Sabina as she swept out.

'More's the pity,' said Peter when he'd closed the

door behind her. He turned to Celeste. 'What made you say all those things? Does it really matter to you what happens to Hildegard? Why would Anna want to look after her as well as you? Think, child! This is the fever speaking, not you.'

'I don't have a fever,' Celeste said. 'It just has to be that way.'

Peter shook his head. 'I don't understand. I don't know what the girl did to you, but I do know you'd be dead if Viggo hadn't found you. Yet still you want to go back to that house.'

'It doesn't make sense, yet it isn't senseless,' said Celeste.

'What if Anna doesn't agree?' said Stephan.

'She will,' said Celeste. 'I know she will.'

Viggo had said nothing.

After Stephan had carried Celeste back to her bed, Peter said to Viggo, 'You might be able to convince her that it is one thing to have Anna with her again. Quite another to be living at Madame Sabina's house with Hildegard.'

Celeste was relishing the tingling feel of cold sheets and soft pillows, knowing they would soon be conquered with warmth, when Viggo sat down beside her.

'Why have you never asked how I found you – how I brought you here?' he said.

Celeste was taken aback. Why hadn't she thought to ask? It should have been her first question. It would have been Maria's.

'Do you want to know?' said Viggo. Celeste nodded. 'You were covered in snow and at first I thought it was a bundle of clothes left on a step.'

'What made you look?'

'Do you want to think like a grown-up?'

'That's a strange question,' said Celeste. 'What has that to do with you finding a bundle of clothes that was me?'

'Perhaps nothing, perhaps everything,' said Viggo. 'I knew a girl who was identical to you. Her name was Maria. It wasn't Celeste.'

'I know that. I want you to tell them to call me Celeste. I am Celeste.'

'But why do no grown-ups realise it? Maria could dance, you say you can't. Maria hardly spoke – she was a quiet one.'

'Maria is my twin,' said Celeste.

'I've worked that out,' said Viggo. 'But my uncle hasn't and neither has it occurred to any of the other grown-ups. I think adults are blind to the gaps between time. They accept the hours of the day, they see only what they think they should see.'

'How did you find me?' asked Celeste.

'She didn't say her name,' said Viggo. 'She was dressed in the same costume as when she danced at the dress rehearsal and I realised it was Maria. I'm not sure if she is a ghost. I hope she isn't. But she looked very ghost-like to me. Is she dead?'

Celeste looked around. 'If I told you the truth, you wouldn't believe me.'

'I take that as an insult,' Viggo said.

'I don't mean it to be. But what has happened is strange – bizarre.'

'Try to explain.'

'I woke up in the costume basket from a dream about a man in an emerald green suit...'

And Celeste told him all she remembered. When she'd finished, Viggo said, 'This game – the Reckoning – how is it played?'

'I don't know, but three things are needed. In what order I can't tell. One is a song, two is a play, three is a light. Maria thought one was a dance, but it wasn't. The man in the emerald green suit told me that if I wanted to save the sleepers—'

Viggo interrupted her. 'Do you know who the sleepers are?'

'Our mother and father are there. And others...' She stopped.

'Go on – what else did he want?'

'He told Maria she wouldn't have to play the

game if she could guess his name. But she doesn't trust him. He's not like Rumpelstiltskin.'

'How do you know all this?' said Viggo.

'Maria isn't dead, she's not a ghost. She played the game first.'

CHAPTER 15

Anna's return felt to Celeste as if the sun had come out of hiding. Now everything would be all right again – it had to be. It was just a matter of explaining what had happened – that she and Maria had somehow swapped places. Anna would surely remember that she and Maria were identical twins.

On an evening just two days after Madame Sabina had visited them, Stephan brought Anna to the flat. He looked so proud when he entered the room with her that Celeste saw Anna as a bride returning from the church with her groom, rather than a suspect released from police custody.

'I wasn't sure if you would be walking so soon, my little treasure,' Anna said to Celeste, kneeling down to look at her.

Celeste thought she would tell her later that it was Maria who had encouraged her to walk, Maria who had sat on the chair and said, '*Come on, you can do this. One step, two steps...*'

'It hurts,' Celeste had said.

'*At least you can feel pain,*' said Maria, '*which is more than I can.*'

That had made Celeste laugh. She hadn't noticed Peter standing in the doorway, watching her.

'I thought there was someone in here with you when I heard you talking,' he said.

'Only to myself,' said Celeste.

'You must take things slowly.' He'd helped her back to bed. 'Tomorrow Anna will be released.'

The evening of Anna's return had been one of the happiest Celeste could remember. But as her memory didn't seem to go back very far, she didn't know if there were happy memories that she'd forgotten.

Peter and Viggo gave a small party to welcome Anna. There were plates of pickled herring, cured meat and wine. Mrs Marks, the doctor's wife, brought a cinnamon cake. The table was alight with candles and when Anna saw the trouble everyone had gone to her eyes filled with tears.

Later Peter took out his accordion and there was dancing. Celeste had watched until she fell asleep at the table. She had woken up in bed to hear the others deep in conversation. There was no more laughter.

With some difficulty, she climbed out of bed. Her feet were frozen on the bare floor as she listened at the door.

'When did this begin?' she heard Anna say.

'When Viggo found her,' said Peter. 'After she recovered she insisted we call her Celeste. Dr Marks thinks that it's due to the accident that she's confused. The other day I was sure I heard her talking to someone but when I went to look there was just Mar – I mean Celeste – holding onto a chair, trying to walk.'

'An imaginary friend?' said Anna.

'Yes, you could call it that,' said Peter.

'It's most unlike Maria,' said Anna. 'Perhaps the doctor's right – it's to do with the accident.'

'I wouldn't be concerned,' said Stephan. 'Children make up all sorts of stories and fantastic games. I know I did when I was small.'

'Perhaps. But it's out of character.'

'The main question,' said Peter, 'is how do you feel about working for Madame Sabina?'

Celeste was too cold to listen any more. She turned to see Maria sitting on her bed, in her costume from *The Saviour*, her wings shimmering. Celeste sat next to her.

'*It's no good,*' said Maria quietly. '*They'll never believe you.*'

'Viggo does,' said Celeste.

'*One person, a boy not much older than us,*' said Maria. '*It's not a battle won.*'

'I wish I felt stronger,' said Celeste, 'then I'm sure I would be able to convince Anna that you are here with me.'

'*I can't help you because no one can see me – only you and Viggo, if I try very hard. I think Anna has forgotten that there were two of us; she used to say we were mirrors of each other's souls, that we are different and yet we are the same. Mirrors of each other's souls.*'

Celeste lay down, Maria beside her.

'I believe in you,' whispered Celeste, 'with all my heart. I believe that together we can win the Reckoning.'

'*I hope so,*' said Maria, and she faded away.

Next morning, as Viggo opened the door to leave for work he came face to face with a pile of boxes. Below the boxes was a long skirt and boots that curled at the toe. Viggo recognised the boots, not the boxes. They belonged, along with the skirt, to Miss Olsen.

'To what do we owe the honour?' said Peter who was putting on his coat.

Miss Olsen huffed and walked into the apartment followed by a boy weighed down by more boxes of various sizes.

'Has Christmas come early?' said Viggo.

Miss Olsen rested the boxes on the table and straightened her hat.

'Wait on the landing until I call for you,' she told the boy. 'Well,' she said, addressing Viggo and his uncle, 'Don't you have somewhere you need to be?'

'What's all this?' asked Anna, coming into the room, followed slowly by Celeste.

'Madame Sabina expects you to be well turned out when you go to her house tomorrow.'

'And Celeste too?' said Anna.

'I don't know anyone by that name,' said Miss Olsen.

'Well, you do now,' said Anna. 'She used to be called Maria and now, with her new life, she wants a new name. Where's the harm in it?'

'I've never heard such rubbish,' said Miss Olsen, as she unpacked dresses and petticoats from layers of tissue. 'I hope you are not encouraging the child.'

'Is all this for me?' asked Anna.

'Two dresses for day wear,' said Miss Olsen. 'Two pairs of detachable collars and cuffs, two sets of petticoats and bloomers. One coat, one hat, gloves and a hard-wearing pair of boots. One tea dress for special occasions and shoes to match.'

Even though the clothes were not of the best quality and the fabric far too thin for the weather, Celeste saw that Anna was transformed into a governess.

Miss Olsen stepped back to examine her work. Through a mouth full of pins, she said, 'Though I say it myself, you look very smart. Just right for the part. The coat is on the thin side, but I had to work to a tight budget.'

It was Celeste's turn. Her legs were weak, and she stood and stood and longed to sit down. At last Miss Olsen had finished and Celeste went back to her room to rest.

As the wardrobe mistress gathered up everything, Celeste heard her say, 'I still can't explain the difference in the measurements.'

'What are you talking about?' said Anna.

'Measurements,' said Miss Olsen, adjusting her hat again in the mirror. 'I take pride in my measurements, I have an eye for waist, hips and height. I measured Maria when she came to the ballet school and again when she was to be Camille's understudy. I'm never out, not by a millimetre. Yet the costume we made for her didn't fit. It was made for someone taller. Hmm,' she said. 'Perhaps

I measured a ghost.' She paused a moment and then decided that was quite witty. She called to the boy who had been waiting outside and then she and the many boxes were gone.

After lunch Anna stoked the stove and swept and tidied the apartment until it gleamed. She asked Celeste to sort out the end of the table that was heaped high with sketch pads, boxes, small models and designs for sets.

When all the clutter was organised into a neat pile, Anna took off her apron and looked round. 'This is much better, Maria.'

'I'm not Maria,' said Celeste. 'Maria is my twin. Miss Olsen had measured Maria, not me.'

There was a silence between them filled with unspoken words. Then Anna took from her pocket a tiny cut-out Harlequin and placed it in one of Peter's model sets. Celeste picked it up.

'This is mine,' she said.

'Your clothes were returned to me when you left hospital and I found it in your pocket,' said Anna. 'Are you sure it's yours?'

'Yes,' said Celeste. She studied the little figure and a memory flickered across her mind's eye: her toy theatre. It was made out of wood, beautifully painted with an elaborate proscenium arch and a painted red curtain. A play too small for actors, she thought. The man in the emerald green suit had told her that was one of the things he wanted. I could put on a play, not performed by actors, but by cardboard characters. She was so lost in thought that she jumped when Anna said, 'Mr Gautier told me that when the crystal galleon began to fall you were at the edge of the stage. He shouted at you to run – why didn't you?'

'Because everything was so wrong. The chandelier was wrong, you were wrong. You thought I was Maria, that I could dance. You didn't recognise me.'

'Maria… Celeste. This has to stop,' said Anna. 'You are far too old for childish games. I know you are Maria and I will call you Celeste if you insist. But this is foolishness and we won't talk about it again.'

'You are wrong,' said Celeste.

But Anna was no longer listening.

CHAPTER 16

As Viggo had supper with his uncle and Anna that night, he could see Celeste making shadow puppets on the wall in the other room. She hadn't wanted to join them at the table, preferring to stay in bed. Who could blame her? he thought. It must be more than frustrating that the one person who should believe in her and didn't was Anna. If she didn't, then he doubted that any other grown-up would believe him when he told them that Celeste was not Maria.

Viggo had always considered his uncle to be terribly old. But as most children have no concept of how long or how short life is, anyone with white hair and a white beard could fall into the ancient category. Many a child had mistaken Peter for Father Christmas.

As they were finishing the meal there was a knock at the door. Viggo left the table to answer it. Stephan stood there, shaking snow from his jacket.

'I've brought beer and flowers,' he announced.

'Go on, lad,' said Peter to Viggo. 'You needn't help clear up. Sit with Celeste – I think she could do with some company.'

Celeste lay with her face to the wall.

Viggo sat down next to her, saying, 'I know how you feel.'

'How?' asked Celeste. 'How, when everyone knows you are Viggo? No one says you're not Viggo. Everyone thinks I'm Maria and I'm not.'

She turned to look at him, sat up, wiped her eyes and blew her nose defiantly into a handkerchief.

'I do know,' said Viggo, 'because I have no one apart from you who I can talk to about my very good friend, Maria. My friend who knew me well and is now a thing of smoke and shadow.'

'I'm sorry, Viggo, that was a stupid thing to say. Maria is my mirror, her right to my left. Quieter than me. I talk more and listen less. She is stronger than me and has bounce in her legs. And...'

They were quiet for a while before Celeste asked, 'Would you mind me asking – what happened to your parents?'

'That's not a very happy subject. I've...' He stopped. 'I've told Maria,' he continued, 'but I've never told you.'

'You don't have to.'

They could hear laughter and chattering in the next room.

'No, I want to,' said Viggo. 'The story goes that I was found at sea bobbing about in a pirate's chest.'

Celeste laughed. 'No!'

'That's better,' said Viggo.

'No, I don't believe you,' said Celeste.

'Oh dear – you don't believe me. Then the story goes that I was found at sea, bobbing about in a tin bath. Do you believe that?'

'Which one should I believe?' said Celeste.

'Neither. I was born at sea, my father was the captain of a merchant brigand, the *Skylark*. He had sailed to the Indies, where he met and married my mother. They were on their way home with a cargo of cooking oil. It was New Year's Eve. My father had written in the ship's log that the sea had begun to freeze. His last entry was: "On the brink of midnight we find ourselves again at the same point we set off from this morning. At least I can report that the crew are healthy, my darling wife is in good spirits and my son is flourishing. Tomorrow, if there is a fair wind, we should be home."'

'You can remember all that?' said Celeste.

'Yes. I'd had enough of people asking me what I remembered so I thought it would be easiest to remember something solid.'

'I don't think this is going to end well,' said Celeste. 'But go on.'

'No one knows what happened. The *Skylark* never arrived here in C—. And she wasn't the first ship that had gone missing. The ship was found drifting in frozen waters. I was discovered in my parents' cabin. Otherwise, the *Skylark* was abandoned. It was said that when the sailors came aboard, they found the milk in my bottle warm, the stove hot and on the table in the living quarters, a fish pie that was about to be served, the spoon still in it. My father's pipe, my mother's sewing… it was as if they'd been there a moment before and had suddenly vanished.'

'That's so mysterious,' said Celeste.

'Yes, it is. And I think I like best the idea of being found floating in the sea in a pirate's chest.'

'Why such solemn faces?' said Peter, coming in to see how they were doing. 'Come, Celeste, come into the other room. There is hot chocolate and gingerbread.'

He lifted her up, carried her to the sofa, sitting her next to Anna who put her arm round her.

'Tell us a story, Uncle Peter,' said Viggo. 'A ghost story – a really frightening one.'

'We have ladies present,' said his uncle. 'They don't want to be frightened.'

Celeste looked at Viggo and said, 'I already am. Viggo's just told me about his parents.'

'Well, that's not so much a ghost story as the unsolved mystery of the *Skylark*,' said Peter.

Stephan looked up. 'I've heard that story. It's happened to other ships too. Some say that in a stretch of sea that sailors call the Devil's Cauldron, ships have been found abandoned.'

'I suppose the greater mystery,' said Peter, 'is what happened to the *Empress*.'

'What did happen to her?' asked Celeste.

Peter smiled. 'Oh, Celeste,' he said good-humouredly, 'everyone in the city of C— knows that story. It's the reason the galleon chandelier hung in the opera house. But enough of solemn things. I have a cheerful story. Viggo came—'

'Uncle Peter, no – not again,' said Viggo.

'Viggo came to live with me,' continued Peter, 'when he was two years old. I would say, if I'm asked, that I invented him.'

Viggo clapped. 'Bravo, maestro, thank you.'

'I watched this great invention of mine grow and grow. Then when he was seven years old, a woman—'

'A wicked witch with ice shoes,' said Viggo. 'She told Uncle Peter that I had to go to school. I stayed there less than a month.'

'Why?' said Celeste.

'Because I knew something was wrong,' said Peter. 'At school you learn your times tables, your ABC, not, as Viggo told me, the history of the snail.'

'I was a very imaginative little boy,' said Viggo.

'I went to the school to see what they were really doing. There I heard a man shouting loudly. It was a spring day – flowers in the meadows, warm sun. I crept nearer and saw Viggo lined up with twelve other little boys, their hands outstretched, and I saw the schoolmaster with his cane.'

'What did you do?' asked Celeste.

'He took all of us back to the opera house,' said Viggo, laughing. 'And he gave us a lesson – on the history of the snail. And then we each made one.'

Viggo went to fetch a box marked SNAILS. He opened it and put thirteen of the oddest shaped clay snails on the table.

'This was mine,' said Viggo. 'Here – you can have it, Celeste.'

'Thank you,' she said. 'I'll treasure it always.'

'That's the tragedy of children,' said Peter. 'They are taught and brought up by giants – some good, some bad and some thoroughly wicked.'

'Uncle, do your magic trick,' said Viggo. 'Make the snails disappear.'

Anna suddenly stood. She was pale.

Peter had taken out a huge scarf, ready to perform his bit of magic.

'That used to be my trick,' said Anna, quietly. 'I used to be able to make things disappear.'

'I didn't know you could do magic,' said Celeste.

'Neither did I,' said Anna.

CHAPTER 17

Hildegard was surprised when her trunks were unpacked and her new school uniform was taken away.

'Am I not being sent to boarding school?' she asked her maid, who did not reply.

Hildegard went to find her mother. Madame Sabina's bedroom door was open, but Mama was nowhere to be seen.

'Mama,' she called softly, to make sure she wasn't there, and was about to leave when she saw the emerald ring lying in a glass dish on the dressing-table, glinting brightly in the gaslight.

She picked it up and tried it on her middle finger.

'What are you doing?' said a voice and quickly Hildegard hid the ring in her pocket before turning to face her mother's maid.

'You shouldn't be in here, Miss Hildegard,' said the maid.

Later that morning her mother summoned her to her study. The walls were papered deep red, the colour of rage, thought Hildegard. Mama hardly looked up. Hildegard gripped the ring in her pocket, wondering if the maid had said anything about it. She held her breath.

But Mama, as if she were Benevolence herself, said, 'I'm going to give you another chance.'

Whatever the other chance might be, Hildegard thought, it must be cheaper than sending her to boarding school.

'You are to have a governess who will look after you and the girl.'

'The girl? You mean Maria?' said Hildegard. This news was even more horrifying than the thought of being sent away. 'Why? Why her?'

'You know why,' said Madame Sabina, who possessed not one jot of forgiveness towards her daughter. 'And you must now call her Celeste.'

'She will be horrible to me, whatever I call her,' said Hildegard. 'And when the governess knows what I did, they will both be horrible to me.'

'I don't care,' said her mother.

'Send me to boarding school, Mama,' Hildegard pleaded. 'At least there I will be with girls from my own class. Please, Mama.'

'What have I told you? Never call me Mama again.'

It stuck in Hildegard's throat, but she stuttered the words. 'Please, please, Madame Sabina, I would rather go to a boarding school than live with Maria – or Celeste.'

'No. I've decided. And once I've made up my mind, I do not change it,' said Madame Sabina. 'I am not interested in your whining. The wickedness in you must be punished until it withers on the vine. You are very lucky that you weren't arrested for attempted murder.'

'Will you believe me when I tell you that she, the girl, is…' Hildegard hesitated, trying to find the right word and failed, '… she is dangerous.'

Hildegard was annoyed to find there were real tears in her eyes, a lump of rage in her throat, her vision blurred.

'How is she dangerous?' said Madame Sabina.

Hildegard held tight to the ring in her pocket. She was astonished that her mother hadn't missed it. No matter what happened, she wasn't giving it back, not to 'Madame Sabina', never. To her mama, perhaps.

'I'm waiting,' said Madame Sabina.

'It's nothing,' said Hildegard, running her finger over the facets of the emerald.

'Nothing?' repeated Madame Sabina. She looked hard at her daughter's face. 'I don't think so.'

There was a knock on the door.

'The new governess, Madame,' announced the butler as a smartly dressed young woman in a dark green coat entered. Her face was framed by a small fur scarf and she wore a hat with a jaunty feather in it.

Madame Sabina was surprised and for a moment wasn't sure if she was really looking at the woman who'd been arrested for causing the chandelier to fall. She lost any interest in questioning Hildegard.

'Wait outside,' she ordered her, as if she was one of her servants. 'And close the door behind you.'

On a chair in the hall sat Celeste, wearing a pale blue coat and muffler. Her brand-new buttoned boots still had the price tag on them. Her wavy hair was plaited and from where Hildegard stood she could hardly see the scars on her face.

'Hello,' said Celeste.

'Are you going to punish me for what I did?' Hildegard asked. She lowered her voice and hissed, 'I'm not sorry and I'm never going to say sorry. So there.'

Celeste said, 'I don't want your sorrys. I want to thank you, for without your help I would never have found my way to Peter, and Anna wouldn't have been released. She is to be our governess.'

Has the world gone completely mad? thought Hildegard. She was to be left in the charge of a woman who her mother had said often enough should be locked up – if not in jail, then in the madhouse. The study door opened, and Hildegard shrank as Madame Sabina came out with Anna.

'If there is anything you need,' she said to Anna, 'you're to let me know.' Then, noticing Celeste, she added, 'Quite charming.'

She waited for the butler to open the front door. 'Go along with Anna and Celeste, Hildegard,' she said. 'Your trunk is in the carriage.'

Hildegard bit her lip and walked down the steps to the waiting carriage, followed by Celeste and Anna. The front door closed behind them with a silent thud and Hildegard felt like screaming.

In the carriage, Celeste said, 'I won't be horrible and neither will Anna, I promise.'

'Where are we going?' asked Hildegard. The carriage had set off in the direction of the opera house.

'Madame Sabina has rented an apartment for us,' said Anna.

'Why am I to live with you?' said Hildegard. 'She said you were mad. She must hate me to do this.'

Nothing was any better when they arrived at the apartment. It was hideous and cold and, worse still, there were no servants. There was nothing but dust and a dead stove. It was warmer outside.

I know what I'll do, Hildegard thought. I will sell the ring and run away to the Americas.

Anna had already taken off her coat and rolled up her sleeves. 'I'll light the stove and we'll soon be warm.'

'I wish I was dead,' said Hildegard as a mouse scurried across the floor.

She sat and watched as Anna scrubbed and cleaned while Celeste polished.

When it was dark a boy arrived. He was followed by a white-haired man he called Uncle Peter who carried a long roll of scenery that had attached to the other end a young man by the name of Stephan.

Hildegard decided she wouldn't speak to them. She curled up on one of the beds in the other room and fell asleep. When she woke the apartment had been transformed – she was lying in an enchanted forest and she could see that the room next door had become a ballroom. She stood up, amazed. Round a table in the ballroom sat the boy, Celeste, Anna, Stephan and Peter.

'Come, join us,' he said pulling out a chair for her.

'What do you think?' said Celeste.

'Won't you be in trouble for taking the scenery?' asked Hildegard.

'No,' said Peter. 'These are bits that can't be used. We've just pinned them up. In daylight you can see the cracks in the canvas.'

'I'll happily paint them over,' said the boy. 'I'm Viggo, by the way.'

Slowly Hildegard took her seat at the table. No one reproached her for not having helped clean the apartment or asked how she could have left Celeste in the cold. None of those dreaded questions came her way. She picked up her fork. For days her only food had been bread and water. The fish pie tasted delicious.

That evening Hildegard had to admit that she was enjoying herself. Enjoying herself not because of something bought for her, or something given to her but because she was a part of something. Perhaps this was better. She was no one's child. Her fingers felt for the emerald ring and the knowledge that she had it made her smile.

CHAPTER 18

'A constellation of stars,' Anna called them. Celeste thought that her scars, white marks that pinpricked her skin, made her look strange. They covered her body, some clustered together, some further apart. She wondered if there was a pattern to them that was more than random marks.

'You're as pretty as you always were.'

'That was Maria,' said Celeste. 'She is prettier than I am.'

Anna ignored that. 'They will fade, my little treasure – they have already begun to fade.'

'My eye won't,' said Celeste.

To which Anna could say little, except that her eye made her unique. It was, without a doubt, the most striking thing about her. Celeste wasn't convinced. Her right eye looked like a green-grey marble.

'You can see out of it,' said Anna.

'Yes, but sometimes light comes from it.'

'Celeste,' said Anna, 'where do you get these notions?'

Celeste had discovered this just after Anna had told her that she didn't believe that she wasn't Maria. Celeste had gone into her bedroom and closed the door. She felt an intense pain in her right eye and a beam of light crossed the room. It came from within her eye. Quickly she had put her hands over her face and waited until the pain had passed. Ever since the accident her fingers tingled and she felt full of a curious kind of strength.

If only Maria was here to talk to, thought Celeste. Perhaps she could explain what was happening, but since they had moved to this apartment, Maria had only appeared once, on the night they had arrived here. It worried Celeste that she'd not returned. What if they had missed the moment, missed the gutter in time? But if that was the case surely she would have met the man in the emerald green suit again. He would have been blunt, telling her that she'd lost the game, that he'd won the Reckoning.

She knew she had once had a mother and father who had loved her. Their love had left an imprint on her heart that no story could wash away. She didn't believe she'd been left as a baby on the steps of the opera house; that was a lie. At night she would lie awake and push her mind to think further back into the past. It always arrived at the same spot: the toy theatre. Could it be that this was the point at which the past met the present, that this was the gutter in time? But why and when and where had she been when she played with the toy theatre? She was certain that the Harlequin was hers. Her only memory was of being on board a ship; after that, just inky blackness.

'Maria, where are you?' said Celeste. 'I'm incomplete without you – half of who I should be.'

She felt angry. Why had this responsibility fallen on her? It was too much. She couldn't save Mother and Father and the rest of the sleepers if she didn't know what the play was, or where to find the song of a bird who can't sing, or a light that blinds the seeing.

There was a piano in the apartment. It was out of tune, and to while away the long evenings after supper Anna would play and Hildegard would sing. The first time they heard her sing, Celeste and Anna were astounded. Celeste had imagined that Hildegard would have a high voice. It was anything but. Deep, rolling, it was a wave of sound.

'You have a voice, Hildegard,' Anna said. 'To have a voice that stirs the soul is quite something.'

Hildegard herself seemed surprised at the effect her singing had on Celeste and Anna.

'You're making fun of me,' she said. 'Telling me I'm good because you don't think I'm good.'

Anna was stunned. 'Why would I do that?'

'Because Mama thinks that when I sing, I sound like boots marching on gravel. She says I'm out of tune, that it's indecent for a girl to have such a low voice.'

'Then your mama is a nincompoop,' said Celeste.

'If you think that being nice to me is going to make me change my mind about sharing a room with you, then you're very wrong,' said Hildegard.

From the day they'd moved into the apartment, Hildegard had refused to share a bedroom with Celeste.

'It'll only be for a short time,' Anna had said to Celeste as they'd moved Hildegard's bed to her own room. 'She just needs to get used to being with us.'

Hildegard was still sleeping in Anna's room and there was no more talk of changing back.

'Do my scars really make me look so frightening?' Celeste asked Hildegard.

'No,' said Hildegard. 'You don't look frightening – just odd. That eye makes you look a little bit crazy.'

'Then why are you scared of me?'

Hildegard looked at her, amazed. 'You are asking me that? That's a silly question. You know why.'

'No, I don't,' said Celeste.

Hildegard lowered her voice. 'I've seen what you can do.'

'What can I do?' asked Celeste.

'You know,' said Hildegard.

'I really don't,' said Celeste.

'That day in the hall,' said Hildegard, 'when you were angry, and you went to get a hat and coat from the cloakroom. You remember – don't pretend you don't. You lit up – all those pinpricks of light came from you.'

'That's not true,' said Celeste, with a sickening feeling that it was.

'Do you know what the doctor said to my mama?' said Hildegard. 'He said that he didn't think you would live. He said it would take more than a miracle, it would need magic for anyone to survive such an accident. Then when you started to get better, he told Mama it would be at least a year before you'd be able to walk again. Look at you – you're well, you're walking, and light beams from you. That's why I don't want to share a room with you, and you know it.'

One evening while Anna and Celeste were

preparing supper, through the open door Celeste saw Hildegard pick up the snail that Viggo had given her and put it in her pocket. Again Celeste felt a burning pain in her eye. She was furious. How dare Hildegard touch her possessions. She had stolen the doll – the gift from the king – she was not going to have the snail as well.

'Here,' said Anna handing Celeste the knives and forks, 'go and lay the table.'

'What are you doing?' asked Celeste as she went through to the dining room. Hildegard now had her hand on the little Harlequin. 'Give me the snail. I saw you take it.'

Hildegard, hearing Anna busy with pots and pans in the kitchen, knew she was safe.

'If you do anything frightening,' she said, backing away, 'I will scream, and Anna will come rushing in. Then how will you explain yourself?'

Celeste felt her right eye twinge. Without knowing what she was doing she held out her hand and light came from her fingertips, and from every scar. She felt the energy inside her and had no idea what it meant except that it scared her.

Hildegard went a ghastly green and fainted just as Anna came into the room.

'What's happened?' she asked, putting a plate of bacon and roasted potatoes on the table. She bent over Hildegard, loosened her collar and told Celeste to get some water.

'She stole my snail and put it in her pocket,' said Celeste, handing Anna the glass. 'I asked her to give it back, but she wouldn't and then she fainted.'

After that Hildegard stayed well away from Celeste and clung to Anna.

'It's ridiculous,' said Anna to Peter one evening when he was paying a visit. 'I've been woken two nights running by Hildegard's nightmares.'

She didn't doubt that Hildegard was genuinely scared of Celeste but she had no idea why.

'Perhaps it would be best if Celeste stays with us for a while – until Hildegard has settled,' said Peter.

CHAPTER 19

The first time Celeste met Mr Albert Ross, she was outside Madame Sabina's dressing-room, a few days after she'd moved back to Peter's apartment. She had accompanied Anna and Hildegard to the theatre through a snowstorm.

'It's as if we're in a snow globe,' said Hildegard. Celeste was extremely cold and could feel the frozen ground through the soles of her boots. Hildegard's boots were new and her coat was lined in fur. 'I like our apartment much better now there are only two of us,' she added.

She put her arm through Anna's, and Anna absently patted her gloved hand.

'At least you slept, my dear,' said Anna. 'No more nightmares.' Anna saw Madame Sabina's carriage draw up outside the theatre. 'Oh dear,' she said, 'this will never do. We're supposed to be there first.'

For the past week Madame Sabina had insisted that Anna and her two charges were at the theatre first thing every morning. Madame had arranged for their use of a dressing-room, far from her own, where Anna was supposed to give the girls their lessons. Lessons in what, Anna didn't know. She had been given no school books or pencils – that would have been an expense too far for the great soprano. Some days Anna read to the girls but more often than not they were left on their own as Madame Sabina required Anna to perform any essential tasks that flitted moth-like across the diva's mind.

Every morning Hildegard would say, 'Today, Mama will want to see me,' and she had always been disappointed. Every evening Hildegard would return to the apartment downcast. This morning she felt optimistic.

At the stage door, Anna was given a list of items that Madame Sabina wanted picked up from various shops. Among them was Holme's Hats and she felt a flicker of something forgotten. She glanced at the snow, which fell in fast, fat flakes, and with a sigh she set off.

The man at the stage door leaned out of his wooden cubicle. 'Miss Petrova, your mother wants to see you.'

'I was right,' said Hildegard, with the hope of a drowning man seeing a ship on the horizon. She ran up the twisty stairs that led to Madame Sabina's dressing-room. 'What did I tell you?' she said to Celeste who trailed behind her. 'Most probably I will be leaving the apartment today to go back to live with Mama.'

Celeste noted that she hesitated before knocking on the dressing-room door. There was a long pause before she was told to come in. Celeste waited for her in the chilly corridor as people hurried past. She shifted from one foot to the other in an attempt to warm up and it was then she saw a man with a stick.

'Out of my way, out,' he shouted, loudly enough for all to hear.

He wore goggles with leather sides to them. His nose was long and his lips were thin; all his features were well etched but it was the goggles that dominated his face. The glass in them, sea-green in colour, was too thick for Celeste to see his eyes. His old-fashioned frockcoat was cut to fit him, a white cravat at his neck had an emerald pin stuck in it and his waistcoat was of a bright green fabric. On his head he wore a tall top hat.

To Celeste's surprise, he stopped in front of her and said, 'I saw you thinking. You were thinking that there would be a wooden fish in my hat.'

'Why wooden, sir?' said Celeste. 'Why a fish?'

'A good question,' said the man. 'One with meat on its legs.' He lowered his voice. 'Can you see into my top hat then?'

Celeste looked at him again, more carefully.

'No one can see into your hat, sir,' she said.

'A good point. I am Albert Ross.' He held out a mittened hand. 'Glad to make your acquaintance, very glad indeed. And you are the littler dancer, Maria, are you not?'

Celeste hesitated before shaking his hand. She would have said he was oily. It was the only word she could think to describe him.

'I caught another silver fish of your thinking,' said Albert Ross. 'Let me think... that goes with fish – oily fish.' Celeste felt herself go red. She would like this man to go away. 'Come on, play the game. What have I in my hat?'

Play the game. His words worried her. Quickly she glanced around. She didn't like this man, and although he appeared blind, she feared he could see all too well.

'You don't know the answer,' he said.

'No,' said Celeste.

'Go on, make a guess. A guess is free, as free as a wish. A guess might be wrong, a wish never be undone.'

Celeste looked once more at his hat.

'Well,' he said, 'go on, guess.'

'You have a wooden fish in your hat,' said Celeste. She hadn't a clue what such a hat might hold, but as Albert Ross had suggested she saw a wooden fish, she hoped agreeing with him would bring the conversation to a close.

'That was your thought, all your thought. It was your thought that put a wooden fish in my hat. What else is in there?'

'Nothing,' said Celeste.

'What kind of fish is it?' he asked.

'I don't know.'

'Make a guess – salmon? Cod? Trout?'

'Trout,' she said and wondered if it might not be best to knock on Madame Sabina's dressing-room door. Even if the diva was angry it would be better than talking to this fish of a man.

'No,' he said. 'She won't be pleased to see you. So there!' He laughed. 'I caught you thinking, caught that silver fish of thought, did I not?' He took off his hat and opened the crown as if it were a lid. 'See for yourself. Go on.'

Celeste reluctantly put her hand in the hat and pulled out a wooden fish and a tiny book.

'Well? Can you read?' he asked.

'Yes,' said Celeste.

'It was as I thought. Even before I knew there was a tea to be had in the word crumpet.'

'Do you always talk nonsense?'

'Always to anyone who can see what's in my hat,' said the man.

Hearing footsteps, he cocked his head. 'Can't abide clowns,' he said. 'They make comedy tragic.' He took back the wooden fish and said, quietly, 'Keep the book.' Then, almost in a whisper, 'Magic is but a sleight of tongue, a sleight of hand.'

And with that he appeared to walk through the door to Madame Sabina's dressing-room. But Celeste was not sure what she had seen and all of it was vague, as if it had happened long ago. The only anchor she had was in her hand – a tiny book of fairy tales.

'You're in the wrong place if you're here for the auditions,' said a man in a Harlequin costume. 'They're taking place on stage. You'd better hurry – only three more to go and they'll be over, thank goodness.'

With that happy remark the Harlequin disappeared. The dressing-room door opened and Celeste expected Albert Ross to be thrown out. Instead it was Hildegard, a bundle of sobs.

'Come on,' said Celeste, taking her arm. 'We don't want anyone seeing you like this.' She took Hildegard to their dressing-room.

'What happened?'

'You aren't going to do anything weird?'

'No,' said Celeste. 'Please stop saying that.'

'No one can hear us?'

'No,' said Celeste.

'I asked Mama – oh, it's so silly, I shouldn't have asked.'

'Asked what?'

'I asked if we were shipwrecked and she could only save one person, who would she save? She said it was a stupid question.'

Hildegard let out a great sob.

'Which it is,' said Celeste. 'A very stupid question.'

'She said, why would she bother saving anyone but herself?'

'It's a stupid question that only a stupid woman would answer,' said Celeste.

That at least made Hildegard smile. 'She is going to America in the New Year, and she's not taking me. She says I must stay here with Anna.'

'And me,' said Celeste.

As they spoke Celeste saw that Hildegard was fiddling nervously with an emerald ring.

Hildegard put the ring back in her pocket and said, 'You won't do anything horrid if I tell you something? Promise-double-promise-promise to infinity?'

'Whatever that means,' said Celeste.

'It means no matter how angry it might make you feel, you will keep your promise.'

'I don't know,' said Celeste. Hildegard stared at her boots and Celeste felt her heart sink. 'All right, I promise.'

'I told Mama about the light that came from your scars. Now you hate me, don't you?'

Celeste burst out laughing. 'No, but tell me, why do you have in your pocket the emerald ring that you nearly choked on? Did Madame give it to you, or did you steal it?'

'I took it – because I hate my mama. I hate her.'

'If that's so,' said Celeste, 'why don't you do something that will truly upset her? I shouldn't think she's even noticed the emerald ring has gone.'

'She hasn't,' said Hildegard. 'But what can I do? What can anyone do if their mother doesn't think they're worth saving in a shipwreck?'

'Sing,' said Celeste.

CHAPTER 20

Every year the Royal Opera House put on a Christmas pantomime. Usually it was *Mother Goose*, but this year, in honour of the great clown Quigley, the director, Mr Gautier, had decided a new show was required to celebrate his talents. Quigley was one of the most famous clowns of his day and he was to play the Harlequin. Mr Gautier had commissioned Peter Tias to design the scenery and costumes. Massini had written seven beautiful songs, all with memorable tunes.

The auditions had gone well but Mr Gautier hadn't yet found a girl who could play the part of Columbine – and, most importantly, a girl who could sing.

Much against his better judgement he had been forced to ask Madame Sabina if she might consider the part.

Unwisely, he had said, 'Of course, the role will have to be rewritten for an older singer...' and the diva had grabbed a vase and thrown it at him, missing him by a whisker.

Mr Gautier instantly remembered why he never wanted to work with the wretched woman again.

'You expect me – ME – to share the stage with a cheap, fairground clown?' she'd shrieked.

This referred to the fact that every summer Quigley performed to a packed theatre in the park in the city of C—. More people had seen him perform than had ever seen Madame Sabina Petrova.

Mr Gautier had hoped that there might be a nightingale in the wings that morning. He had been bitterly disappointed to find flocks of web-footed ducklings, their pushy mothers all hissing that their little loves were about to turn into swans. The last girl had a voice that a seagull would have been ashamed of and she and her mother left in tears.

The director sat in the auditorium in a sea of red plush velvet. Next to him was Quigley, a long, gangly man who had the gift of carving the air around him into geometric shapes. It was said there wasn't a bone in his body that couldn't bend two ways. He was in his Harlequin costume, as he was every morning, without the mask but wearing the clown's hat.

'Surely,' he said, 'in the whole city of C— there must be at least one child with a voice that doesn't sound like fingernails on a blackboard.'

'I don't know where these children come from,' said Mr Gautier. 'Have any of them even had a singing lesson before they think they can take to the boards?' He called to Massini who was seated at the piano on stage. 'I've had enough. Time is against us. Perhaps we'll have to rethink the songs.'

'No,' said Massini. 'You can't do that to me.'

'I could sing them,' said Quigley.

'Absolutely not!' shouted Massini.

Quigley laughed. 'Come on, Massini. You can't be so serious all the time. This show is supposed to be—'

'Lunch,' said Mr Gautier, gathering up his gloves, hat and coat from the seat next to him. 'We'll meet back here, at… let's say… two.'

'Wait,' came a voice from the wings.

Celeste had been standing there, listening, Hildegard's hand gripped in hers.

'Hildegard can sing,' she called, stepping onto the stage.

'Is that you, Maria?' said Mr Gautier. 'It's good to see you're walking. How do you feel?'

'Much better, thank you. Please, Mr Gautier, will you let her audition?'

'My dear girl, I've had enough for one morning.' Then she heard him say to Quigley, 'Working with the mother is bad enough. I think we'll leave it. Lunch, my old friend.' He patted the clown on the back.

'They don't want anything to do with me,' said Hildegard to Celeste.

The footlights were blinding, and Celeste wasn't sure if the director and the clown had already left the auditorium.

But still she spoke into the darkness. 'Please, Mr Gautier, at least hear her. You won't be disappointed.'

There was no answer but Massini handed Hildegard a song sheet.

'You can read music, can't you?' he said.

'Yes,' said Hildegard.

'Try *Columbine's Lament*,' he said.

Celeste had seen a flash of light as the door at the back of the auditorium was opened and closed. She was about to say there was no point as Mr Gautier and Quigley had left, but Massini sat down at the piano.

'When you're ready, Hildegard,' he said.

Hildegard had been shaking with nerves but stopped the second Massini played the first notes.

Celeste watched her as her voice, hesitant to begin with, took flight. With every breath, Hildegard's confidence grew. She closed her eyes as her voice soared, filling the auditorium with a glorious, rich, velvety sound before it fell with a sob that was at the heart of the song. Her voice rose once more, higher than before, and without a single wrong note the song became hers.

Even those working backstage, who usually took little notice of what was happening out front, stopped to listen. This was a voice with freshness to it, a sound that shivered one's soul. Hildegard was transformed from an awkward girl into a singer who filled the song with so much yearning and emotion that even the composer was moved to tears.

When the last note died there was complete silence in the auditorium. Massini sat at the piano, unable to move. Hildegard opened her eyes, surprised to find herself where she was.

'Bravo!'

'Magnificent!'

Mr Gautier and Quigley shouted from the darkness and started to clap. 'Bravo, Hildegard, my dear girl!' said Mr Gautier. 'What a voice, what a talent. The part is yours. We start rehearsals tomorrow. Can you be here?'

'I don't know,' said Hildegard. 'Mama says I can't sing.'

Massini stood up at the piano and bowed to her. 'You have a voice given to you by the angels,' he said.

Quigley giggled. 'Which is a lot more than can be said for your mama.'

Mr Gautier cleared his throat and tried to control his excitement.

'Can you learn the songs tonight?' he asked.

Hildegard almost dared not speak in case the magic was broken. She nodded.

'Very good,' said Mr Gautier.

Hildegard came off the stage in a daze. 'My feet – are they touching the ground?' she asked Celeste.

'Yes,' said Celeste. 'Well, not quite. You did it – you even made Massini weep.'

'What shall I do now?' said Hildegard. 'What will Anna say? We might all be in terrible trouble.'

'I don't think so,' said Celeste. 'Mr Gautier has given you the part of Columbine – what can your mama do? Anna, I know, will be very proud of you.'

Once they were back in the dressing-room, Hildegard said, almost in a whisper, 'Thank you.'

'I didn't do anything,' said Celeste. 'You did, though.'

Hildegard stared at herself in the mirror.

'I look the same,' she said, 'but inside I don't feel the same. I think I could fly.'

'Try not to,' said Celeste. 'I'm going to find Viggo.'

'No, no, please – you can't leave me,' said Hildegard. 'Shouldn't we wait for Anna together? What if Mama...' She stopped. 'If I have a voice as they – as you – tell me, I promise one thing. I will never be like my mother, never. I think I've been horrid to you and I'm sorry.'

Celeste laughed. 'No, you won't be like her. You'll be like Hildegard.'

CHAPTER 21

Anna knew that it was neither the cold nor the fact that she hadn't eaten that had caused her to pass out in the hat shop. The young man with wire-rimmed glasses who had served her had been kind and had given her a chair and brought out smelling-salts. Anna had recovered, though she had the distinct impression that somehow the shop didn't look as magical as it had done when she had entered. Everything was too organised, the enchanting higgledy-piggledyness of all the various hats was gone. But when she had asked the young man where Mr Holme was, he had looked at her as if she were speaking a language which he didn't understand.

Anna tried to explain.

'He was helping me with the hat – the black one in the window.' She pointed to the window and couldn't see any black hats.

The young man didn't know what to make of Anna.

'I think it's the cold,' he said. 'I've heard it said it can make people see all sorts of things. If you don't mind me saying so, what you're wearing is not appropriate for such weather as we're having.'

Anna looked so pale he sent his assistant to the theatre to get help. He couldn't let her leave the shop in the state she was in.

'Thank you,' she said, rising. 'I'm sorry to have been a nuisance. If you would be kind enough to thank Mr Holme too.'

There was an awkward silence.

'Unfortunately,' said the young man, pushing his glasses up his nose with his index finger, 'no one can thank Mr Holme. My grandfather was one of the many passengers and crew who were lost on board the *Empress*.'

'The *Empress*...' Anna repeated, as if dreaming. 'That's impossible, I was just...' She hesitated. No, she thought, that isn't right. He was here, I was talking to him, he wanted me to have the black hat in the window, told me that I had often looked at it and... 'The *Empress*,' she repeated.

'It happened two years ago,' said the young man. 'I run the shop now for my grandfather. It's foolish, I know, but I still hope that they might all be found.'

Anna held tight to the counter. She felt her legs losing their strength and the young man once more helped her to the chair.

He said, 'We were invited to the theatre with the other bereaved families to see the chandelier being hung in the auditorium. It was terrible about the accident that injured that young girl – they say it's a miracle she survived.'

Anna stood up unsteadily. 'I must go. I need some fresh air.'

Forgetting her parcels, forgetting everything except getting away from the shop, Anna fled. It was still snowing. Her boots disappeared into the fresh fallen snow and her feet instantly lost the heat they'd gained indoors. She took a last look at the shop window. There were many festive hats displayed and not a single black one.

'Anna, Anna!'

She heard her name being called and saw Stephan and Viggo. She felt Stephan's strong arms about her as Viggo ran into the shop where the young man stood holding a number of hat boxes.

'I hope she'll be all right,' he said.

Stephan said to Viggo, 'Go and tell Miss Olsen that Anna has become ill with the cold then come back and meet me at...' Snowflakes landed on his eyelashes as he looked around. '... at that café on the corner.'

Viggo sped off and Stephan picked up Anna's parcels and led her to the café. He found them a table near the stove and rubbed her hands to get some warmth into her fingers.

'I think I'm going mad,' she said.

'No, you're not,' said Stephan. 'It's the cold. You shouldn't have come out in this...'

He saw tears welling in Anna's eyes and stopped. He ordered hot chocolate and the plate of the day.

'I was to pick up a head-piece for Madame Sabina – that's the reason I was in the hat shop. I didn't ring the bell on the counter because old Mr Holme was there. He said, "Good morning, how can I help you?" I had a slip of paper to give him. Then he said, "Are you still thinking about the little black hat in the window?" I was – it being such a simple and elegant hat. "Yes," I said. But as I had only seen it this morning I couldn't think what he meant by his use of the word "still". He took it out for me to try on. It had the prettiest black veil and I had the oddest feeling that I'd tried it on before. Mr Holme moved the mirror on the counter so that I might see myself. He said he was surprised I hadn't yet bought the hat as I'd looked at it so many times. And, as he'd told me before, he would sell it to me for a reasonable price. I was about to say he was mistaken, that it was the first time I'd ever seen the hat, when Mr Holme laughed and said, "The last time, you came in with two little girls." He said he even remembered their names, and that one wanted to dance and the other, the smaller one, said she had just been given a Harlequin by a clown. He said we were off to choose a toy theatre. "They were twins," he said, "the daughters of a great singer."'

Stephan gave Anna a handkerchief. A blast of cold air rushed into the café along with Viggo.

'What have I missed?' he said, sitting down, but seeing the look on Stephan's face and the tears in Anna's eyes, he thought it best to keep quiet.

Anna continued. 'Mr Holme said the most chatty of the two girls was Celeste, who told him that they were going to put on a show for their parents. He said the quiet girl who could dance was called Maria. And then Mr Holme said something so strange that it unsettled me – as so much of what he had said has unsettled me.'

'What did he say?' asked Stephan.

'He said it could all have been so different if they had never left Copenhagen. I felt the room spinning.

I said that there's no city of that name and then I fainted. When I came around the young man told me old Mr Holme had been lost on the *Empress*. Am I mad?'

'No. I think you were dreaming while you were awake,' said Stephan, 'and the dream was brought on by the cold, and your anxiety about Celeste.'

'Anna,' said Viggo, 'do you now believe Celeste when she tells you she isn't Maria?'

Anna paused, then nodded. 'Yes – perhaps. But where is Maria?'

'That's hard to explain,' he said. 'But I see her.'

'You see Maria?' said Anna.

'Yes,' said Viggo. 'Each time I see her, she's become paler. Celeste thinks it means that time is running out for them.'

'I don't understand,' said Anna. She felt that all she knew was slowly becoming unpicked, that time was rewinding itself to be knitted into an altogether different garment.

'Viggo,' said Stephan, 'whatever this mystery is, it will be best if you just come out with it.'

'Maria would tell it much better than me,' said Viggo.

'Maria isn't here, so you must try,' said Stephan.

'All right,' said Viggo. 'Celeste and Maria both

found themselves in the cave of dreams and sleepers. Maria played first.'

'First?' interrupted Anna. 'What do you mean by "first"?'

'Maria was the first to play the game. Celeste took over from her and the man in the emerald green suit didn't notice because he doesn't know Maria has a twin. He calls the second part of the game the Reckoning. If Celeste wins then the sleepers will be returned to their rightful places. But first she has to find three things. Umm – a play too small for actors, a light that blinds the seeing and… and I've forgotten the third. I think it's to find out the name of the man in the emerald green suit.'

'It still makes no sense to me,' said Anna.

To Viggo's surprise, Stephan said, 'I've heard old seafarers' tales of the Reckoning.'

'You have?' said Viggo, ridiculously relieved. Stephan would be able to explain it in a way that a suspicious grown-up might understand.

'The legend goes that there is a great bird,' said Stephan, 'of such immense size that it has the power to hold a ship still with its talons. Its wings are so vast that they smother the mast and sails in darkness and when the great bird takes flight again the crew and passengers are gone, leaving behind the abandoned ship.'

'But what has this great bird to do with the game – the Reckoning? And who is the man in the emerald green suit?' asked Anna.

'Some sailors believe the bird is the soul of a drowned mariner, others that the great white bird rescues a drowning sailor, plucks out his eyes and takes his soul that he may do its bidding,' said Stephan.

'That's a fairy tale,' said Anna. 'I know it well. You have just told it differently. It goes like this: once upon a time there was a great white bird that flew over sea and land searching for souls. When it saw a ship or a city it would come down and in the shape of a man it had the power to snatch you from your bed. But only if you woke and caught the clock at twelve minutes to midnight for that was the time he could make you disappear. But it isn't real. It can't be real.'

'How does the story end?' said Stephan.

'A young girl and her sister outwit the great bird.'

'How?'

'By finding the three impossible things he asks for.' Anna shook her head. 'That's a story, just a...'

'Maria thinks we are in the gutter of time,' said Viggo. 'And that if Celeste can find the moment – as you said, the very hour, the minute when the great bird arrives – then the man in the emerald green suit must let the sleepers go.'

'Has that ever happened?' asked Anna.

'I don't think so,' said Viggo. 'I don't know. The man in the emerald green suit told Celeste that he always wins the Reckoning.'

'Then it's hopeless,' said Anna.

'Only if you believe it to be so,' said Stephan.

CHAPTER 22

'Who are you talking to?' said Hildegard.
'Myself,' said Celeste.

'You're doing that a lot,' said Hildegard. 'Does it mean you are going to light up and be scary?' They had been waiting for Anna in the dressing-room for what Hildegard considered forever, but must only have been an hour or so.

'My tummy is rumbling. I'm hungry. Are you hungry?'

I can hear Maria, thought Celeste, and that is more than enough.

For the first time since she'd begun to play the game, Maria felt there was some hope of winning. They'd both come to realise that they didn't need to be with one another to be able to communicate and for both of them there was great comfort in knowing that the other was there. Maria could talk to Viggo but for that she had to be visible in his presence and it was becoming harder to take on her ghost-like form.

'*When Anna comes back*,' Maria was saying, '*ask her where she's been. But do it when you're alone.*'

Then:

'*If Anna now believes you're not me, she mustn't tell anyone we are twins.*'

And:

'*You must be careful of Albert Ross. He is not to be trusted.*'

'Do you know who he is?' asked Celeste.

'*No, but I keep thinking of the fairy tale.*'

'I wonder if Mama knows about the pantomime yet,' said Hildegard.

Just then Anna burst in carrying an extravagant number of parcels. 'I've been to Mr Holme's hat shop,' she said. She put the parcels on the dressing-table and sat down, dusting snow off her petticoat.

'Do you know,' she said to Celeste, 'I feel more clear-headed than I have done for ages. Have you two had anything to eat? When we get home I'll make you something delicious.'

'Let's leave now,' said Hildegard.

It was Celeste who told Anna about the audition. She sensed the change in Anna, that she was no longer reciting as if from a script.

'Is this true, Hildegard?' Anna said, laughing. 'You have the part of Columbine in the Christmas pantomime?'

Hildegard nodded.

'Why, that's wonderful. Does Madame know?'

'No,' said Hildegard, 'and I don't think we should tell her – not today. You see, I wouldn't have done it if it hadn't been for the shipwreck.'

Anna was puzzled. 'What shipwreck?' she asked and Hildegard explained.

'Madame Sabina should be told straight away about Hildegard's taking the Columbine role,' said Anna. 'Better now than later.'

'*Miss Olsen has told her,*' Maria said to Celeste.

'Madame Sabina has already been told,' said Celeste to Anna.

'Then we should leave the theatre now,' said Hildegard.

Anna gathered up the parcels from the dressing-table. She didn't do it with care but as if they were cannonballs to be fired at the enemy.

Smiling, she said, 'Come on, let's pay a visit to your mama.'

Celeste saw in the way Anna moved that she was the Anna she remembered – strong-minded, determined, no one's servant. She made Celeste feel brave too.

'Our Anna, the old Anna is back,' said Celeste to Maria in her head.

Another memory escaped the iron box of forgetfulness: the hat shop. Anna had looked at a black hat every day for three weeks, taking detours in order to stare again at the hat shop window. And Celeste remembered the kind old gentleman telling Anna that she looked so pretty in the hat. She remembered it was on the day she chose the toy theatre; it was a Christmas present from her parents. It was Christmas.

'*Christmas,*' repeated Maria. '*Of course. It was Christmas and afterwards we were going on the* Empress.'

'Why were we?' said Celeste.

'Why were we what?' said Hildegard.

'Nothing,' said Celeste.

They were nearing Madame Sabina's dressing-room when they heard the tap-tap-tap of a cane.

'Out of my way, out of my way,' said the piano tuner as he passed them.

Celeste pulled up abruptly for she was sure she heard him mutter, 'Time is not your friend.'

'What did he say?' asked Hildegard.

'I don't know,' said Celeste and turned to watch him walk away.

Again, she had a strange feeling that he had disappeared into nothing.

Outside Madame Sabina's door, Hildegard tugged Anna's sleeve. 'Please,' she whispered, 'can't we go home?'

'There's never going to be a good time to do this,' said Anna gently. 'Just a time which is now. Let's slay the dragon.'

Madame Sabina was sitting at her dressing-table, powdering her face. She was in a foul temper. The moment she saw Anna she snapped.

'There you are – at last. Miss Olsen came with some feeble excuse that you had fainted in the hat shop. Are my parcels safe? You didn't drop them? You will have to pay for any damage.'

Anna said nothing but didn't take her eyes off the furious diva. Hildegard clung to Celeste.

'You should have been back hours ago and if you had been doing your job properly this nonsense with Hildegard would have been stopped before it got out of hand. I've told Gautier that he will have to look again for a singer. I will not have my daughter appearing in a pantomime.' Another thought fuelled her fury. 'You should be locked up in a madhouse – I never should have persuaded myself to trust you.'

Celeste listened with a growing sense of rage. How dare she talk to Anna – or to anybody – in such a manner.

'And after all my kindness to you, Maria – Celeste – or whatever you call yourself,' Madame Sabina continued, 'you go behind my back to the director and...'

Anna had still said nothing, nor had she moved. Suddenly she let the carefully wrapped packages fall to the floor. The noise they made was satisfying and the sound of glass breaking came from one of them.

Madame Sabina looked horrified. 'You will pay for that!' she screamed.

Anna replied without raising her voice, 'I have seen how you treat your daughter, how you cast her out, letting her know that she's not important, making her fully aware that you do not care for her. Far from encouraging an extraordinary musical talent, you told her that her voice sounded like gravel, and you have done your best to ruin her confidence. You are not the spirit of this city, you are a cruel, jealous woman.'

'I will take my daughter back immediately,' said Madame Sabina. 'As for you, you witch, you can pack your bags and leave the apartment. You will have nothing more to do with Hildegard.'

Hildegard backed away, but Madame Sabina took hold of her and raised her hand to hit her. Celeste was enraged. She couldn't help it – beams of light shone from her scars, powerful enough to push Madame Sabina across the dressing-room. Then, Celeste calmed herself, and the beams turned to flickers, dimmed and died as Mr Gautier entered the dressing-room. He had heard Madame Sabina's tirade as had most of the theatre and was furious.

'I am sure,' he said, 'the newspapers would be delighted to know exactly how the great diva, Madame Sabina Petrova, punishes her daughter for winning a starring role in the Royal Opera House's Christmas pantomime. You would no longer be hailed as the spirit of the city, would you?'

'Did you see the light that came from the girl?' gasped Madame Sabina.

'No, but I heard every word that came from your lips.'

Celeste wished it hadn't happened, not in front of the diva. Anna hadn't moved; Hildegard was holding her hand and they looked as if they would not be separated, regardless of what Hildegard's mama might demand. Mr Gautier gathered them up and accompanied the three of them to the stage door where he called for a cab.

'Don't worry,' he said to Anna. 'I'll deal with it. Just bring Hildegard to rehearsals tomorrow morning.'

They sat quietly in the cab, lost in their own thoughts. Hildegard found it hard to believe that her own mother could be so jealous of her.

Anna couldn't get out of her mind the image of Celeste disappearing in the brilliant lights that came from her scars. And she feared what Madame Sabina would make of it. She must speak to Celeste later when they were alone.

Inside Celeste's head, Maria was silent.

At the apartment, Anna went to light the fire and make the tea.

'I didn't think Mama would be so very angry,' said Hildegard. 'Did you?'

'Yes, I did,' said Celeste. 'Now, tell me – which of us is more frightening – your mama or me?'

Hildegard burst out laughing and so did Celeste.

CHAPTER 23

Celeste couldn't quite describe how she communicated with Maria, but she did her best to explain it to Anna as they walked to Peter's apartment. They had left Hildegard to learn her part. To their surprise, Madame Sabina had sent a maid and the coal buckets were full and the apartment warm.

'I hear Maria in my head,' said Celeste. 'It isn't me – her voice is very Maria-ish.'

Anna laughed. 'She keeps her words short and sharp.'

'Yes – unlike me,' said Celeste, pulling her muffler tight about her neck.

Anna had to admit they were both dressed poorly for the weather. 'We'll soon be there,' she said, putting her arm round Celeste. 'I'm sorry I didn't believe you. You're not like Maria at all. You might be identical in looks but you are the mirror opposite of each other in personality. I should have known straight away when I saw you eating with your left hand. Maria is right-handed. Tell me about the beams of light.'

'I don't know what to say,' said Celeste. 'It only happens when I'm angry.'

'Is it what scared Hildegard?' asked Anna.

'Yes. She told Madame Sabina and now Madame Sabina has seen it for herself.'

'This is what worries me. I think Madame has sent the maid to spy on us and tell her if it happens again.'

'Which it won't, I promise,' said Celeste.

'It's a good thing that you're staying at Peter's.'

'Madame Sabina looked frightened when she saw the lights,' said Celeste.

'Yes, but before we know it, she will have you on stage, starring as the Living Chandelier.'

They both laughed.

'Bet I can beat you to the corner,' said Celeste.

And still laughing, they ran until they reached the end of the street.

'What else do you remember, apart from the hat shop?' asked Celeste, out of breath.

'I have a vague memory of the ship – the *Empress*. It was Christmas but I didn't take any days off – I imagine I didn't want to.'

'Do you have a family?' said Celeste. 'I expect I used to know that.'

'No, I was brought up in an orphanage,' said Anna. 'Perhaps that's why I believed the story I was told about us – I mean Maria and me – living in poverty. I didn't question it, not until today in the hat shop. Today I feel I'm me again.'

'I think once you start remembering, you remember much more than you think,' said Celeste.

'It appears that I do. It was the 27th of December when we boarded the ship. It was night. It wasn't going to be a long voyage, but you insisted on bringing your Christmas present – a toy theatre. You told me you would have to find a role for the Harlequin because he didn't belong in the play... but after that there's nothing more. It's as if my memory runs out of road and into a fog. I thought I would write it all down when I go home and see if it helps me remember anything else. But I keep thinking about Madame Sabina. There's no bond between her and her daughter at all. I feel sorry for Hildegard.'

'Madame Sabina's horrid,' said Celeste, 'and envious.'

The streets were full of people weighed down with parcels. The shop windows glowed honey-bright and all the goods on offer seemed to have been dusted with magic. They stopped and looked in the window of a toy shop. There was a tin train set complete with rails, a station, a porter and a tunnel. Every time the train went through the tunnel it let out a hoot and a puff of smoke. But it was what was in the middle of the display that had both Celeste and Anna fixed to the spot.

'That's...' Celeste couldn't finish what she was about to say.

It was just like the painted wooden toy theatre that she remembered choosing that Christmas. The scene within the small proscenium arch showed a watery cave painted in greens and blues. A figure of Neptune rose from behind the rocks and before him stood a little girl.

'I don't remember a scene in a cave,' said Celeste.

'Celeste!'

It was Viggo.

'You're late and Uncle Peter sent me to see if Anna is all right. He gave me the right amount of money for a cab.'

'Look,' said Celeste, pointing to the toy theatre.

Viggo peered in the window.

'The theatre? It's beautiful,' he said.

'It's exactly like the one I remember,' said Celeste.

'The one her parents bought for her,' said Anna.

'If I had enough money,' said Celeste, 'I would buy it.'

'Let's go in and have a look at it,' said Viggo.

And before Anna could think of a good enough reason to say no, he had pushed open the shop door and an inviting warmth drew them into the toy shop. It was a kaleidoscope of a place, filled with well-heeled and warmly dressed ladies and gentlemen who could afford expensive presents for their children.

'Could we see the toy theatre, please?' said Viggo to a shop assistant.

'There's only the one,' said the assistant, 'and it's part of our window display. I'm sorry but it's not for sale.' She was about to serve a customer but stopped when she saw Celeste's marbled eye. She stared at the scars on her face, then lowered her voice. 'Forgive me for asking, miss – are you the girl who was injured in the accident at the Royal Opera House?'

Celeste nodded.

'What a brave girl,' she said. 'Wait a moment.'

She went up to a smart-looking gentleman in an embroidered waistcoat. He seemed to be the owner of the shop. For a few minutes they were deep in conversation and occasionally the shop owner glanced in their direction.

'Perhaps we should leave,' said Anna.

But then the shop owner came over to them and, bending down so he was the same height as Celeste, said, 'Would you like to have the toy theatre?'

'Oh, yes, very much,' said Celeste. 'But I don't have any—'

'It will be yours,' he said. 'After all, Christmas is a time for magic.'

He delicately took the theatre from the window, packed it in a box and wrapped it in Christmas paper. Then, to the cheers of the customers and shop assistants, he handed the rather large box to Celeste and said, 'This is a gift from my toy shop to a very courageous young girl. And it's not to be opened until Christmas Eve.'

'Thank you so much, sir,' said Celeste.

Viggo was holding open the door thinking they should leave before the shop owner changed his mind, but he walked out in front of Celeste and Anna, hailed a cab and paid for it.

Celeste found herself with the box on her lap, seated with Anna and Viggo and being driven home with her chilly feet in bags of straw for warmth. Inside her head, she heard Maria's voice.

'A toy theatre is too small for actors.'

'Thank you, Viggo,' Celeste said.

'I didn't do anything,' said Viggo.

'Yes, you did,' said Anna, laughing. 'I would never have had the cheek to do what you did!'

CHAPTER 24

No one talked much as they ate that evening. Peter was unusually serious but Celeste thought little of it. He had a lot of work to do on the pantomime and perhaps he felt he should be at the opera house rather than cooking supper.

'He wants to know what's going on.'

'Should I tell him?' asked Celeste, but Maria didn't answer.

After we've finished supper, Celeste thought, I'll have time to talk to Viggo and Maria alone, and I might even see her.

'It's one thing to talk to you in my head but I would much rather see you in front of me.'

Celeste was lost in these thoughts and was only vaguely aware of the grown-ups. A plum pudding was served with fresh cream, and after they'd eaten it, she asked if she and Viggo might be allowed to leave the table.

To her surprise, Peter said, 'No. I think the time has come for us to be honest with each other. No more secrets behind closed doors. Stephan has told me Anna's story and he has his own far-fetched fairy tale, and I've yet to make up my mind as to what I believe. I'm not a fool – though I may believe in the ancient history of the snail. So please – what is happening here?'

Everyone was quiet. Celeste waited for Maria to speak to her.

'Well?' said Peter.

'*Tell them. Perhaps they can help.*' Celeste was about to start when Maria said, '*First show them what you can do.*'

'No,' said Celeste out loud.

'No?' said Peter. 'You aren't going to explain?'

'I am, yes, I am. I was just... I didn't mean "No."'

'Good. Would you start then?'

'I don't know where to begin.'

'The beginning, I'm told,' said Peter, 'is a good enough place.'

'That's the trouble,' said Celeste. 'You won't believe the beginning and if I start where I think I should, it won't make any sense.'

'Begin where you need to,' said Anna.

Celeste took a deep breath and told them about all that happened with the man in the emerald green suit, about the cave of dreams and the sleepers. She told them about Maria and the gutter of time and how they were sure that as long as the man in the emerald green suit didn't find out they were twins they stood a chance of winning the game that he called the Reckoning.

When she had finished, Peter and Stephan looked very solemn.

'I think,' said Celeste, who had grown used to the sound of her own voice, 'I think I have two of the things the man in the emerald green suit wants.'

'You have?' said Peter.

'Yes. The song of a bird who can't sing.'

'Hildegard can sing like a bird,' said Anna. 'And her mother says she can't.'

'Go on,' said Peter, sounding dubious.

'And the second, a play too small for actors,' said Celeste. 'I think it's the toy theatre I was given in the toy shop. It's far too small for real actors but I can put on a play with cardboard actors.'

Stephan suddenly said, 'I must see that toy theatre.'

'I'm not supposed to open it until Christmas Eve,' said Celeste. But the idea of opening it there and then was thrilling.

'Why, Stephan?' said Peter.

'To see if it's the same.'

'The same as what?' said Anna.

'The one that was found on the *Empress*,' Stephan said, softly.

'How would you know?' asked Anna.

'Because I was the first to board the ship when she was found. And in the saloon was a toy theatre. I would recognise it.'

Carefully, so that it might be wrapped up again, Celeste opened the Christmas present.

'Oh!' said Anna, remembering. 'We did this before. You were so excited and knowing what it was, you begged me to let you open it. I said you could but it would have to be wrapped again and put under the tree.'

'You did,' said Celeste. 'I remember too.'

'*So do I*,' said the voice in her head.

'You rehearsed a play,' said Anna. 'You were going to perform it for your mother and father on—'

'New Year's Eve,' said Celeste.

'That's right,' said Anna. 'You made up the story.'

'*We made it up together*,' said Maria to Celeste.

Peter and Viggo assembled the theatre. There were tiny holders for small candles to go in and wire sticks to hold and move the figures with.

'There,' said Peter as he lit the candles.

'It looks as if it belongs in fairyland,' said Viggo.

'I'm sure it's the very same theatre,' said Stephan. 'It's the one I found two years ago on the *Empress*.'

Anna, Celeste and Viggo turned to look at him.

Stephan started. 'We had set sail for the Americas on a clipper, the *Mary Bell*. It was nearing New Year's Eve when we found ourselves in a stretch of uncharted waters. It had begun to freeze and we longed for a good wind to blow us back on course. Then out of a sea-fret we saw her, the *Empress*. She was flying her flags and making her way under her own sail. But she seemed deserted and there was no answer to our signal. Our captain decided that we would go aboard. It wasn't an easy manoeuvre to go alongside her. It was growing dark when to our surprise every light on the ship went on and as we drew nearer we could hear music. By then many of our sailors were terrified. They believed her to be a ghost ship – we are a superstitious lot and the sea rarely gives back alive what it has taken.

'I was First Mate and, along with one of our deck hands, was the first to board her. Everything I saw that evening was unreal. As I said, in the saloon there was a toy theatre, it was lit up, just like this one. On the floor, in front of it, was a silk shawl. I saw chairs that had been recently sat on and beside them glasses filled with champagne, the bubbles still sparkling. In short everything was as it should have been, except there was no one on board. The deck hand and I didn't know what to make of it. But our job was to secure lines from the *Empress* to the *Mary Bell*, which we did, and we resumed our voyage. That night, only me and the deck hand stayed aboard the *Empress*. About three in the morning we heard the sound of tapping and I went to see what was causing it. The noise grew louder and it sounded like a blind man tapping the walls with a cane to guide himself. The sound stopped in the saloon. I felt my heart in my mouth. The saloon door was shut but then I heard the tap-tap-tapping, coming from inside. When I opened the door there was no one there.

'Next day was New Year's Eve. The *Mary Bell* had been slowed down towing the *Empress*. The deck hand refused to stay aboard her that night and the captain asked if I was willing. It was nearly midnight when the tapping started again. I was on the bridge and I remember I looked at the clock and saw it was twelve minutes to twelve. The sound stopped right outside the door. I shouted, "Who's there? Show yourself," and at that moment a fog descended. I was never to see the *Mary Bell* again.

'When the fog cleared she was gone and the *Empress* was surrounded by small boats. She was towed into the harbour of the city of C—.

'I spent nearly a year in prison pending further enquiries. No one believed my story; no one had any knowledge of a clipper called the *Mary Bell*. I wasn't released until every item on the *Empress* had been accounted for. But I'm guilty of taking one thing from the *Empress*. This was on a writing desk in the saloon.'

Stephan took from his wallet a photograph and put it on the table.

Celeste knelt on a chair to look at it. Anna gasped. It was a studio portrait of Anna with Maria and Celeste, the twins wearing sailor dresses.

'When I found you in the dome of the opera house,' said Stephan, 'I recognised you and thought that perhaps I wasn't alone in the madness. I soon realised you had no memory of the *Empress*. But then, later that day, I was watching from the fly tower just before the chandelier fell. I heard Celeste say what I've thought since the day I arrived in this city – "This is all wrong."'

'When did you pick up the photograph?' asked Celeste. 'Before or after you heard the tapping?'

'Before. When I first went into the saloon.'

'That's good,' said Celeste.

'*That's good*,' said Maria at the same time.

'Where was the *Mary Bell*'s home port?' asked Anna.

'Copenhagen,' said Stephan.

CHAPTER 25

After Stephan had finished his story, silence fell over the gathering. Only the clock could be heard steadily ticking away the minutes.

'Are we all ghosts?' asked Anna.

Peter leaned back in his chair and said, 'From what Celeste said, I understand that the gutter of time is the moment when things could have been different – such as when you take a wrong turn and meet the right person. Let me try to explain it another way. The time when my brother was coming home with his new wife and baby: that moment, before I knew what had happened, was filled with multiple possibilities. If my brother and his family had arrived, Viggo wouldn't be living here with me and everything that has happened since would in some unimaginable way be changed. We are not ghosts, though we may well be puppets of time and perhaps time doesn't work on a straight line.'

Wearily, Anna stood up. 'I don't understand any of it,' she said. 'All I know is I must get back to Hildegard. Goodnight, Peter, and thank you for supper.'

Stephan followed her into the hall where Celeste could see him helping Anna with her coat. There was a cold breeze as they left the apartment and their voices faded down the stairwell. That night she dreamed of the man in the emerald green suit.

Tiny pages from a book waver around him, the words and illustrations floating away. Celeste sees they are from the fairy tale about the great white bird.

'I can't talk for long,' the man says, lighting another set of candles. 'Too much to do. Need to find time, to beat time, to keep time from running out. New Year is fast approaching. Are you any closer to bringing me the three things I want? Do you know my name?'

'Albert Ross,' says Celeste.

The man rubs his hands together and opens the ledger.

'Wrong. Very wrong, missed the point completely.

Jumbled it up, swallowed it whole, without reading the story. Only looked at the pictures.'

'Does that mean I've lost?' Celeste asks. She can't see his face.

'I thought you would be cleverer. Go on – another guess.'

'No. I'll stick with my first guess. I'm sure it's right.'

'As sure as sure as the sandy shoreline?'

Celeste nods, not trusting herself to speak.

'Well, here is a conundrum. Could be, should be. Sorry, it isn't the answer I'm looking for today. Perhaps yesterday it might have been the right answer, but today it's all wrong. Diddly-dum.'

I'm still in the game, Celeste thinks. Otherwise he would've told me.

'Not saying a word. The cat's got your tail. I suppose you think you can win. Most unlikely, near impossible. You have to ask yourself a question. No, make that five questions and roll them into one. Can I be trusted? No, nothing? Then how would I best describe your predicament without using the word "like"?' You are not *like* a rickety boat, no, you are in a rickety boat that has sprung a leak, alas, and two guesses won't mend the hole. If I might agree with what I am about to say, which is no cradlesong, both you and the leak are doomed.'

He opens his desk and takes out a large sand clock. 'Keeps time even underwater,' says the man in the emerald green suit. 'It seems my generosity is about to run into the sands of time. This year is on its last page and soon I can write it off, start again with clean white paper, no mark upon it until I write.'

'What will you write?' says Celeste.

'That you failed, of course. Oh dear, don't look so sad, the children always fail. I can never save them, no matter how hard I try to help them. There. I've told you the truth. It's fruitless. You can never win. Do you still want to go on with the game?'

Celeste nods.

With great speed, the pages that have been floating about gather together and with a twist of his wrist the man hands the book to her. It's the one she'd taken from Albert Ross's hat, the tiny book of fairy tales. She had forgotten all about it.

'No cheating,' he says. 'That would never do.'

And he blew the candles out.

Celeste woke with a start, gasping. It was dark outside and the snow was lightly falling. She climbed out of bed with a sense of dread. Had she given away one of her guesses? Or was it nothing more than a dream? She found her clothes and rummaged in the pocket in which she'd put the tiny book. Taking it out, she saw that all the writing was gone, the pages blank. Celeste sat on the bed and cried. When she'd wiped her eyes, Maria was sitting beside her.

'Have I given away a guess? Have I?' said Celeste.

'*Yes*,' said Maria.

'I told myself it didn't count because I was asleep,' said Celeste.

'*But it does*,' said Maria.

'So we have two guesses left. There is hope.'

In the morning the sun shone and the snow glimmered with different colours.

As she sat in the tram with Peter and Viggo, Celeste thought of the dream.

'You're very quiet this morning,' said Viggo. 'Aren't you feeling well?'

Celeste sighed. 'I'm cold, that's all.'

'Here, have my gloves.'

'No, you keep them.'

Viggo lowered his voice. 'Maria is all right, isn't she?'

'Yes. I saw her last night.'

'Good,' he said.

The tram rattled along and Celeste, on the verge of tears, looked out of the window. At the next stop a group of people, eager to board, shoved and pushed their way into the car. Only one person was left behind on the pavement. Albert Ross, in his frockcoat and his tall top hat, stood quite still, holding his cane. As the tram started off, Celeste turned to catch a last glimpse of him. She was sure she saw him wave to her.

'He makes my blood creep,' said Viggo. 'He talks in riddles.'

'I think he sees more than he lets on,' said Celeste with a shiver.

In her head, she waited to hear what Maria had to say. It was short and sharp.

The man in the emerald green suit lied. He is Albert Ross.

'Mama used to say that I would only be allowed to go in a sleigh if I became less clumsy,' said Hildegard. 'Now look at me – and I'm still a bit clumsy. Would you like to ride with us in Mr Quigley's sleigh? I could ask him. He's very kind. Celeste, you're not listening.'

Hildegard and Anna had arrived at the theatre in style that morning in the clown's horse-drawn sleigh.

'Yes, I am. What did you say?'

'Oh, it doesn't matter. Why did Anna come home so late?'

'Did she?' said Celeste, only vaguely interested.

'Yes. And I have a secret.'

'What is it?'

Hildegard started to hum in a rather irritating manner.

Anna found to her surprise that Hildegard had been given Madame Sabina's dressing-room. Hildegard stood nervously outside.

'It's a mistake,' Hildegard said to Anna. 'I think we should ask Mr Gautier.'

Even when Anna reassured her there had been no mistake, Hildegard insisted Anna and Celeste went in first in case Mama was waiting to pounce on her upstart daughter. The dressing-room was tidy and calm without the chaos of Madame Sabina's many unnecessary possessions. Anna hadn't realised before that there was a piano.

'Perfect,' she said as Hildegard followed them in.

'You can practise here when you're not needed in rehearsals.'

She lifted the lid and ran her fingers up and down the keys. It was out of tune.

'I could stamp my foot and say it must be tuned,' said Hildegard.

'I hope you won't,' said Celeste.

'No, I won't. Mama would.'

Mr Gautier had heard the last part of the conversation as he came in.

'Of course it will be seen to. Now – are you ready?'

'Is this it?' said Hildegard, looking solemn. 'We're going to start rehearsals?'

'Yes, we are,' said Mr Gautier. 'Anna will chaperone you.'

Hildegard took Anna's hand and they disappeared down the corridor.

Celeste supposed she was free to do what she wanted. She went to watch Peter and Viggo at work, but the paint shop was freezing. Then she wandered off to the wardrobe department where Miss Olsen, with a mouthful of pins, was standing at a large table covered in fabric. Celeste waved and walked on. Just before lunch, not knowing what else to do, she returned to the dressing-room.

Albert Ross was there, his top hat resting on the piano and his ear to the keys.

He didn't look up when Celeste entered but he said, 'Have you read the book I gave you?'

'Yes and no,' said Celeste. 'I expect it's the fairy tale that everyone knows – the one about the great white bird.'

Albert Ross laughed. 'Left it too late,' he said, and she noticed three of his teeth were silver-capped. He tapped his front teeth. 'All from dead sailors' chests.'

Suddenly Miss Olsen poked her head round the door. 'Mr Ross,' she said, making Celeste jump. 'I've been looking for you everywhere.' Then seeing Celeste, she added, 'Albert, what have you been doing? Frightening the child witless by the looks of it.'

'Three guesses, one gone. Hard to strike the right note,' said the piano tuner and played A flat.

'What nonsense you speak,' said Miss Olsen. 'Come along, if you're finished here.'

It was then that Celeste heard Miss Olsen say, 'You and those little books.'

'You've never read them,' said Albert Ross.

'How do you know?' said Miss Olsen.

CHAPTER 26

The following morning, Peter found a group of children gathered round a horse-drawn sleigh outside his apartment building.

'Look, Mr Tias,' a young lad shouted.

Peter couldn't help but look. Quigley, in his conical hat and wearing a fur-lined coat over his Harlequin costume, was standing beside one of the most elaborate four-seater sleighs Peter had ever seen. It was painted red and gold, complete with a swan figurehead. Anna was sitting at the front looking awkward. Hildegard was sitting at the back looking thrilled.

'Good morning, Mr Tias,' said the clown.

'Good morning. That is quite a sleigh,' said Peter.

'The only red swan sleigh in the whole of the city of C—,' said Quigley.

Celeste came out of the apartment building, followed by Viggo. Quigley gave a bow.

'Your carriage awaits, my lady. May I help you up?'

Celeste sat next to Hildegard. Quigley saw Viggo watching them, and said, 'Young man, with your uncle's permission, would you like to ride with us? There's plenty of room for you. Move up, ladies.'

Viggo climbed in, looking delighted.

He saluted Peter, and saying 'Farewell' to the children, flicked the reins and off they set.

'I would like to travel in this every day,' said Hildegard.

'That's because you have a warm coat and fur-lined mittens,' said Celeste.

Celeste, looking at Hildegard's rosy cheeks and happy expression, knew she meant well. Hildegard took Celeste's hands in hers to warm her up. 'You are rather chilly,' said Hildegard.

'Did you say Celeste is silly?' said Quigley, over his shoulder.

'No,' giggled Hildegard. 'I said Celeste is chilly.'

Quigley turned to look at his passengers.

'Soon be there,' he said.

Hildegard put her arm round Celeste.

'You know, if you were living with Anna and me at the apartment, I would've given you my other mittens – to keep.'

'Thank you,' said Celeste.

'Really, I would love it if you did come back.'

'It's much better this way,' said Celeste. 'You have Anna to yourself and she can help you learn your lines.'

'You aren't jealous?' said Hildegard. 'And you don't mind terribly staying at Peter's a bit longer?'

'No, not at all. You need Anna at the moment.'

'I'm very lucky to have you for a friend.'

'And I'm lucky too,' said Celeste and she meant it. But what she didn't say was that she had to stay with Viggo and Peter because she and Maria had a play to write.

She had told Peter that she thought that the man in the emerald green suit and Albert Ross were the same person.

'If that is the case, then you need to be doubly careful,' said Peter. 'He hears everything and is very close to Miss Olsen.'

'Why is he so close to Miss Olsen?' Celeste asked. Or rather Maria asked and Celeste spoke her words.

'A good question,' said Peter, 'and one I have no answer to. Perhaps they are both lonely.'

Celeste was thinking this over as the sleigh sped through the snowy streets of the city of C—. It was such an enchanting sight that people smiled and waved as they passed and Hildegard waved back.

'When you have my spare mittens, you'll be able to do this,' she said to Celeste. 'Wave, I mean.'

Anna, sitting up front with Quigley, couldn't hear them, but Hildegard, enjoying the drama of what she was about to say, cupped her hand and whispered, her breath warm in Celeste's ear.

'Don't you want to know my secret? I saw Stephan kiss Anna! You're not to tell.'

'Who could I tell?' said Celeste, puzzled. 'There's no one apart from Viggo and I don't think...' She stopped. She could see Hildegard was deflated.

'I thought it was a good secret,' said Hildegard.

'It's not really a secret,' said Celeste.

'What are you two whispering about?' called Anna.

'Nothing important,' said Celeste.

Having nothing else to do, Celeste stayed in the dressing-room. It was warm, and she curled up on the day-bed and snoozed.

'There you are.' She woke to find Viggo looking down at her. 'Come on,' he said.

'Where are we going?'

'It's a surprise,' he said, taking her hand.

He led her to where Anna was waiting by the stage door.

'Viggo,' Anna said, 'what's this all about? I really shouldn't leave Hildegard.'

Viggo didn't answer but took them out to a waiting cab. Celeste and Anna stopped when they saw it.

'Madame Sabina didn't send it, did she?' asked Anna.

'No,' said Viggo, trying to hide his excitement. 'Hurry, there isn't much time.'

They climbed in and found Quigley the clown sitting in the corner, his chequered suit glimmering in the gloom of the cab.

'We're going shopping,' he said. And seeing Anna on the point of protesting added, 'No buts. "Buts" don't keep you warm. This is my pleasure. Let's say we are dressing you for a part. Anna, you are playing the smart young governess, a lady who knows her mind and is going to protect her young charges from a dragon.'

Celeste and Viggo burst out laughing. 'What part is Celeste going to play?' asked Viggo.

To Celeste's surprise, the clown said, 'She is the light.'

The dress shop, like the hat shop, awoke memories. Celeste and Anna had been there many times. Celeste remembered going with Mother to buy clothes for the voyage. They were to spend New Year on the king's ship... Mother was going to sing for him. Except... except...

'*Except the king never came,*' Maria finished her thought. '*He was ill and his doctors forbade him to leave his bed. The ship sailed with the prince and all his guests – the king wanted everything to carry on, just as if he was there.*'

And those guests are the sleepers, thought Celeste, and again the enormity of what she was trying to do overwhelmed her.

Anna and Celeste were shown to two chairs in front of a slightly raised platform. Quigley and Viggo stood behind them. Before them was a model wearing the latest creation and a small man with mincing hand movements described the gown.

'This dress is made from a wool fabric, printed with flowers and richly trimmed. We have used a goodly volume of material for the flounce. The skirt is almost straight as you can see, and blossoms behind into a mountainous mass of folds. It is lavishly decorated with horizontal panels, finished at the hem with vertical pleating and trimmed with several tucked and ruched bands of the same material.'

'All that in one dress?' said Quigley. 'Does it dance a jig as well?'

Anna said nothing but held tight to Celeste's hand for this was the dress that the girls' mother had bought her especially for the trip on the *Empress*. Next they were shown a sailor dress, modelled by a grumpy-looking young girl. It was made of rich blue velvet and trimmed with a wide red sash that ended in two red pompoms. It was the same costume Celeste and Maria had worn when they were photographed with Anna. Celeste remembered that her sash had been tied to the left and Maria's to the right. She had liked the pompoms – they were the best thing about the outfit.

'We need hats, mittens and stout boots,' said Quigley. 'And,' pointing to Viggo, 'a waistcoat for this young helper of mine.'

'This is all too much,' said Anna.

'That's what I have – too much, and nothing much to spend it on,' said Quigley. 'What is money for if not for burning?'

He took out his wallet, flipped it open and flames jumped from it before he shut it with a snap.

'How do you do that?' asked Viggo.

'You're a clever lad – I bet you can work it out for yourself.'

Anna and Celeste knew that all the clothes that were bought that day they'd once had in a life that was lost to them. The mittens, boots, stockings and petticoats were things they'd owned, and today they were wrapped in tissue, boxed up and tied with ribbon. Brand new.

The cab took Anna and the parcels to the apartment, while Viggo and Celeste returned with Quigley to the opera house. Celeste hurried into the warmth of the theatre.

Hildegard was nowhere to be seen and Celeste eventually found her lurking in the corridor that led to the wardrobe department.

'Where's Anna?' said Hildegard.

'Taking some parcels to the apartment,' said Celeste. 'Mr Quigley took us shopping and...' The look of anguish on Hildegard's face stopped her. 'What's happened?' she asked.

'It's Mama. She's come to take me home – but I don't want to go home any more.'

Just then they heard Madame Sabina on the stairs, shouting.

'Olsen, Olsen – have you seen my daughter?'

'Oh no,' said Hildegard. 'She never usually comes up here. What can I do? Where can I hide?'

Celeste looked around.

'The costume basket,' she said.

She'd spotted it outside Miss Olsen's door. Celeste quickly lifted the lid and both girls climbed into the basket, closing it just as a taffeta skirt swished past them.

CHAPTER 27

'Where is she?' shouted Madame Sabina. 'Where is my daughter, Miss Olsen? Do you know where she is?'

Through the weave of the costume basket, Celeste saw a group of ballerinas stop to watch the diva. She pushed them aside and one nearly tripped over the basket. Miss Olsen sent a seamstress to move it into her workshop.

'You can't leave it there for anyone to fall over,' she snapped.

'It's blooming heavy,' muttered the seamstress as she pushed it into the workshop.

'Olsen!' shrieked Madame Sabina. 'Do you know where Hildegard is?'

'Madame,' said Miss Olsen, 'I believe she is either in rehearsal, or with Anna in her dressing-room.'

'HER dressing-room? Hers?' said Madame

Sabina. 'You mean MY dressing-room. And she's not there. Go and find her – now.'

'No, I'm sorry, Madame. I cut and make costumes. I don't chaperone children. And I am in no way responsible for your daughter.'

From the costume basket, Celeste could see the chubby hand of the diva as it made a violent move. There was a clatter. She had flung to the floor everything that had been on Miss Olsen's worktable.

Celeste hardly dared breathe as a seamstress bent down, inches from her face, and picked everything up.

'Olsen, you are a two-faced witch,' shouted Madame Sabina.

The girls felt a jolt as the seamstress moved the costume basket so part of it was under the high cutting table. Now all they could see through the weave of the basket was the hem of Miss Olsen's skirt and her well-polished, curly-toed boots. Hildegard stuffed a leg of a pantaloon into her mouth to stop her teeth chattering with fear.

'You should be careful how you talk to me, Madame,' said Miss Olsen, who now had the wind of injustice in her sails. 'I know where you came from and what you did. And if ever you dare talk to me like that again, I won't hesitate to speak out. I have been at your beck and call long enough. And I'll tell you this for a barrelful of tar: your daughter has the makings of a great singer – far greater than you.'

The seamstresses began to giggle.

Madame Sabina let out a little scream and flounced from Miss Olsen's workshop. Just when the girls thought they might be able to escape, to their horror they felt a cane tap the side of the basket.

'There you are, Mr Ross,' said Miss Olsen. 'Coffee's ready.' Then she said to her seamstresses, 'You can go for lunch. Don't be back late.'

Celeste and Hildegard heard the sound of the seamstresses' boots disappearing rapidly down the stairs.

'And tell the stage door keeper to send up two porters,' Miss Olsen called after them. 'This costume basket is to go to Mr Quigley.'

There was a silence in the workroom which felt to Celeste as if it went on forever. It was long enough almost to make her think that Miss Olsen and Albert Ross might have left too.

Her tummy tumbled when she heard Albert Ross say, 'You're a kind woman, Miss Olsen. Kind, very kind. A kind of woman is you.'

'More of your gibberish, Mr Ross,' Miss Olsen replied.

'Albert, call me Albert.' There was a tinkle of

china cups and then he said, 'There's no one else here, is there?'

'No, Albert, you saw me send them away.'

'You heard her?' said Albert Ross, 'the so-called Madame Sabina.'

'Yes,' said Miss Olsen. 'The whole opera house could hear her. It was the best performance she's given in a long while. Now, Albert, you were telling me what happened after the ship was wrecked. You never finished your story.'

Celeste heard two plops in a china cup. Sugar lumps, she thought as a spoon stirred vigorously.

'Go on then,' said Miss Olsen.

There was silence then Albert Ross said suddenly, 'There is someone in here.'

'Where?' said Miss Olsen.

'In that basket.'

Celeste and Hildegard buried themselves as much as they could under the pile of clothes. The lid of the costume basket was opened then shut.

'Nothing,' said Miss Olsen. 'Just your imaginings. If you don't start, there will be no time for you to finish, which would be a pity. Is the coffee to your liking?'

Now the girls had a view of Miss Olsen's bloomers and black stockings as she rested her boots on a chair in front of her.

'You told me about the cabin boy you tried to save – what was his name…? Oh, yes, Noah Jepson. What happened next?'

'We were returning, limping, from the battle and made it to these icy waters. A storm did what the cannonball could not and we went down with all hands. That sea, even when the sun has been on it, is only ever the temperature of the devil's blood. Ice cold. One by one the sailors drowned.'

'Wait,' said Miss Olsen. 'Only yesterday you told me it was a passenger ship.'

'It was both and neither, neither and both. And I hear two hearts beating.'

'Drink your coffee, Mr Ross. There's no one here.'

Celeste stifled a gasp when the basket was tapped again.

'You haven't been telling anyone else my stories?' said Albert Ross.

'Don't be daft. I had a father who was a sea captain and he talked much nonsense about the great albatross. He said it was the soul of a dead sailor.'

'Not far wrong. Not far wrong was your father.' Celeste could hear Albert Ross sniffing the air. 'There is someone here.'

'Where, Mr Ross?'

'In that basket.'

'But how do you know?'

'I can hear two hearts beating, beating too fast.'

'I want to know how your story ends. What happened to the lad you were trying to save?'

'The cabin boy was only a little chap with wonky legs. I did my best to keep him alive, finding bits of the boat for him to hold onto. Noah Jepson. Written on my heart, that name. He couldn't swim. He kept asking me if Neptune was a kind man, because he was certainly heading that way.'

'Did the boy live?'

'I gave up my soul, my sight, to save him and still he drowned. He didn't even try to save himself.'

'No, no,' said Miss Olsen, 'that's fairy tale nonsense. So the boy died?'

'Yes, he died.'

'Where does the albatross come into your story?'

'I told you that. You weren't listening. The boy was lost and I was about to follow him to my watery grave, when a great albatross came swooping down, pecked out my eyes and took my soul.'

'Rubbish! No bird could do that. Fairy tales are for children – I'm far too old for such silliness.'

'So I came home to my wife and daughter,' said Albert Ross.

'Now that's more the ticket,' said Miss Olsen,

getting to her feet. 'I'll put a drop of rum in your coffee – to warm the cockles of your heart.'

'Some would say I haven't got one,' said Albert Ross. 'I came home to my wife and daughter a blind and broken man and learned to be a piano tuner. But my wife wanted more. She wasn't a good woman, my wife. She left me. I followed her. I know her.'

'Do I know her?' said Miss Olsen, sitting down again. 'Who is she?'

Albert Ross laughed.

Celeste's legs were stiff and Hildegard had cramp in her foot. They were both wondering how much longer the torture would go on for when they heard the porter's voice.

'Miss Olsen,' he said, 'we've been sent to collect the costume basket for Mr Quigley.'

'Sometimes, Miss Olsen', said Albert Ross, 'it's best you leave the story be.'

'The basket for Mr Quigley, Miss Olsen?' repeated the porter.

Suddenly Miss Olsen's boots moved with speed.

'Oh dear, I nearly forgot. I mended his jacket.'

She opened the lid of the basket again. Hildegard could see her quite clearly and if Miss Olsen had happened to glance down she would have seen Hildegard's terrified face staring up at her. But instead she dropped the jacket into the basket, closed the lid and fastened it. The girls felt themselves moving.

Before Miss Olsen's voice faded away entirely, they heard her say, 'I have some very nice fabric for a new waistcoat for you, Mr Ross. Come on, finish the story.'

The porters struggled down the stairs to the clown's dressing-room, Celeste and Hildegard trying not to fall on top of one another.

They heard the porter knock on the door.

'We never close,' called the clown. 'Come on in, it's open house.'

The porter pushed the costume basket inside.

'What have you got in there, Mr Quigley?' wheezed the porter. 'The crown jewels?'

Celeste put her hand over Hildegard's mouth to stop her giving their hiding place away. But knowing the basket to be fastened shut was too much for her. The second she heard the door close, she screamed.

'Let me out, ple-e-e-ase, Mr Quigley. Please let me out.'

Quigley opened the basket and burst out laughing when he saw the girls.

'You two could work this up as a comedy act – the audience would love it.'

He laughed again at their solemn faces. 'Come on, girls, worse things happen at sea.'

Quigley escorted Celeste and a very shaken Hildegard back to what once had been Madame Sabina's dressing-room. Anna had been anxiously looking for them.

'They're all right,' said Quigley. 'Just a little crumpled after hiding in my costume basket.'

Anna gathered up the girls.

'I'm so sorry I wasn't here – it won't happen again,' she said. 'I'll stay with you all the time, I promise.'

It was too much for Hildegard. She burst into tears which became sobs, her whole body shaking.

She managed to say, 'Mama isn't here, is she?'

'No,' said Anna. 'Mr Gautier took her home. He assured me that she promised not to come to the theatre again, not while the pantomime is on.'

'Mama's always nice to other people. Until she knows their secrets, then she turns on them.' Hildegard blew her nose and said, 'I've just thought of something cheerful.'

'What?' said Anna and Celeste together.

'Celeste didn't light up when we were in the costume basket. That would have been terrible. If she had, we would have been discovered straight away.'

Anna dried Hildegard's tears and she lay on the day-bed and fell asleep.

Celeste said very quietly to Anna, 'Albert Ross was once married and had a daughter.'

'Is that important?' asked Anna.

'I don't know. We heard him tell Miss Olsen that his wife wasn't a good woman. Miss Olsen asked if his wife was someone she knew. He didn't answer but I wondered if he was talking about Madame Sabina.'

'That's a ridiculous notion,' said Anna.

'Is it?' said Celeste. 'Do you remember I told you about the box of chocolates? When Madame Sabina saw who it was from, she threw everyone out of her dressing-room, including Hildegard, who had nearly choked on an emerald ring. On the card was written, *To Hildegard from Papa*.'

An opera house is a place of gossip, a small world where minor incidents become major events. The seamstresses made sure that Madame Sabina's performance in the wardrobe department that afternoon was the subject of most conversations in the opera house that evening.

CHAPTER 28

After that, the days had a pattern to them of sorts. Celeste would go to the opera house with Peter and Viggo and spend the day watching the rehearsals. Hildegard and Celeste often had lunchtime to themselves and sometimes Celeste would take Hildegard up to the dome.

'Why?' said Hildegard, when they first climbed the stairs.

'To look out over the city. And for you to hear your voice.'

Hildegard had not been much impressed. The place, she thought, was cold and miserable.

'How could you possibly live up here?' she'd said. 'It's horrid.'

'We didn't have any choice,' said Celeste. 'Now – sing.'

Hildegard did and her voice, which in the

rehearsal room sounded muffled, took full flight in the cavernous dome.

Hearing her was a great comfort to Celeste. What she couldn't tell anyone – not Hildegard, nor really Anna – was that Maria had gone. Celeste no longer heard her in her head and it made Celeste feel that it mattered little if she had any of the three things the man in the emerald green suit wanted if she didn't have Maria. Not for the first time she felt panic. Time was running out and Maria's absence was a void filled with nothing but heartache.

'Are you unhappy because you don't live with us?' asked Hildegard.

'No. Why?'

'It's just that Anna looks worried, and Stephan doesn't come to see us because she thinks the maid Mama sent will tell her about him. But I've decided to be cheerful. Being cheerful is a good thing, isn't it?' She thought for a moment and then said, 'But I would be very miserable indeed if my mama came to the theatre again. Perhaps happiness is stepping stones across the river and sometimes you get your feet wet finding them.'

Celeste laughed.

'I did ask Anna about Stephan,' said Hildegard. 'I wasn't sure how to say it so I just asked if she'd seen him and she said, "No," as if she were sweeping broken china under the carpet and hoping no one would notice. Then she said that thing that a grown-up always says when she wants there to be a big distance between you, "You wouldn't understand".'

Maria's vanishing had started slowly. The best part of the day for Celeste had been before Peter and Viggo came home, when she let herself into Peter's apartment. It was then that she'd had time on her own with Maria in her head. The moment she entered the hall, Maria was talking to her. As Celeste stoked the fire and laid the table for supper, the conversation continued. Maria thought they should concentrate on the play and as the days passed Celeste refused to acknowledge that Maria was hardly speaking at all. It had been Celeste who'd suggested that they stay true to the scenery that came with the toy theatre. Act One was a palace. Act Two was a street scene where one of the houses was on fire. The flames were painted in bright reds, yellows and oranges. Act Three was a scene on board a ship. And the finale was a green, watery cave, the scene that had been displayed in the window of the toy shop. It had been Maria's last and final suggestion that the play should in some way be about the man in the emerald green suit.

The time came when Celeste knew Maria had gone. There was no voice in her head, Maria had vanished altogether.

'Don't leave me,' Celeste said to the empty room. 'Maria, I can't do this on my own – I need you.'

Silence.

That was how Viggo had found her when he and Peter had returned home that evening: standing in the middle of the apartment in the dark.

'What's the matter?' asked Viggo.

'She's gone,' said Celeste. 'Maria's gone.' Her eyes filled with tears that she had no power to stop. 'It's hopeless – all hopeless.'

They tried to comfort her, but Peter felt awkward and didn't know what to say. If he was honest with himself, he wasn't convinced by the story Celeste had told about the cave of dreams and the sleepers and about Maria. Its only weight was Stephan's account of his own experience. That alone made Peter think there may be something in it. After all, many a sailor had brought back a strange tale from the sea.

Viggo said, 'Why don't you go and make supper, Uncle.'

'Good idea,' said Peter, disappearing into the kitchen.

Viggo gave Celeste his handkerchief.

'There's a huge empty space that Maria once filled,' Celeste said. 'A noisy silence is all I hear in my head.'

Viggo took Celeste's hand.

'Maria said to me that her strength was in you now,' he said. 'The trouble was that you didn't know it. But that's why you recovered so fast – you let her in. I don't believe she's left you. You can't hear her, you can't see her, but you know that doesn't mean she's not here. You have to believe that.'

'You're a good friend,' said Celeste.

'And I'm fond of you,' said Viggo. 'But Maria is still my favourite.' This made Celeste smile.

'It's hard to explain what I feel,' she said. 'I don't think anyone who isn't a twin would completely understand – but you're doing well.'

When they sat down to eat, Celeste watched the candles' reflection in the window. She longed to glimpse Maria there, but she didn't.

'I've been thinking,' said Peter. 'We should have a party, after the pantomime has opened on Christmas Eve.'

'Most people will go home to their families,' said Viggo.

'If they have families,' said Peter. 'Christmas is often a very hard time for people who don't. We'll have a party here. I thought I would invite Anna and Hildegard, and of course, Stephan. Mr Gautier and Quigley, if they'd like to come. And Massini – he always strikes me as a lonely one.' He stopped. 'And I thought that perhaps we should ask Miss Olsen and Albert Ross.'

Celeste had been lost in her thoughts but at the mention of Albert Ross, she looked up.

'Are you sure?' she said.

'Yes, said Peter. 'It's better to face the devil and ask him to dance than the other way round. What do they say about friends and foes? I have made some invitations and tomorrow, Celeste, I would like you to hand them out.' Then before Celeste could say anything else, he clapped his hands together. 'I know what we're going to do this evening – we're going to see a run-through of your play.'

'Oh, yes!' said Viggo.

Peter carried the theatre into the main room. When he lifted it up high to put it on the table, Viggo bent under it to clear a space.

'Uncle, stop,' said Viggo. 'The theatre has writing on the bottom. I've never seen it before.'

Celeste crouched to look.

'What does it say?' said Peter.

Viggo read it. *'To our darling girls, with love from your mother and father. Christmas 18—.* And it says underneath that it was made in Copenhagen. This is proof that there is a city called Copenhagen, just as Stephan said. That was the *Mary Bell*'s home port.'

Peter put down the theatre.

Celeste was filled with hope. This was undeniable proof that she and Maria had a mother, a father, and that they had been together for Christmas in Copenhagen. She may have no memory of it but now no one could doubt her or Stephan.

Her thoughts were still dancing with joy when Viggo said, 'Stephan heard from some sailor friends that the *Empress* was towed into the harbour today. She has been expensively refitted and the owner is looking for a crew.'

'The *Empress*?' said Anna. 'Is she going on a voyage? Why would anyone want to take her out to sea?'

'I wish I could see her,' said Celeste, quietly.

'Come on, Madame Director,' said Peter. 'Forget about the *Empress* for the time being and let's see this play of yours.'

Celeste couldn't forget. Perhaps the pieces of this impossible jigsaw were finally coming together. Perhaps, just perhaps, as in the fairy tale of the great white bird, she could win the game.

Peter pulled up the chairs and blew out the

candles so that the stage was lit by the flickering footlights of the wood and cardboard theatre.

'It may be a good sign that the *Empress* is in the harbour,' said Celeste to Viggo.

'The play, Celeste, the play,' said Peter. 'Are you ready?'

'Yes – cue drum.'

Viggo banged a saucepan by way of a drum and the little painted curtain shimmered as it rose to reveal the palace scene. The Harlequin made his entrance.

'Bravo,' shouted Peter when it was over. He stood and clapped his hands.

Viggo said, 'All you need is for Hildegard to sing.'

'It was wonderful – very moving indeed,' said Peter. 'If only every production went as well as this.'

Celeste sighed. 'But is it enough to win the Reckoning?'

'Celeste,' said Peter, 'you are clever and brave. And what I've learned from life is that only brave hearts win.'

CHAPTER 29

By lunchtime Celeste had delivered all Peter's invitations except two: Miss Olsen's and Albert Ross's.

Reluctantly she climbed the stairs to the wardrobe department. The young seamstresses gleefully looked up from their work.

'What are you doing here?' said Miss Olsen, not glancing away from the cutting table. 'This is not the place for you. Please leave.'

'I have an invitation for you,' said Celeste.

She held out the envelope.

Miss Olsen sniffed. 'Who is it from?'

'Peter,' said Celeste.

Miss Olsen sniffed again as if by smelling the envelope she would know what was inside.

'You mean Mr Tias. There's no need to stand there. Now you've delivered it you can go.'

Celeste ran back down the stairs, bumping into Albert Ross as he came up.

'There you are, there you are,' he said. 'I knew it would be you, skittering around, trying to dance your way to the bottom. You're not going to ask me what I have in my hat?'

'Not today,' said Celeste. 'I have an invitation for you.' She handed it to him and was about to leave, only to feel his hand grasp her dress.

'Now, how can I read it, tell me? How can I know what is in this envelope unless you help me?'

Celeste freed herself and moved away from him. She took back the envelope, opened it and gave him the card.

'What does it say?' asked Albert Ross.

'Mr Tias is having a Christmas party at his apartment.'

'What's that to me?'

'He has invited you to the party.'

'I don't like parties,' he said. 'Why should I go?'

'Because parties are fun?' she suggested.

'No, no, they're not. They are full of people I don't know and who have never said a word to me, and I am expected to talk to them. That's not fun. So I'm not going.'

He put his mittened hands up to his little round goggles and adjusted them.

'I'll keep the invitation, though,' he said, 'and the envelope. You never know when it won't come in useful.'

Miss Olsen appeared at the top of the stairs.

'Albert,' she called down, 'I have coffee on for you. You, girl, be gone. You're not wanted up here.'

Viggo found Celeste as she was about to go back to the dressing-room.

'I have the afternoon off,' he said. 'And something to show you.'

He took her hand and led her to one of the empty dressing-rooms. Hanging on a hook was a boy's suit of clothes – hat and muffler, and on the floor a scruffy pair of boots. For a moment it reminded Celeste of the sleepers in the cave of dreamers.

'Put them on,' said Viggo. 'Don't take too long.' He could see that Celeste was on the point of asking questions and added, quickly, 'Do you want to see the *Empress* or not?'

Unnoticed, they slipped out of the auditorium through one of the exit doors into the empty street. It had been a sunny morning with no snow but by the time they'd arrived at the harbour it was getting dark.

'Do I look like a boy?' said Celeste.

Viggo studied her.

'Not completely,' he said honestly. 'Pull your hat down over your eyes, bring your muffler up past your chin. Whatever you do don't speak. Let me do the talking. Your voice would give you away.'

Celeste felt a tingle of excitement. This was an adventure. She walked purposefully beside Viggo.

'Is this dangerous?' she asked.

'I suppose it is,' said Viggo, kicking a pile of snow and feeling himself to be as grown-up as ever he would be.

The harbour was not far from the theatre nor hard to find for the masts of the ships rose above the houses and pierced the sky. Steamboats, cargo and passenger ships lined up, waiting hungrily for tides and anchors to set them free. The jangle and jingle of the rigging sang with the longing for adventure and above the hurly-burly was the scream of seagulls. Celeste breathed in the smell of tar, of wooden timbers soaked in seawater. The harbour was busy with passengers arriving and leaving, porters unloading and loading ships, and amid the bustle no one paid any attention to two young lads. Viggo asked several people where the *Empress* was.

A porter said, 'Out of bounds for the likes of you. Now skedaddle.'

It wasn't easy, but they found her. Compared to the others, she was a small ship of an elegant design, and at the same time Celeste thought she looked a vulnerable vessel. They waited, hidden behind some crates, watching the comings and goings. The gangplank was down but as far as they could see, there was no one aboard the ship. She looked quite deserted.

'Is she how you remember her?' asked Viggo.

'I don't know,' said Celeste. 'It was night when we went on board and I never really saw her from the outside. If I could see inside I think I would know if this was the ship we were on.'

'That's too risky,' said Viggo. 'You'll just have to... Celeste... no!'

Celeste had moved swiftly and was approaching the gangplank.

Viggo could think of some very rude words but as he joined her, he just said, 'Be careful.'

'I only want to see inside the saloon,' said Celeste. 'Then I would know for sure. I'll only be a minute and then I'll be out again.'

It had grown dark and there were hardly any lights on the ship. Once on board Celeste felt her heart beating fast. Those were the steps that led down to the saloon – she remembered them. She could see very little and had to feel her way. There was something about the ship that was eerie, she thought. She looked in the saloon. It was hard to make it out in the gloom but occasionally the ship moved and a light of sorts shone weakly through a porthole.

Yes, thought Celeste, this is the ship. I remember the saloon, and the table was here... She crept to where it had been put so that her toy theatre could be placed on it. She had almost forgotten the danger she was in and too late felt someone grab her.

'Well, what've we got here?'

She couldn't see the sailor's face but his clothes were rough and his manner rougher. 'I'm taking you to the First Mate. Do you know what he does with little stowaways like you?'

Celeste said nothing but her mind was racing. Where was Viggo? Had he been caught too?

The sailor marched her to the upper deck and then said, 'On second thoughts, I don't think I'll bother the First Mate. I'll throw you overboard. Who'd miss you? No one. Just another accident, happens all the time.'

Celeste felt a warm feeling of fury. How dare this brutal man threaten her? As always, she was unaware of the effect of her anger. Light poured from her scars and the sailor jumped back, a look of fear etched on his face.

'What kind of demon are you?' he said. He took a pistol from his belt and aimed it at her. 'If you're a ghost this won't hurt you. If not, you'll be dead.'

'Leave her be!'

Viggo could see the pistol as he jumped out of his hiding place. He ran to Celeste, saw a flash of fire and heard the bang. He stumbled, pulling Celeste down with him. All the light in her had gone out. Viggo felt a sharp pain in his arm.

'What's going on, Andersen?' said a voice.

'We've got snoopers. I'm dealing with it.'

To Viggo's amazement – and relief – it was Stephan Larsen who was kneeling beside them, holding a lantern.

'They're children,' he snapped. He brought the lantern closer and saw that the faces were those of Viggo and Celeste. Viggo was obviously in pain and Celeste's eyes were closed.

'What have you done?' he shouted. 'Don't stand there, man, get help.'

'I didn't mean to shoot anyone,' said Andersen. 'But it wasn't human, what the lad did. There was light beaming from him. I've seen many things but I've never seen that before. Honest, Mr Larsen, I didn't mean to kill him.'

CHAPTER 30

Peter arrived out of breath at his apartment to find the door open and half the occupants of the building crowded on the landing.

'Terrible,' said one woman.

'It looked bad,' said another neighbour. 'There's blood on the stairs.'

Peter had received a message at the opera house saying that he should go home straight away as there had been an accident. That was all he knew. Fumbling with his key, he let himself in.

'Viggo?' he called as he pulled off his outer coat, his hat and boots. Anna appeared carrying a basin of bloody water. 'Where's Viggo?' said Peter. 'What's happened?'

'He's hurt but he'll be fine,' said Anna. 'Dr Marks is with him.'

'Dr Marks… oh, my word,' said Peter.

'The bullet—'

'The bullet?' said Peter. 'What bullet? You mean he's been shot? This is worse than I thought possible.'

'Please, Peter,' said Anna, 'you must compose yourself.'

Stephan came into the main room.

'They're both going to be fine,' he said.

'Both?' repeated Peter.

'Celeste was with him,' said Stephan.

'Celeste was shot at as well? Who shot them?'

'A sailor on the *Empress*. But Celeste wasn't shot.'

'Viggo was on the *Empress*?' said Peter. 'This is making no sense. He had the afternoon off and I gave him money to go and buy decorations for the party. He never said anything about going to see the *Empress*.'

Stephan explained what had happened as far as he knew. Peter, completely baffled, scratched his head.

'He was immensely brave,' said Stephan. 'If he hadn't moved as fast as he did, Celeste would have been shot.'

'They should never have been there,' said Peter. 'I let him have one afternoon off and...'

He stopped as Dr Marks came into the room, rolling down his shirt sleeves.

'Hello, Peter. I've set the arm and it will mend – it's not a major break. A hair fracture, and his shoulder will hurt for a while but it's clean and as long as there is no infection all will be well.'

'What are you saying?' said Peter. 'I thought he was shot.'

'Viggo has broken his arm. The bullet only grazed him. Celeste has slight concussion and is resting in her room.'

Celeste had been knocked unconscious by the fall and, much against her will, Anna took her home to their apartment. She felt dizzy and wasn't sure what had happened but she knew she was in trouble and that as far as everyone was concerned it was her fault. She asked three times if Viggo was all right before falling asleep in the enchanted forest.

It was two days to the dress rehearsal and that morning Celeste woke to find that Hildegard had moved her bed back into her room.

'I thought I should stay with you in case you needed anything in the night,' said Hildegard. 'And anyway, I rather like this painted scenery. I wish we lived together in a real forest.'

Anna, on the other hand, was not in such a

loving mood. She made it quite clear that Celeste was to stay in bed while she went to the opera house with Hildegard, and that the maid on no account was to let anyone in.

'I'm not ill,' Celeste protested.

'That is by the by,' said Anna.

'If I had the toy theatre I could—'

'No,' said Anna from her own bedroom.

'Couldn't I go and see Viggo?' Celeste called.

'No,' came the reply. 'You have caused quite enough trouble as it is.'

Celeste heard the front door close and then open again and Hildegard came into her room.

'I made an excuse to come back for my gloves,' she said. 'They're in my pocket. Mama would call that a white lie.'

'She's wrong,' said Celeste. 'A lie is a lie.'

'Oh,' said Hildegard. 'Well, what I wanted to say is, it's not your fault that Anna is cross. She's cross with Stephan.'

'Hildegard,' called Anna.

'I'll tell you everything later,' said Hildegard and, taking her gloves from her pocket, she ran off.

Reluctantly, Celeste lay back on the pillows. A whole day with nothing to do, she thought. No Maria to talk to, no Viggo for company – and I'm not even ill.

She weighed up exactly how much trouble she would be in if she did leave the flat and go to see Viggo. It added up into a whole load more, about double. The hours ticked by and she wondered if she stayed very still indeed and did nothing, what would happen to make her move. Would time stop?

'A chicken pie for lunch,' said the maid.

A chicken pie, thought Celeste, and time ticked on.

Viggo was faring better as he was seen as a hero, which in a way he was. Also, it wasn't his fault that Celeste had gone onto the ship. Even as he thought that he knew it wasn't completely true. He should have known that Celeste wouldn't be satisfied with seeing the outside of the *Empress*.

Peter had taken the day off work to look after him.

'There are more important things in life than a pantomime,' he said. 'Like you, nephew.'

By lunchtime Viggo felt much improved and told his uncle that staying in bed was plain dull. He, like Celeste, wondered if time would stop if he lay still and did nothing.

Peter said, 'I remember when I was little I hated

being in bed when I was ill unless, of course, I was very ill. I used to think being in bed made you worse.'

'I'd like to go and see Celeste,' said Viggo.

'No,' said Peter. 'You stay in bed and I'll go and get Celeste. I'll take a carriage and leave a note for Anna at the stage door. After all, it's nearly Christmas.'

And for the rest of the day the three of them made Christmas decorations. Or rather Celeste and Peter did while Viggo, his arm in a sling, sat in an armchair wrapped as warm as a Christmas parcel. He played director and made suggestions as to what decorations should be made and where they should go. Over the years Peter had collected useful items, from broken wooden toys to sweet wrappers, and kept them in boxes marked BITS AND PIECES.

Celeste and Peter made paper angels, Father Christmases and stars.

They stuck the legs back on wooden sheep, painted them and gave them halos. They put wings on many of the small cardboard characters that Peter had kept from model sets of different productions. Celeste stuck cloves in oranges until her finger hurt and Peter suggested she use a thimble. Then they baked biscuits which they decorated. These were to go on the tree.

They hadn't spoken about what had happened on the ship until Viggo said to Celeste, 'How did you do that?'

'Do what?' she said.

'Light up.'

'No one can light up,' said Peter, smiling at the idea.

'Celeste can. That's what saved us on the ship. She became so bright that I could hardly see her. It was incredible, Uncle.'

'Show me,' said Peter.

'I can't,' said Celeste. 'I mean, I need to be angry and even then I'm not aware I'm doing it.'

Peter scratched his head. 'In all honesty, I don't know what to make of that, apart from saying it sounds impossible.'

Anna, looking none too pleased, arrived later with Hildegard.

'Viggo was bored,' said Peter, 'and he wanted to see Celeste so I went to pick her up.' Anna sat down. 'Everything is all right, Anna.'

Celeste glanced at her and thought her face said everything was far from all right.

'Come,' said Peter to Anna. 'Help me make supper.'

And the two of them went into the kitchen.

Hildegard was much taken with the fancy

decorations that they'd made. 'You did this this afternoon? I love the way the angel's wings shimmer. How did you make the birds?'

'From bits and pieces that Peter has kept,' said Celeste.

'Oh, it's magical,' said Hildegard dramatically. 'You're so clever. I'm nowhere near as clever as you are.'

'No,' said Celeste. 'You're only singing the lead role in the pantomime and that's not clever at all. Or is it?'

'Show me how you make those birds then,' said Hildegard.

'It's not difficult,' said Viggo. 'Though it is a bit if you only have one hand.'

The three of them could just hear Anna and Peter talking in the kitchen.

'I think,' said Hildegard, 'this is about Stephan and what happened yesterday.'

'What did happen yesterday apart from Viggo getting shot?' said Celeste.

'Stephan turning out to be the new First Mate of the *Empress*,' said Viggo.

'Anna is upset because he didn't tell her he'd left the opera house and had signed up to be a seaman again,' said Hildegard.

'When I'm grown up,' said Viggo, 'I'm never

going to be that foolish. If I like someone I will tell them and…' He stopped, then said, 'I wish I had told someone.'

Hildegard, although she didn't know it yet, was a born romantic. She said, 'Who do – who did you like?'

'It doesn't matter,' said Viggo.

'Perhaps,' said Hildegard, 'you could do your play. I'd love to see it. And I'll sing the song that you've written.' She looked down at Celeste's writing. 'It's a pretty title: "To Heal the Wounds of a Dove".'

So that evening Peter and Anna both watched the run-through of the play. It moved Anna to tears.

When it was over, she said, 'I know what I did when the play had finished.'

'What did you do?' asked Celeste.

'I stood up and said, "I can make all this disappear".'

'Sometimes,' said Hildegard, in the silence that followed, 'you are so clever that I haven't a clue what any of you are talking about.'

CHAPTER 31

It snowed the day of the dress rehearsal. A blizzard blew in and the city of C— froze. Icicles hung from the buildings and it felt to everyone as if they were in a pocket of time that was lost from the history books.

Hildegard was so nervous that morning that she hadn't eaten breakfast and her face had come out in red blotches. Nothing Anna said could calm her.

'I know I won't be able to remember my lines. What if I open my mouth and nothing comes out?'

Anna had assured her that it wouldn't happen.

Hildegard cheered up only slightly at the sight of Quigley's red and gold sleigh waiting to take them to the opera house. The clown wasn't driving them today as he had been called for an early rehearsal and had taken his carriage.

Hildegard sighed as Celeste climbed into the sleigh.

'What's the matter?' she asked.

'I have a delicate throat and I'm sure this cold air is not good for it.'

'When did it start, your delicate throat?' said Celeste, trying not to laugh.

'This morning, about the same time I knew I would forget my words. I want to go home. I feel sick.'

'It's nerves,' said Celeste. 'You have to overcome them.'

'And how do I do that?'

Celeste didn't really know but suggested, 'By being brave.'

'Oh dear,' said Hildegard, pulling her muffler tight about her delicate throat. 'I don't know if I'm good at that.'

Mr Gautier, on the other hand, was in an excellent mood as he walked to the opera house. Yes, it was snowing badly but surely that only added to the charm the city. Tomorrow's Christmas Eve performance was sold out. For the first time in a long while he was certain that he had on his hands a show to be proud of. He wasn't alone. The company felt the same and there was a genuine excitement about the pantomime. The scenery worked and looked enchanting, the costumes were beautiful, and everything was in place.

Or was it? Hildegard's costume for Act One was missing.

'What do you mean – missing?' asked Miss Olsen.

'It's not there,' said Hildegard's dresser. 'I've looked everywhere for it. I know it was there last night. I left late after making sure everything was as it should be. And the wig is missing too.'

Half an hour before the curtain was due to rise on the dress rehearsal, the costume was found by the stage door keeper. It had been left outside by the bins in the snow. He also found the wig. It had been dipped in purple dye.

'All that work ruined,' said Miss Olsen. She sniffed and sniffed again. 'I smell a rat.'

At such short notice nothing could be done. Hildegard would have to wear the costume for Act Two. The dresser discovered that it had been torn but not so badly that it couldn't be mended in time.

As for the wig, it was decided that Hildegard would wear her own hair, which was thick. And as Hildegard said, a lot less itchy.

'You don't think,' she said, 'that someone is trying to jinx my performance?'

Anna looked at Celeste. The look said, 'Don't say a word,' for both had a nasty feeling they knew who was responsible.

'I'm sure it's nothing like that,' said Celeste.

Hildegard wasn't sure. She felt it was a sign. Perhaps her voice was too weak to fill the theatre.

'Celeste,' she said, 'will you go up into the gods and see if I can be heard from that high up?'

Celeste was pleased to leave the panic of the dressing-room and grateful to have something to do. It was a long way to the upper circle. She could almost touch the ceiling once she was there. She stopped once to watch Quigley make his first entrance. She had seen him do it many times in rehearsal and it always got a laugh. From the wings he threw one of his legs out, wriggled his foot around, and then threw the other leg so it looked as if he was floating, only to march on to the set. Except this time he stumbled, nearly fell and saved himself by somersaulting. There was a gasp from those watching. He stood up and put out his hand to stop the orchestra.

'There was a wire across my entrance in the wings,' he said. Then walking to the front of the stage he stared into the dark auditorium and called, 'Mr Gautier?'

'Yes,' said Mr Gautier from a seat in the stalls.

'I think we would like some assurance that Madame Sabina Petrova isn't in the theatre,' said Quigley. 'If she is, kindly make sure she leaves now before she causes any more trouble. Being funny is a serious business.'

'I'm sure she isn't here,' said Mr Gautier. 'I had a firm word with her.'

Celeste was now seated high up in the auditorium looking down at the tiny figure of the clown who seemed miles and miles away. She was thinking how disappointing it would be for anyone to have to see the pantomime at this distance, when she heard the all-too-familiar voice of Madame Sabina. She was talking in hushed tones to Albert Ross.

'I can see what you're doing,' said Albert Ross. 'I don't need two eyes, the eye in the middle of my forehead sees it all.'

'You always talk such nonsense,' said Madame Sabina. 'Doesn't it exhaust you, those stupid words you use that mean nothing? I am up here only to see if my daughter's voice carries. I fear it is a little too low and weak.'

'How dare you speak of our child in such an empty-headed manner. Aren't you proud of her?'

I was right, thought Celeste. It wasn't a ridiculous notion. But poor Hildegard to have a living nightmare for a father as well as a witch of a mother.

'Proud – why should I be proud?' said Madame Sabina. 'She is a child. This is just a passing talent that will disappear by the time she grows up. Unfortunately, she doesn't even have the looks to save her – her nose is far too big for her face. And she is clumsy. This cheap show is filling her head with false hope. As for her voice, it's far too deep for the role of Columbine.'

'Do you not have one kind thing to say?'

'I am doing this in her best interest. What is the point of her thinking she could be an actress or a singer when it's obvious she hasn't the talent?'

At that moment Hildegard began to sing *Columbine's Lament*. Her voice filled the auditorium and what Celeste could see on stage was a charismatic young lady who had a genuine innocence.

'Pitch perfect,' said Albert Ross as the music swelled.

It was while Hildegard was singing that Albert Ross said something to Madame Sabina that Celeste didn't quite catch.

What she thought she heard was, 'When you next try to sing your voice will sound like the screaming of seagulls.' Whether he had said that or not she wasn't sure, but whatever it was made

Madame Sabina very angry indeed for she slapped him round the face.

'Leave me alone,' she hissed.

Now Celeste heard every word that Albert Ross said. 'The emerald ring was meant for Hildegard, not you. Perhaps you should have let her read the card.'

'That ring nearly choked her. Were you trying to kill her?'

'I hope she has it with her. It has the power to protect her from her jealous mother. A power she might need.' He turned away from Madame Sabina and walked down the aisle, tapping his stick. 'Tiggerly-tum, tiggerly-tum,' he hummed. He stopped at the front row and called down to the stalls.

'She's up here. Up here is Madame Sabina Petrova. Up here.'

Celeste heard the diva curse Albert Ross and make a quick exit through the door at the rear of the gods.

'I can see you, little dancer,' called Albert Ross. 'Don't think I can't. Did you hear all that, little dancer, did you hear it?'

CHAPTER 32

Viggo hadn't been allowed to go to the dress rehearsal and no amount of pleading had changed Peter's mind.

The day dragged on. Usually Viggo never noticed the hours or how many there were of them. He must have slept, and this is where his confusion lay for he was not sure if he had actually seen Maria or if he had dreamed that he saw her. It was a strange, vivid dream in which the colours were too bright and everything was lopsided. He was walking through a painted city not unlike the scenery in the toy theatre. As he walked he grew bigger and bigger and Maria danced beside him, her feet not touching the ground. She still wore the costume from *The Saviour*. His words sounded awkward.

'I meant to tell you. And I forgot. No, I didn't forget. I didn't know how to tell you.'

'Tell me what?' said Maria.

'That you mean everything to me.'

He heard her say something but couldn't quite catch her words. He thought she said, 'Are your feet wet?'

And, as is the way with dreams, he found himself underwater. Fishes swam past him, but he had no trouble breathing. He knew he shouldn't be there and had a slight dread that his uncle might see him. He searched desperately for Maria.

When finally he found her, he said, 'Maria, what are you doing here? You must come home.'

She put her finger to her lips to silence him.

Only then did he notice Albert Ross in his round green goggles. He was wearing an emerald green satin waistcoat and seated at a barnacle-encrusted piano, holding a sand clock to his ear.

'New Year is coming,' said Albert Ross. 'A new page to be written. Rip up the old, ring in the new. Hurry, hurry, find your place before the last chime strikes twelve, strikes you out, buries you forever in a watery grave.' He paused and brushed away a school of fish. 'I did tell the girl. I told her I always win the Reckoning.'

Viggo woke, his heart racing. Panic flooded him as if the dream might have been a warning.

He lit all the candles but still the images stayed with him.

He jumped when he heard the key in the door. A green object pushed its way into the hall and it took Viggo a moment to make sense of what he was seeing. It was the top of a Christmas tree.

Viggo, wearing Peter's dressing-gown which trailed on the floor, watched Celeste guide the tree into the main room while Peter carried the other end.

'Feeling better?' said Peter.

'Yes, thank you – and I'm very pleased to see Celeste,' said Viggo. 'Very pleased.'

Peter was trying to make the tree stand upright and didn't notice Viggo's anxious face.

'How did the transformation scene go?' asked Viggo.

'A mess. We'll sort it out tomorrow morning. I'm counting on you helping me.'

'Yes, good,' said Viggo.

'Not that you can use your arm, but you might have an idea of what's causing the mechanism to jam.'

'Madame Sabina Petrova,' said Celeste. 'I would guess that she interfered with it. Look what she did to Quigley.'

'What did she do?' asked Viggo, and the

normality of the conversation pushed the dream further and further away from his mind.

While Peter was getting supper ready, Celeste told Viggo what she had overheard when she went up to the gods to hear Hildegard sing.

'Does Hildegard still have the ring?' he asked when Celeste had finished.

'I think so,' said Celeste.

'Then it went to the right person,' said Viggo.

He thought better of telling Celeste about the dream because he knew that hearing about Maria would upset her. Anyway, the dream had begun to fade with the business of the evening meal: plates and knives, a serving dish and 'We need pepper,' and the dream was nearly gone.

Later they ate spiced brown biscuits and drank hot chocolate as they hung the decorations. Peter stood on a ladder to place a star at the top of the tree, and when all the candles in the little tin candle holders were set on every branch, he said, 'Shall we light them to see what it looks like?'

When the candles were lit the three of them stood spellbound by the Christmas tree, the decorations glowing in the candlelight. They said nothing, all lost in their own thoughts.

Celeste wondered if this would be the first Christmas she'd ever spent without Maria. She had no way of knowing except an instinct as strong as breathing that told her that they had never been apart until now. Viggo thought about the dream.

CHAPTER 33

There is an enchantment to Christmas Eve, a magic that no other day of the year can boast, full of the dreams, hopes and wishes of a wintry world holding its frosty breath.

'I want to go home,' Celeste said quietly to Anna when Hildegard was out of the room. 'I want to see Maria. And I'm frightened.'

Anna gave her a hug. 'I too want to go back to Copenhagen,' she said.

Hildegard came and joined them at the table. 'Where's that?' she said, brightly. 'I've never heard of anywhere called Copenhagen. Is it a puzzle?'

'Sort of,' said Celeste. 'It's a very hard one to crack.'

Celeste was relieved that Hildegard immediately lost all interest in the subject. Hildegard was worried that no one would come to the pantomime.

She talked all through breakfast, talked while they put on their coats and hats and talked to fill the silence left by Celeste.

'A penny for them,' said Hildegard at last.

'For what?' said Celeste.

'Your thoughts.'

'Oh, they're not worth that much,' said Celeste. Which wasn't true, but how could she explain that if she won the game, she might never see Hildegard, Viggo and Peter again? And if she lost? That didn't bear thinking about.

'I'm worried,' said Hildegard. 'What if it all goes wrong?'

'If worry was a colour, what would it be?' said Celeste.

'Is that a riddle?' said Hildegard.

'No,' said Celeste.

Hildegard thought for a moment. 'Grey,' she said. 'The colour of slush when the beauty of the snow melts.'

They were halfway down the stairs when Anna said, 'I've forgotten something. Wait in the hall,' she called as she disappeared into the apartment again.

As soon as she was out of sight, Hildegard whispered to Celeste, 'Anna still hasn't spoken to Stephan and the *Empress* is about to sail. That means he might not even come to Peter's party.'

'What are you whispering about?' said Anna as she came downstairs again.

'You,' said Celeste, truthfully.

The sun had managed to turn the snow pink and with Quigley's red and gold swan sleigh parked in it, the street looked as if it were a scene from a Christmas card. Anna and the girls were disappointed to see that again the sleigh had come without its owner. The driver helped them in and covered their legs with thick, warm blankets. They set off, bells jingling, and Celeste tried to remember if she had seen a sleigh like this in Copenhagen.

'I think it's good to arrive at the opera house in style,' said Hildegard.

There was a holiday atmosphere in the streets and, instead of taking the tram, Peter and Viggo walked to work, admiring the shop windows and their displays of Christmas goods.

As they approached the opera house, they saw there was a long queue of people outside.

'What are they doing here in this freezing weather?' asked Viggo.

'They're buying tickets, I suppose,' said his uncle. 'That's what happens when you have a successful show on your hands.'

'But how do they know it's successful if they haven't seen it?'

'Word-of-mouth,' said Peter, sounding unconvinced.

Even the stage door keeper was in a jolly mood. He was surrounded by bouquets of flowers and an eager little lad was carrying them to the dressing-rooms.

'The power of the press, eh?' said the stage door keeper to Peter who had no idea what he was talking about.

He and Viggo went onto the stage where the mechanism for the transformation scene at the end of the pantomime was still not working.

'It must be spectacular,' said Peter. 'And it is anything but.'

He saw Mr Gautier coming towards him, waving a newspaper as if it were a flag. Peter assumed the director wanted to talk to him about the problem with the mechanism and started to tell him that all would be well, but Mr Gautier interrupted him.

'Have you seen this? It shouldn't have happened but a reviewer from one of the newspapers sneaked into yesterday's dress rehearsal. Listen...' and he began to read. '"The soprano, Madame Sabina Petrova, has a secret and the secret is finally out. Her daughter, Hildegard, aged thirteen, is the true star of the family. Where the diva's voice has struggled lately to reach the high notes her daughter has a voice given to her by the angels. Anyone lucky enough to have a ticket to see this production is in for a treat." And it says a lot more about me, of course, and Quigley, and other things. Oh, and Peter,' Mr Gautier added, 'your designs are mentioned too.'

'The bit about Madame Sabina,' said Peter, 'don't you think it might upset her?'

'I don't care, as long as I never have to work with the wretched woman again. Remember,' he said as he walked away, 'I want a spectacular transformation for the finale. Make that scenery work.'

The moment he'd gone, Peter sent Viggo to buy a newspaper. 'I want to read what Mr Gautier left out,' he said.

Viggo was returning to the stage when he bumped into Celeste. She was waiting at the foot of the stairs for Hildegard.

'What are you doing?' he asked.

'I'm not allowed to go up there,' said Celeste. 'Hildegard is having her new costume fitted by Miss Olsen.'

'Where's Anna?'

'Making sure that Madame Sabina isn't hiding in a wardrobe,' said Celeste.

'Madame Sabina will blow her top when she reads this newspaper,' said Viggo and showed Celeste the article.

'Oh, my word!' she said. 'Did you see that about

Hildegard being banished from her mother's home to live with a governess? It's not at all sympathetic – in fact, quite the opposite. Who would have told a reporter this? Oh dear, if Madame was angry before, she'll be furious now.'

'That's what Peter thinks too,' said Viggo.

Just then Hildegard came down wearing her new Columbine costume. Her face was painted white, with rosy cheeks and red, heart-shaped lips. Viggo and Celeste stared at her.

'What do you think?' she asked.

'I think you look wonderful,' said Celeste.

'Spectacular,' said Viggo.

'You don't think I look clumsy and fat?'

'No,' said Celeste. 'Absolutely not, that's a foolish idea. What makes you say that?'

Hildegard handed Celeste a card.

'It came with a bouquet of *dead* roses,' said Hildegard. 'There is no name on it, but I know who it's from.'

Without thinking, Viggo said, 'Do you think Madame Sabina is a witch and we just haven't realised it?'

'Even if she is a witch, she's still my mother,' said Hildegard.

'Sorry,' said Viggo, 'I didn't mean... I... er... have to go...' and he disappeared.

'Mama is right. I shouldn't be doing this,' said Hildegard miserably. 'I don't think she will ever speak to me again. Then what will I do? I mean, I can't live with Anna forever, as much as I'd love to.'

Celeste could see she was on the verge of tears and said, 'You can't think about that now. You must concentrate on your performance.'

Hildegard looked down at her shoes, which were shiny and pretty. 'I don't have much instinct about things, not like you, but still I have a terrible feeling that Mama is in the theatre.'

'No one has seen her,' said Celeste.

'No one saw her at the dress rehearsal, and yet she ruined my costume and my wig, and the transformation scene.'

'True,' said Celeste.

'Will you stay in the wings the whole time and watch me and make sure...' Hildegard stopped as she saw Anna coming towards them. 'Make sure I'm safe.'

'There you are,' said Anna, gathering Hildegard to her. 'They've called "Act One beginners".'

CHAPTER 34

The first half of the show was an uproarious success from the moment the orchestra started to play. When the curtain came down at the interval, Mr Gautier could not have been more delighted. Hildegard's confidence had grown with every scene. The audience loved her, and the combination of the Harlequin, played by Quigley, and Columbine together was both funny and touching. Hildegard received a standing ovation when she sang *Columbine's Lament*.

In the interval Mr Gautier went to find Peter, only to learn there would be no transformation scene. Peter had tried his best with the damaged mechanism but could do nothing with it. Mr Gautier was in far too good a mood to let anything upset him.

'I'm sure you have another trick up your sleeve, Peter. Something that will impress His Majesty.'

Before Peter could answer there was a commotion at the side of the stage as the door that led to the Royal Box opened. To everyone's surprise, the king came onto the stage. No one in the company could remember the last time he'd been seen in the house. His presence caused quite a stir.

'Very well done,' he said to no one in particular. 'I would like to meet Mr Quigley and Miss Hildegard Petrova.'

Mr Gautier introduced them. The clown bowed and Hildegard curtsied.

'You have a unique voice,' said the king to Hildegard. 'A voice such as yours is a rare gift. It turns up in unexpected places. I hope your mama is immensely proud of you and encourages you in every way.'

Hildegard could think of nothing to say, so she said nothing and curtsied again, which seemed to be the right thing to do.

'Wonderful,' said His Majesty. 'I look forward with great anticipation to the second half. And Mr Gautier tells me that something spectacular is in store for us at the end of the show.'

With that he disappeared up the stairs to the Royal Box.

Hildegard was returning to her dressing-room when Mr Gautier stopped her in the corridor.

'There will be no scene transformation at the end, so do your very best to make up for it.'

It struck Hildegard that sometimes she had absolutely no idea what Mr Gautier meant. What was she supposed to do if the scenery didn't work? She was about to ask him, but he had gone.

As soon as Hildegard had changed into her second costume, the call went up, 'Act Two beginners.'

Celeste, who was wearing one of her new dresses for the occasion, walked with her to the wings.

'I meant to tell you,' said Hildegard. 'When I came out of Miss Olsen's workroom after the costume fitting, Mr Ross was waiting for me. He asked if I had the emerald ring. I thought he was going to call me a thief. I didn't say if I did or didn't, and he said, "Keep it safe – it will protect you." How does he know about the ring?'

'You have got it safe?' asked Celeste.

'Yes – on a ribbon round my neck. I don't think Mama has noticed that it's missing.'

'The curtain's about to rise,' said the stage manager. 'Break a leg!'

Hildegard gave Celeste's hand a squeeze. 'You'll stay where you were? You gave me a lot of courage.'

As she took up her position on the stage, the orchestra started to play, the sound as rich as the red velvet curtain that rose on a market square. The scene was given a round of applause and Quigley somersaulted onto the stage. The audience burst out laughing. He was followed by a troupe of little dancers.

It was nearing the end of the show when Celeste became aware of a noise backstage and the noise turned into the unmistakable voice of Madame Sabina Petrova.

'Let me through,' she was shouting. 'I demand you let me through.'

The stage manager tried to stop her and she pushed him away. He stumbled and fell backwards, and the noise was loud enough to make Hildegard look into the wings. The moment she saw her mama she forgot her lines. Her mouth opened but no sound came from her. The orchestra played the introduction again, waiting for her to sing, but she was unable to move. Quigley tried to cover for her, but it was no use. Hildegard looked as if she was on the point of passing out. Now the audience too could hear the rumpus in the wings and wondered if it was part of the show.

When Celeste saw Madame Sabina, the injustice of what this woman had done to her daughter filled her with anger. Suddenly Celeste became aware that Sabina Petrova was no longer coming towards her but backing away and Celeste knew that beams of light were radiating from her many scars. The more she thought about Madame Sabina the brighter they shone. The diva raised her hands to shield her eyes.

Hildegard still hadn't moved. Quigley turned a cartwheel into the wings and the audience started to clap.

'You have to help,' he said to Celeste. 'She'll be unable to do this unless you help her. Make it look as though it's part of the show.'

For the first time in days Celeste felt Maria was with her and she found she remembered the simple dance steps Maria had once tried to teach her. The beams that shone from her disguised a slight clumsiness as she joined Hildegard on stage and took her hand.

'It's all right,' she said quietly, 'I'm here.'

Quigley was improvising, making a comedy of pretending to conduct the orchestra. The audience roared with laughter.

Hildegard turned to Celeste, her eyes filled with tears. 'I can't remember anything.'

'Yes, you can,' said Celeste. 'You can do it.'

And then Hildegard stepped forward and sang the final song, *When the Sun Shines.*

Thinking hard about Madame Sabina, Celeste used her anger to make her light stronger and brighter, beaming into the gods, into the upper circle and down into the stalls, until the audience couldn't see Celeste for her light.

Before the last note had died away, the entire audience was on its feet.

Mr Gautier addressed the assembled company afterwards. 'Spectacular is a sad word when it comes to describing what I've just witnessed.'

Viggo whispered, 'Uncle, you must say something.'

His uncle was dazed. 'Is this what she did on the ship?' he whispered.

'Yes,' said Viggo. 'But not as bright as tonight.'

'My word,' said Peter.

'Go on,' said Viggo. 'Say something, otherwise it will be impossible to explain.'

'Ah… you thought the finale worked?' said Peter to the director.

'Worked? It was magic.'

'It took a lot of preparation,' said Peter, warming to his subject. 'We weren't sure about it, were we, Celeste?'

Celeste said, 'No, we weren't sure. Not sure at all.'

Hildegard had to suppress a giggle.

The king came onto the stage again.

'That was quite the most remarkable thing I've

ever seen in the theatre. And if I may say so, the most moving. It had an element of poetry to it. Very well done.' He turned to Celeste. 'You are the little dancer who was injured in that terrible accident with the chandelier.'

'Yes, sir,' she said.

'I sent you a doll.'

'Yes, thank you, sir. I loved it.' Then she added, 'Hildegard and I both loved it. Didn't we, Hildegard?'

'You never came to tea,' said the king. 'I did invite you to tea, didn't I?'

Beside the king stood a man who Celeste hadn't noticed until then. No one else seemed to have noticed him either. Celeste thought afterwards it was as if he'd appeared from the king's frockcoat. He carried an important-looking leather-bound notebook and a pen. A pair of the smallest of spectacles rested on his nose.

'Make a note that this young lady – it's Maria, isn't it? What is your last name?'

'I don't know,' said Celeste, which was honest.

'Of course you don't,' said the king. 'You are the little dancer. Yes, make a note that Maria and Hildegard are to come to tea at the palace. Good. Well done all of you.' And then he left.

CHAPTER 35

'He's quite a magician,' said Quigley when they were on their way to Peter's party.

Hildegard was holding a huge bouquet of flowers that had being given to her by a well-wisher. 'Who's a magician?' she said, from behind the foliage.

'Mr Peter Tias,' said Quigley. 'I'd love to know how he did that lighting effect. Can you tell us, Celeste?'

'No,' said Celeste. 'I was sworn to secrecy.'

'Intriguing, very intriguing,' said Quigley.

Hildegard sneezed and Anna took the flowers from her.

'They are rather big,' said Anna.

'This is just the start,' said Quigley. 'Flowers today, jewels tomorrow.'

'I won't let it go to my head. I won't,' said Hildegard as if saying it once wasn't enough.

'It's none of my business, Hildegard,' said Quigley, 'but I would be very cautious if I were you for I suspect that tomorrow, Madame-Your-Mama will insist you return home. If she does and if you do, then you,' he turned to Anna and Celeste, 'will be homeless again.'

'No!' said Hildegard. 'No, that won't happen.'

'My dear girl, you are too young to stop it.'

'It will be all right,' said Anna.

'Of course it will be all right,' said Quigley. 'Here,' he handed Anna a card, 'this is the address of an apartment I sometimes use which at the moment is vacant. It's available for you and Celeste.'

'Thank you,' said Anna, putting the card safely away as the carriage pulled up outside Peter's apartment building.

The sound of the party filled the stairwell.

'Here come the stars of the show,' said Mr Gautier, the moment the four of them entered the room.

Everyone stopped talking and raised their glasses. To Hildegard's surprise, Massini took her hand and kissed it.

'To a true artist,' he said, raising his glass. 'I will only ever write my music for you.'

A cheer went up and three members of the orchestra played the melody from *Columbine's Lament*.

Viggo, who was looking very smart in his new waistcoat with his arm in a red satin sling, said to Celeste, 'You were extraordinary.'

'Thank you,' she said. 'I couldn't think how else to stop that dragon from ruining everything.'

'I keep reminding Uncle Peter not to let slip that you made the beams of light by yourself,' said Viggo.

And I've got to find a way do it again and again, thought Celeste. But she looked around her and said, 'I don't think I've ever seen the room look as magical as this.'

She was about to say more when Viggo said, 'Look who's arrived – Miss Olsen.'

Celeste went to greet her, certain that she would turn her back on her. But she didn't.

'I saw what happened tonight,' said the wardrobe mistress. 'It was most brave of you to go on stage to help Hildegard. I was touched. I've spoken to Mr Gautier about a costume for you, and Peter is going to give me a design. It should be ready for the next performance, the day after tomorrow. Can you come for your costume fitting around six o'clock?'

'Yes, I can,' said Celeste. She wanted to ask her where she lived and much more besides, but Miss Olsen said she had to leave. 'So soon? Oh please don't,' said Celeste.

There was a ringing of bells and again everyone

stopped talking. Mr Gautier had borrowed a costume from the wardrobe department and was dressed as Father Christmas.

'I would like to thank everyone who worked on the production,' he said to cheers from the company. 'Wait, wait, I haven't finished!'

'When do you ever finish?' called one of the musicians, and laughter rippled round the room.

'Secondly, I want to say a huge thank you to the stars of our show, one of whom I'm proud to say I discovered – Hildegard Petrova. The other is, of course, our very own Quigley, the greatest clown this fine city of ours has ever produced.'

Another loud cheer went up as he handed presents to everyone.

Then Mrs Marks' maid brought in a goose on a platter followed by her second maid with two roast ducks.

'I didn't know we had a duck,' said Peter. 'Or ducks,' he added, seeing there were two.

'They're Mrs Marks' present to us,' said Viggo. 'And so are the rice puddings.'

'My word,' said Peter, as bowls of red cabbage and boiled potatoes, jugs of sauce and gravy manifested themselves and the table groaned with food. 'A feast. Eat, everyone, and be merry.'

His guests needed no encouragement.

Whether Hildegard realised it or not she was the star of the party. Everyone congratulated her on her performance and when she was out of hearing everyone talked about her mother.

Peter spent the evening trying to sound mysterious about how he had projected the beams of light from Celeste. Viggo rescued him countless times.

'Remember, Uncle,' he would say. 'You swore you'd never talk about it to anybody.' Finally he said, 'Why don't you play your accordion?'

There was singing and dancing until about half past eleven when people began to go home or to the midnight service. Just as the last goodbyes had been said and 'Merry Christmas' shouted again from the street below, Stephan arrived.

'I wasn't sure if you would still be up,' he said. 'Have I missed the party completely?'

'No, you're very welcome,' said Peter. 'Anna and the girls are still here.' He poured him a glass of wine. 'And now I can give you all your presents.'

'And we have presents too,' said Hildegard, 'don't we, Anna? I chose them and you didn't know anything about it, did you, Celeste?'

She gave Celeste a little box. Celeste opened it and there on a blue velvet cushion was a silver ballet dancer.

'Anna thought it might make you sad as you can't dance any more but I thought it would make you remember that you are doubly talented,' said Hildegard. 'I did the right thing, didn't I?'

Celeste hugged her. 'Yes, you did,' she said and pinned the brooch to her dress.

'I have one for you,' Stephan said to Anna. 'I've been an idiot,' he added quietly. 'I should have explained what I was going to do. I hope you'll forgive me.'

Anna opened the parcel to find inside it a shawl. She went ghostly white. 'But this is...' She couldn't finish the sentence.

'The shawl you once owned,' said Stephan. 'The one that I saw on the ship.'

'That makes no sense,' said Hildegard. 'If Anna owned it before, why has she got it new again now?'

Stephan laughed. 'Perhaps she lost it and I found an identical one.'

'Is this to do with Copenhagen?' said Hildegard. 'Celeste said it was a puzzle.'

'It is,' said Stephan. His face suddenly hardened for standing in the doorway was Albert Ross.

They were all so surprised to see him that no one moved until Peter remembered his manners and went to greet him.

'As I'm here,' said Albert Ross, 'I thought I'd

have a biscuit with you and a glass of wine. Then I'll go home.' Peter guided him to a chair. 'Did you light up?' Albert Ross pointed his stick to where Celeste was standing. 'Do you light up? Can you light up?'

'Yes,' said Celeste. 'I did, I do and I can.'

Albert Ross took one of the star-shaped biscuits and ate it as a rabbit might: slowly nibbling the points of the star. He appeared to be lost in thought.

'You lit up like a chandelier,' he said. 'Do you think that will help you in life?'

Celeste didn't answer. Everyone was quiet.

'I like this party,' said Albert Ross. 'I like it a lot when no one is here. Do you know, tonight is the night animals speak to us and we to them? None of you brought the animals presents.' Not waiting for a response, he said, 'I thought not. I had a very good conversation with a dog this morning and one with a rabbit who was lost. Two cats who were giving up hunting in favour of the fireside. And a mouse that I met on the stairs coming up here.'

'What did the animals say?' asked Hildegard.

'Many wishy-washy things but the most important one was the rat. The rat told me that a certain ship – the *Empress* – is going to sail. The rat told me that the king is going to be aboard. The rat told me Maria and Anna would be aboard.' He thought for a moment then he pointed his stick at Hildegard. 'And the rat also told me that you will miss the boat, Miss Hildegard Petrova. But then again, you can never trust a rat. I'd take the word of a mouse any old day. Mice don't lie. The mouse told me your mama would do anything to stop you singing for the king.' He stood up. 'Christmas presents,' he said. 'Let's see if I have anything left for the children after giving presents to my furry friends.'

He took off his hat, put it on the table beside his chair and opened the crown. He pulled out three presents and before anyone had a chance to open them he quickly found his way to the door and left.

Each present was labelled. Gingerly, as if they might bite, Celeste, Viggo and Hildegard took the present addressed to them.

Albert Ross had given Viggo a compass, Hildegard a pair of emerald earrings that matched the ring and Celeste a small cut-out figure. There was no mistaking the figure – it was the little dancer.

CHAPTER 36

Celeste and Hildegard were woken late the following morning by the maid who said there was a visitor waiting. Celeste could hear a conversation and knew by the voice that the visitor was Madame Sabina Petrova.

'Why is she here?' said Hildegard.

'To take you home, I would think,' said Celeste.

'Once I would have wanted to go,' said Hildegard, sadly, 'but not now. Even though it's cold here and the beds are damp and I don't have a maid all to myself, I still would much rather stay with you and Anna. I'll tell Mama that I want to stay. I mean, I'm thirteen, nearly grown up.' But as she rolled down to the end of the sentence, her words sounded less assured.

Her mama's voice was heard in the heart of her abandoned daughter.

'I made a terrible mistake and I am humbly sorry for what I did,' said Madame Sabina.

A little too loudly, thought Celeste, a little too theatrically. But Celeste could see the effect it had on Hildegard and who could blame her? Every child wants to know that to their mother at least they are the most important creature in the world.

'I am determined to concentrate on Hildegard's talents,' Madame Sabina was saying. 'There is much I can teach her. I thank you for looking after her, Anna, though I do believe you overstepped the mark and made...' She stopped. 'But never mind.'

'Shall we go in?' said Hildegard, getting up from her bed. She took Celeste's hand and, still in their nightgowns, together they walked, barefooted, into the cold living room to face Hildegard's repentant mother.

Madame Sabina didn't rise when she saw her daughter. She was dressed more for a funeral than for Christmas and her penitent air appeared well rehearsed to both Anna and Celeste. Staying seated, the diva held out her small pudgy hands to her daughter.

Slowly, Hildegard went to her.

'My darling little mouse,' said Madame Sabina. 'Will you forgive your foolish and jealous old mama? It's very difficult for me to come to terms with the fact that my voice is not what it used to be. It's hard to be overtaken by anybody, but especially by one's daughter. I have wronged you and I ask for your forgiveness. I want to look after you, to love you, to care for you and to make sure that you have a fine career ahead of you.'

With every warm, honeyed word, Celeste could almost see Hildegard's feet melting. Fifteen minutes later, she had dressed and Madame Sabina had her arm round her daughter's shoulders as she steered her out of the apartment.

'Anna and Celeste will be able to stay here, won't they?' asked Hildegard.

'It's taken care of, darling. Now, you go down to the carriage and wait for me like a good little mouse.' The maid escorted Hildegard.

When they had gone, Madame Sabina said, 'I want you out of here in fifteen minutes. You can leave all the clothes I bought you, Anna. Celeste, you may take one dress.'

Celeste went to the bedroom and dressed herself in the clothes that Quigley had bought her. She carefully packed up her toy theatre and tied string round the box so she could carry it. She slipped into her pocket Viggo's snail, the Harlequin and the cut-out figure of a little dancer that looked like Maria.

She and Anna stood in the hall, warmly dressed against the weather.

'Where did you get those clothes?' asked Madame Sabina.

'Mr Quigley was kind enough to buy them for us,' said Anna.

'Quigley has more money than sense,' said Madame Sabina.

She was about to herd them out when a footman appeared in the doorway.

'I have an invitation from His Majesty for Miss Hildegard Petrova and for Miss Maria,' he said.

'Give it to me,' said Madame Sabina.

She tried to take the envelope but the footman gave her a look of such disgust that she let go of it.

'I am here on the king's orders, which are that this invitation is to be handed to Miss Anna, there being no surname.' The footman looked Madame Sabina up and down. 'You are not Miss Anna.'

Anna moved swiftly. 'Thank you, I am Anna,' she said and took the envelope.

'As the invitation includes Hildegard, I should know the details,' said Madame Sabina.

The footman took no notice of her. 'Miss Anna,' he said, 'I have been ordered to wait for your reply, time being of the essence.'

Anna read what was written on the white card

with the gold crest, then said, 'Celeste, Hildegard and I have been invited to join his Royal Highness on a short voyage to commemorate those who disappeared on the *Empress* two years ago.'

She slipped the card into her bodice.

'You will inform His Majesty,' said Madame Sabina, 'that in place of Miss Anna, Madame Sabina Petrova will accompany Miss Hildegard Petrova and Miss Maria.'

The footman unrolled a sheet of paper and looked down the list of names.

'Your name is not on here,' he said.

Anna said quickly, 'I will be delighted to attend and so will Miss Maria.' And before Madame Sabina could say another word, the footman was gone.

'How dare you!' she hissed at Anna. 'You, a nobody. This is not the end of the matter. I don't care what happens to you but money and power will always win over poverty. You will get out of here as soon as I have left.'

She slammed the apartment door.

Anna and Celeste stood motionless. When they heard the carriage drive away they too left the apartment and opened the door onto the frozen street.

'We have to be on that ship come what may,' said Anna. 'And Hildegard must be there too.'

Snow had begun to fall again, bringing with it an eerie silence. Soon the city of C— was covered in a clean blanket of shimmering white.

They went first to Peter's apartment only to learn from a neighbour that he and Viggo had gone to pay a visit to an old friend. Anna remembered the card Quigley had given her and they set off once more through deserted streets, looking in windows at happy scenes of families, and Christmas trees bright with candles. At last they arrived at a house that was painted orange and overlooked the canal. Anna pulled the bell. No one answered.

Celeste shifted the box containing the toy theatre to her other hand. Despite her mittens, the string was cutting into her frozen fingers. Snow had begun to stick to their clothes and they huddled in the doorway as the light faded.

'What shall we do now?' asked Celeste.

Anna looked in her purse and sighed. 'I've enough money for us to stay no longer than one night in a hotel. But it's Christmas and there is nowhere open.'

'Perhaps Peter will be back soon,' said Celeste, her teeth chattering.

It was then that the red and gold swan sleigh drew up in the middle of the road outside the house. There appeared to be no one in it and no one got out until finally the driver climbed down to wake up the sleeping passenger, and there in the gaslight stood Quigley. His face was white and he was dressed in a silvery Harlequin costume and a black conical hat.

'Merry Christmas,' he said as if he had been expecting to see them. 'Come on in. You two look like ice sculptures. She chucked you out, then,' he said, laughing. 'I knew she would.'

Quigley's 'spare apartment', as he called it, was a mansion. It was full of paintings and antiques, and Celeste and Anna were astounded by its grandeur. The servant took their bags and showed them to their rooms.

They joined Quigley in the warm drawing room.

'We rang,' said Celeste, 'but no one opened the door.'

'Of course not,' said Quigley. 'Someone such as myself has to say "Abracadabra" before it will open.'

'Why don't you live here?' asked Celeste as tea was served.

'I do sometimes. Sometimes like now.'

'Where do you live all the other times?'

'In a caravan in the park.'

'Isn't it chilly?'

'It's as cosy as a bug in a rug,' said the clown. 'I was born in a caravan. My parents did touring shows. I was on stage at three, at five I was their star attraction. I would sleep as the caravan went along the roads to the next village, then to the next. We performed in village halls, market squares, in stables and once in a barn where a cow was giving birth. Never have I felt safer or more loved than I did then. But when I became famous and had all this money, I was told I needed a big house to show everybody how wealthy I was. Sometimes I entertain here. Most of the time I want to get away and find a lovely lady who would like nothing better than to live with me in a caravan. But every lady I meet wants to live in this big house with me. And if truth be told, it's the one place I don't wish to be.'

'You've never met the right lady, then,' said Celeste.

'Not only are you a living chandelier,' said Quigley, 'but perhaps you're the wisest little girl that the moon ever shone on.'

CHAPTER 37

The theatre is a small world and the news that Hildegard had gone home to her mother was commented on by some and thought nothing of by others. Most agreed that the daughter would have had to return home sooner or later. But the main gossip was not to do with Hildegard but with who had been invited to the king's New Year's Eve cruise and who had not. The fact that Anna had been invited and not Madame Sabina was believed to have been the reason Anna had lost her job.

As Miss Olsen said, 'No one is allowed to outshine that woman.'

'It's jealousy,' said Peter when he heard that Madame Sabina had thrown Anna and Celeste onto the streets on Christmas Day. 'Nothing but the mean green god. Madame Sabina can't stand the idea of her daughter being talented.'

In fact, there was no one at the opera house who

thought for a moment that the diva had taken her daughter back out of genuine love.

Peter invited Anna and Celeste to stay at his apartment, but Anna felt they couldn't accept as Quigley hated being on his own in the big house.

'He's promised not to kick us out,' she said, laughing.

Celeste had hoped that she might be able to have a word alone with Hildegard the day after Christmas, before the evening performance, but it was impossible.

'That witch,' said Miss Olsen, when Celeste went for her costume fitting.

'Do you mean Madame Sabina?' said Celeste.

Miss Olsen wasn't talking to Celeste but to the head of the wig department.

'No other,' said Miss Olsen. 'The high and mighty queen. She said that if any alterations are to be made to her daughter's costumes, they should be made in her dressing-room.'

That evening, Celeste noticed that Hildegard's voice trembled, and her performance lacked confidence. When it came to the finale, Celeste had only to think of Madame Sabina Petrova and light beamed from her scars, dancing wherever she willed them.

'Are you all right?' she said to Hildegard as the curtain came down, to rise again to great applause.

'No,' said Hildegard.

As the curtain fell again, she flinched as her mother appeared and, firmly taking hold of her arm, pulled her towards the wings.

There was a scuffle and the stage manager said, 'Madame, would you please leave. The audience want another curtain call.'

'One is quite sufficient,' said the diva.

As the stage manager raised his hands in despair, Hildegard stumbled into Celeste who pushed a crumpled piece of paper into her hand. She hid it in her tinsel gown.

Anna could no longer come to the theatre and so Quigley was taking Celeste home in his sleigh. It was snowing outside that evening and there was a crowd of people wanting autographs. Celeste waited by the stage door and as Madame Sabina dragged Hildegard past them, a cry of 'There she is!' went up and people surged towards her. Madame Sabina was having none of it and hurried her daughter into her carriage and, in a whirl of snow and ice, they were gone.

In his sleigh, Quigley sat lost in thought. It was too dark to read Hildegard's letter, though Celeste could feel the words nibbling at her pocket, desperate to be heard.

'Did you notice anything different about Hildegard's performance tonight?' said Quigley at last.

'Yes,' said Celeste. 'She seemed less confident.'

'She fluffed her lines,' said Quigley. 'She has never fluffed her lines. From the beginning, she's been word perfect. That woman will be the death of her.'

'Don't say that,' said Celeste.

'I meant it only as a figure of speech.'

They arrived at Quigley's house on the canal to find lights in all the windows.

'Just a small party,' said Quigley. 'I do it every year.'

Unlike Peter's party, it was full of people Celeste didn't know. She tried to find Anna, and Quigley told her that she was out seeing a certain sailor. Celeste sat in the library and read Hildegard's letter. It made her feel so sad that she decided to go to bed. On the landing she stopped and sat to watch the party through the banisters. A memory came to her of another grand house, and of she and Maria watching as guests arrived too early, looking awkward. She took out Hildegard's letter, smoothed it flat and read it again.

Dear Celeste,

I miss you and the light that comes from you that frightens Mama. I am such a nincompoop. I wanted so much to believe that the good Christmas mother would not disappear in a puff of theatrical smoke. I wish you were here. I wish I could talk to you. I can almost hear you say, do not trust her.

Christmas Day with Mama was strange and uncomfortable. She had bought me toys and clothes that would have suited ten-year-old me. I think I must be stupid. I longed for Christmas magic. I thought there would be a real change in Mama, that she was not just play-acting. I knew when I saw the clothes that they were too small. I felt big and awkward. She showed me a rocking horse she'd bought. It was delicate. If I sat on it, I am certain it would break. After the present-giving, Mama went to rest. Too late I realised I had been a fool to leave the apartment, to leave you and Anna. Now I am here there is no way I can escape, or even talk to you.

The evening went badly wrong. As none of the new dresses fitted, I went down to dinner in what I had arrived in. When Mama saw me she insisted that I go back upstairs and change into one of the dresses she had given me. She said this in front of guests, and that she had spent hard-earned money to buy me clothes and lovely things and this was all the thanks she was given.

There was one dress that was a little bigger than the others and my maid had to sew me into it. I looked truly ridiculous and felt miserable. All the guests worked in opera. She told them that I was in a childish pantomime but that I had to start somewhere. She talked about me as if I wasn't there. I could not eat a thing as I was scared that the stitches might burst.

When dessert was served she told me I was to say good night to everybody.

'There is one little girl who doesn't need pudding tonight,' she said, again in front of everyone.

Then I thought of you. I thought what you would do, and I felt angry and said – and I shouldn't have said – 'I am thirteen, not ten,' and walked out. She followed me into the hall and she smacked me across the face.

Oh, Celeste, she is mad and I am scared of what she might do. She is furious that I have been invited to the New Year's Eve cruise on the Empress. I don't think she will let me go.

I am frightened. Not pretend frightened to get my own way, but really, deep down, scared . . .

Celeste refolded the letter. Tomorrow she would find Viggo and see if they could come up with a plan. She was about to go to her room when she saw Mr Gautier arrive and wondered if he might be able to do something. But when she tried to tell him how worried she was about Hildegard he patted her on the shoulder and changed the subject.

'I thought your costume was perfect tonight,' he said, looking round the room. 'Miss Olsen did a wonderful job.' He spotted an acquaintance. 'Charles,' he called, 'how nice to see you here.' He excused himself and walked away, leaving Celeste feeling powerless.

CHAPTER 38

On 31st December, Mr Gautier read his daily notes again and tried to justify his actions. Why, oh why had he not listened to Celeste on the night of the clown's party? When he thought back to that evening, he had to admit all the signs were there. The stage manager had reported to him that afternoon, before the performance, that Madame Sabina Petrova had lost her temper the moment she had entered Hildegard's dressing-room. The cause had been the many bouquets that had been sent to her daughter by well-wishers. It was two dozen white roses from the king that had caused the episode to become ugly. Apparently the card with them said that His Majesty was looking forward to hearing Hildegard sing on New Year's Eve. The vase had ended up broken and the flowers trampled on the floor.

Mr Gautier had been surprised – not at the diva's violent temper, that was true to her nature – no, what had surprised him was that she appeared to have no pride in her daughter. Perhaps he should have seen the danger signs in that, but he hadn't. He had received an invitation and was relieved that he had a good reason to decline: he suffered badly from sea-sickness. If he was honest with himself, he did not want to set foot on the *Empress*, regardless of it having been refurbished. He was a superstitious man and sea-sickness was a good excuse. He had disregarded the fact that Madame Sabina Petrova would mind very much that she was not invited and that was another mistake.

And yet, he said to himself, what was he or anyone else supposed to do?

At breakfast on 28th December he had read a ridiculous article in the newspaper about the great soprano... he had laughed into his toast... the great pain would be more true... he read on... Madame Sabina Petrova claimed she had dedicated herself to nurturing her daughter's talent.

He had found it rather amusing and he wasn't alone in that. The same day he had noted the matinee and evening performances, and that Madame Sabina had demanded that Hildegard's dressing-room be returned to how it was when she was in residence. Mr Gautier had been called upon to intervene and instead of remarking that Hildegard looked pale and had a blueish tint around her eyes, he had taken a certain delight in telling the diva that this wasn't her show and that never once had Hildegard complained about the dressing-room. Madame Sabina had shouted at the director and he had shouted back. What he said, what she said, he couldn't remember and had made no note of.

The following day, 29th December, there was an evening performance. Madame Sabina had asked to see Mr Gautier, not in the dressing-room this time. No, she wanted a more public space and chose the prompt side of the stage where she could be heard complaining loudly that two performances a day had been too much for Hildegard.

'It is quite simple,' she had said, 'the girl doesn't possess the stamina required for a pantomime. Perhaps you, Gautier, should have considered that before employing an untrained singer.'

She had waved her chubby hands at him and what he had noticed was that she was wearing the emerald ring that had nearly choked Hildegard. Again Mr Gautier had to admit that he had missed the signs. But Quigley hadn't. Unable to avoid hearing the row that echoed around the theatre, the highs and the lows of it, the clown had asked her directly what she was up to.

'I am protecting my daughter,' said Madame Sabina.

'From what?' asked Quigley. 'From being a success?'

Just then, Mr Gautier had seen that behind Madame Sabina, creeping down the spiral stairs from the Royal Box, was Hildegard, supported by Viggo. Celeste was guiding them. When she saw him, she put her finger to her lips. Now when he remembered, he felt like weeping. If only Celeste and Hildegard had run away. If only he had seen what Celeste saw: that Madame Sabina Petrova was extremely dangerous. Before the evening performance Celeste had come to him with a letter from Hildegard. It was addressed to him. He had thanked her and put it in his jacket pocket then forgotten all about it until now.

He read the notes he had written the previous day, 30th December, a day he would never forget. A day when things could have been so different. He had been about to go and watch the opening of the show when he had nearly collided with Viggo.

'What's the hurry?' he'd asked.

'I'm going to get the doctor.'

'Why? For whom?'

Viggo hadn't stopped and hadn't answered.

Thinking back to that moment, Mr Gautier hoped there might be a world of different possibilities, of alternative endings, a place where he played a more honourable part. He should have been on his guard, he should have taken notice of Hildegard, he should have listened to Celeste. Yes, 30th December was a day he would never forget. And he would never forgive himself for what happened.

CHAPTER 39

The finale of the show had by degrees become grander and was now the moment that the audience waited for. Celeste was unaware that she was the star attraction. Every night she was filled with more rage than she knew what to do with and her beams were brighter and stronger as she tried to blind the diva. She had still not been able to speak to Hildegard alone and Hildegard dared not say a word to her. Celeste had attempted to give her a letter from Anna, but she hadn't taken it, terrified her mother might see, for Madame Sabina waited in the wings at every performance and at the end took Hildegard back to the dressing-room.

Celeste saw that the emerald ring that Hildegard had worn on a ribbon round her neck was now on Madame Sabina's little finger. It glinted in the darkness and knowing that it was no longer with

Hildegard made Celeste even more fearful that her friend was in danger. In the last days of the year, she watched Hildegard's face become blanker with each performance as if she believed there was no point in trying.

Viggo had an idea that they should see if Miss Olsen could request a costume fitting.

'Then there might be a chance for you to speak to her,' he said.

'Miss Olsen doesn't like me,' said Celeste, 'and anyway, all costume fittings must be done in the dressing-room in Madame's presence.'

It was Albert Ross who came to their rescue. Celeste hadn't seen him since Peter's party and had thought that he might have gone away. Knowing now that he was Hildegard's father, for the first time she found the tap of his stick reassuring.

'Please, Mr Ross,' she said. 'I must speak to Hildegard.'

'Now what's that to do with me?' said Albert Ross. 'Is it a riddle? It's a dull riddle.'

'It isn't a riddle.'

'Something in the water. Shouldn't be drinking it.'

'Who shouldn't be drinking it?' asked Celeste.

'Why, Hildegard. That's obvious.'

'How do I stop her? I can't even speak to her.'

'The ring is on the mother's finger.'

'Yes,' said Celeste, 'I know that.'

'Soon this will be in the past tense,' said Albert Ross.

She followed him down the corridor to Hildegard's dressing-room.

'Are you going to do nothing?' she asked. 'It seems to me that all adults do is walk away without looking. Anna is beside herself with worry but she's powerless and...'

Before she had finished her sentence, to her utter relief Albert Ross had knocked and walked through the wall into Hildegard's dressing-room. A few minutes later Hildegard appeared.

Celeste took her hand and led her quickly up the stairs towards the only place she knew they would be alone.

'Don't go so fast,' said Hildegard.

Celeste, realising that Hildegard was too weak to reach the dome, remembered the Royal Box. No one would be there. And if the king was hiding in the shadows, he would help. She took Hildegard through the forbidden narrow door to the foyer, then into the anteroom. There was no king. They sat next to one another on the gold spindly chairs, holding hands and looking out at the auditorium.

'I don't have the ring. Mama saw it and said I

was a thief and she took it. Now she wears it. Don't tell me I have to get it back because I can't. I don't want another beating.' She rested her head on Celeste's shoulder, exhausted, battling to keep her eyes open. 'Do you know,' she said, 'I feel so tired that every bone in my body just wants to sleep. I've never felt like this before. I'm so thirsty and all there is to drink is this water that Mama says is good for the throat.'

'What is it?' asked Celeste.

'It has a bitter taste. Mama says it's lemons, but it doesn't taste of lemon.'

'You mustn't drink any more of it. You must spit it out.'

'I don't think it's worth fighting.'

She closed her eyes and was asleep. Celeste shook her awake. 'Hildegard, you must fight.'

'I know it's pathetic and I know you would fight. You are brave. Different from me and brave. But I can't... I'm too tired. I want to sleep. I just want to—'

'Remember the ship,' said Celeste, 'and the invitation from the king. You have to sing for him. Remember the song in my play – we practised.'

'I know. Now you'll be cross with me because I can't sing.'

'I'm not cross. This is not your fault.'

'Where is Anna?'

'She wants so much to see you, but she can't because—'

'Because Mama won't let her,' said Hildegard. 'Tell me – where is Copenhagen? Is it a place or is it made up?'

'I thought this place was made up when I first came here,' said Celeste. 'I know Copenhagen is where we should be, where all would be well. Not here.'

'I hope you're right,' said Hildegard. 'It might be that another Hildegard is living safe in Copenhagen with a mother who loves her and a father who...' Her eyes closed.

'Wake up, Hildegard. Please wake up,' said Celeste.

'My mother is a witch,' said Hildegard. 'Do you think she has a broomstick? I think I am Gretel, and Mama is going to cook me in her oven. Here.' She took from her skirt two letters. 'I wrote this to Anna, and this is for Mr Gautier. Will you give it to him?'

Celeste jumped as the door to the Royal Box opened. It was Viggo.

'Mr Ross told me you were here. We must get her back,' he said. 'Her mama is having a fearful row with Mr Gautier at the prompt desk.'

'Then she will see us,' said Celeste.

'No, she won't,' said Viggo. 'She's got her back to us.'

With difficulty they helped Hildegard down the spiral staircase. Her mother's voice woke her only slightly. She was back in the dressing-room before Madame Sabina, in a fury, marched away from Mr Gautier and Quigley.

Viggo and Celeste ran to the paint shop.

'What shall we do?' said Viggo.

'Tell Dr Marks to come,' said Celeste. 'This note is for Anna but I'm sure Dr Marks will come if he reads it.'

'What does it say?'

Celeste showed him Hildegard's wobbly writing. There were only two words: *Help me.*

CHAPTER 40

Mr Gautier held the letter that Celeste had given him. Still he couldn't bring himself to read it. Instead he read his notes for yesterday, 30th December. Again there was only an evening performance. Hildegard had seemed very tired and he had made many notes on her lacklustre performance, her lapses of concentration. He had watched the first half of the show from the auditorium. He noted that three times she had slurred her words, stumbled on the stage and had come in a beat too late on *Columbine's Lament*. Quigley had done his best to cover for her. Sitting on the swing, she had appeared to fall asleep. The audience laughed as Quigley made a joke of it.

In the interval Mr Gautier heard members of the audience chatting.

'My dear, the girl can hardly sing.'

'I've no idea what all the fuss is about.'

'What was the reviewer thinking of?'

Mr Gautier felt that some firm words were needed and went backstage. There he saw Quigley carrying Hildegard in his arms, Celeste behind him.

'What's happened?' he asked.

'She collapsed on stage,' said Celeste, 'as the curtain came down.'

Quigley took Hildegard to her dressing-room and laid her on the day-bed. Celeste knelt beside her and took her hand. She was stone-still.

'I told Mr Gautier yesterday that my daughter is not up to doing a full run,' said Madame Sabina. 'I think it would be wise if you have an understudy. And as the situation is desperate, I could, of course, step in.'

'So that's your game,' said the clown.

'I'm offering my services for nothing,' said the diva.

'And that's exactly what they're worth – nothing,' said Quigley.

'Get out!' screamed Madame Sabina. 'Get out, all of you, get out immediately!'

Celeste stayed where she was. 'The water,' she said to Quigley.

Quigley went to a side table and picked up a glass of water. He sniffed it.

'What is this?' he asked.

'Water,' said Madame Sabina. 'Water and lemon with a little honey. It helps the throat. Surely you know that.'

'Drink it,' said Quigley to Madame Sabina. 'Drink it now.'

'If you will excuse me, I must look after my daughter.'

'No,' said Quigley. 'I will not excuse you. Drink it.'

Madame Sabina Petrova, faced with the clown's icy rage, did as she was told.

'As you can see, there's nothing in it.'

But Quigley wasn't listening. 'We need a doctor, Gautier,' he said.

'Viggo has gone to fetch one,' said Celeste, and at that moment Viggo showed Dr Marks into the dressing-room.

Dr Marks made a quick examination of Hildegard and said, 'She has been drugged.' He turned to Madame Sabina. 'What have you given her?'

'Why does everyone think I have given her something?' she said.

'What was it? I must know, if I am to treat her,' said Dr Marks, his voice harsh.

Madame Sabina was inching towards the door. 'I have to go—'

'No, you stay put,' said Quigley, blocking her exit, 'and tell the doctor what it is you have poisoned your daughter with. What's in the water?'

The stage manager put his head round the door. 'It's Act Two beginners,' he said.

'No, it's not,' said Quigley.

'She looks drugged,' said the stage manager.

'Precisely,' said Quigley. 'It's the work of her loving mama.'

'There was nothing in the wat... er.' Madame Sabina's words were slurred. 'I would never do...' She took a step, grabbed the edge of the dressing-table and fell.

'Get her out of here,' said Quigley.

Mr Gautier and the stage manager dragged her into an empty dressing-room as if she were a rolled-up carpet.

Dr Marks said to Viggo, 'Would you go and find Anna?'

'Try my house first,' said Quigley, and gave Viggo the address.

'Mr Gautier,' said Celeste, 'there's an emerald ring on Madame Sabina's little finger that belongs to Hildegard. Would you...'

'With pleasure,' said Mr Gautier.

He left the dressing-room and after a minute returned with the ring. Celeste washed it, found a piece of ribbon on the dressing-table and gently tied it round Hildegard's neck.

'She needs it,' she said to Dr Marks, who was mixing a medicine from the contents of his bag.

'I believe she does,' he said.

'Mr Gautier,' said the stage manager, 'I'm sorry, but we have to tell the audience something.'

Quigley straightened his Harlequin suit and put the conical hat back on his head. He took a deep breath.

'Celeste, when I give the cue, can you light up as you usually do? Or do you need Peter to pull a lever?'

'No,' said Celeste. 'I can do it on my own.'

'I thought so,' said the clown. He turned to the stage manager. 'Call the company together, please.'

As they stood for a moment in the wings, Celeste felt tears sting her eyes. She glanced at Quigley and saw that he too was crying.

The velvet curtains rose silently. There was no music, only the sound of Quigley's shoes as the great clown walked on stage and stood in the footlights.

'Ladies and gentlemen, my dear audience,' he said. 'Tonight, you may have noticed that the young star of our pantomime, Miss Hildegard Petrova, was not on top form. The reason is that someone who should have known how to love her and care for her has given her what we hope is nothing worse than a sleeping draught.' There was a gasp of horror from the audience. 'A doctor is with her and your good wishes will go a long way to helping her recover. I hope you understand that in the circumstances, the performance will not continue as planned. However, we would like to perform a finale for you.'

The conductor tapped the lectern and the orchestra started up. All the actors came on stage, stood in a row and sang *Columbine's Lament*. At the end when Celeste's beams of light filled the auditorium, the curtain came down to a standing ovation.

Mr Gautier had run out of notes to read. There was only Hildegard's letter left. He wiped his eyes. It wasn't long. It read:

I'm sorry I have let you down.
Hildegard.

CHAPTER 41

Grey clouds hung heavy over the city of C—
that New Year's Eve morning.

It felt to Celeste, as she sat on the window-seat in the dining room of Quigley's house, that the clouds were tapping on the window, knocking at the door, filled with bad news. Breakfast was laid on the table but she wasn't hungry and to pass the time she watched people walk past, huddled and wrapped tight against the bitter cold.

Hildegard might wake up, she told herself, and feel well enough to go on the *Empress*. But everything felt brittle, hopeless.

'Don't let there be bad news,' she whispered to the frosty window.

Last night Dr Marks had taken Hildegard to her mother's house and Anna had gone with them. The police had arrived at the opera house and arrested a dazed Madame Sabina Petrova and charged her with attempted murder. For a while after Hildegard had gone and Madame Sabina had been taken away, no one knew what to do until at last Mr Gautier told them all to go home.

Celeste had hardly been able to sleep. It had still been dark when she'd got up and for want of anything better to do she had packed her toy theatre, then the dress Anna was going to wear on the ship and the shawl Stephan had given her. On top of the shawl she'd found a piece of card on which Hildegard had written:

Dear Anna,
    I love you very much. I would have been lost without you.
    With love, Hildegard.

PS I wasn't really scared of Celeste, I just wanted you all to myself. But I think you knew that.
PPS The frame is for you to put your wedding picture in. You can take mine out quite easily.

Celeste looked everywhere for the frame, anxious that she might have missed it. When she finally thought to turn over the card she discovered that the card was the frame. Hildegard had made it and had gone to such a lot of trouble. She'd cut herself out from a photograph that originally must have included her mama, and put bright pink paper behind it. Celeste didn't know that Hildegard was good at art and thought that there was much she had yet to learn about her. She wrapped the picture in the shawl. Even as she did it she thought that they wouldn't be going anywhere today, on this the last day of the year, her last chance to meet the man in the emerald green suit, her last chance to win the Reckoning. But without Hildegard, who would be able to sing the song? But then she remembered: 'the song of a bird who can't sing' – it was the song that was important, and the bird can't sing it because she's ill.

How many times had she gone over everything in her mind? A thousand times, perhaps more. She had wondered if the three things had to be in a certain order. Was it the song first, or the play? She felt that becoming invisible must be last. Or was it the first? And did it matter? She heard the doorbell ring as she traced Hildegard's name in the condensation on the windowpane and spun round when the door opened and Viggo came into the room.

'Any news?' she asked.

'No,' he said. 'Uncle Peter sent me here to tell you to be ready.'

'We can't go,' said Celeste.

'My uncle says you have to. He says whatever else happens today, you and Anna must be on the *Empress*. And I agree. I want to see Maria again – I want that as much as you do. Remember, it was you and Maria who explained about the gutter in time – perhaps there is a chance this story will end in a different way. If it doesn't, though I might have no memory of you and Maria and Anna, I will live my life knowing that I never met the person I was supposed to meet, that there is an empty space where she should have been.'

'If I do win the game,' said Celeste, 'and we're all in Copenhagen, you won't know you knew us here. But I've thought about that,' and she took from her pocket the cut-out figure of the little dancer, of Maria. 'If I win the Reckoning, and we meet again, Maria will ask you for this. You won't know why you have it but we will know.'

Viggo put the figure in his pocket as Quigley came in.

'Good morning, Viggo.' He poured a cup of coffee and sat down. 'Any word?'

'No, but my uncle has gone to the Petrova house to collect Anna. She and Celeste mustn't miss the ship's departure.'

'You're right. I believe this day, New Year's Eve, is a very important day.'

'We can't leave if Hildegard isn't with us,' said Celeste.

Quigley thought about this, then said, 'As we're waiting for news and there's nothing we can do but wait, let me tell you a story about my brother.'

'Was he a clown?'

'No, my brother was a tattoo artist. He worked not far from here. He was famous for his designs and many sailors and sea captains came to him. They often had stories to tell and there was one that he heard again and again from those who made their living on the water. They spoke of the great white bird, an albatross, and of the blind man who does his bidding. It was believed that he was once a drowning sailor who, in exchange for his life, had given up his soul and lost his sight to the great white bird. Legend says that this man was allowed back on land whenever there was a Reckoning.'

Viggo looked alarmed and Celeste slipped her arm through his.

'Should I carry on?' said Quigley.

Celeste nodded.

'If there was a child on board a ship from which he had taken the passengers and crew, the blind man felt obliged to play the Reckoning, to give the child a chance to win back his or her life and the lives of everyone else on the ship. Though he boasted that no child would ever win the game. One day, my brother was told this same story by a blind man and he asked the blind man if there was a way a child could beat the albatross and win.

'The blind man laughed and said, "No." But then he thought again. "Identical twins," he said, "that's what the great white bird fears." My brother asked why. "Because two children could play the game as one. It has never happened," he said. And then he had my brother tattoo two names on his arm: Maria and Celeste. My brother asked if they were twins but the blind man wouldn't answer.'

'Who was he?' asked Viggo, though he knew the answer.

'He didn't say his name.'

'When was this?'

'A little over twelve years ago,' said Quigley. He sipped his coffee. 'I, being a curious man and, being a clown, thought too foolish to be taken seriously, asked the blind piano tuner, Mr Albert Ross, if he knew that there was a Celeste at the opera house and that there had also been a Maria. He asked if it was a riddle and I said yes, a riddle of sorts.

'He said, "The answer is that they are one person and the same person, not two people." Now, here is the conundrum: I saw the dress rehearsal of *The Saviour*, and I know that Celeste is not Maria. I will say no more except that you, Celeste, must be on that ship with Anna. You understand? Too many ships have lost their passengers and crew and the more often this happens the more isolated the city of C— becomes.'

Celeste went to the clown and hugged him.

'No, no, no,' said Quigley, laughing. 'And, by the way, I don't want to know how you become invisible in your bright lights. We all need our trade secrets.'

They heard the bell and then the front door opening, and voices in the hall.

Quigley stood up and the three of them braced themselves as if expecting the grey clouds to rush in. Peter came in with Anna who looked beyond tears, and told them what Celeste, Viggo and Quigley never wanted to hear, not this year, not next year and never in all the years to come.

Hildegard was dead.

CHAPTER 42

The *Empress*, her flags flying, was ready to sail. Her passengers were aboard though no one had seen the king arrive and the crowd that had gathered at the harbour wondered where he was. The tide was on the turn and the crew and passengers were eager to be off. They were waiting for a final carriage to arrive.

A sea-fret had blown in and the onlookers watched as the ship disappeared in a fog that clung to her tall masts and decks, turning her into a ghost ship coming out of the mist.

The press was there too, to report on this historic voyage. A photographer was hoping to take one of the first photographs of the king boarding the *Empress*, if he would only stand still long enough for the exposure. Above them seagulls screeched in the fast-fading light of the last day of the year. The crowd cheered when a carriage arrived at the gangplank, but it wasn't the king who stepped out but Anna and Celeste.

'Where is the king?' A murmur ran through the crowd. 'Perhaps he's already on board.'

Stephan helped Anna and Celeste from the carriage, then reached in and lifted out the box containing the toy theatre.

'There she is!' shouted someone in the crowd. 'It's that girl who lights up.'

Finally the photographer had someone to take a picture of.

'This way, ladies,' he said. There was a flash and the image of the young woman and her charge, blurred by movement, was captured on dry gelatine plates.

Once aboard, Stephan showed them to their cabin. They had been given one of the state rooms that looked out the starboard side of the ship. Flowers, a bowl of fruit and a bottle of champagne were waiting for them with a printed card listing the night's entertainments.

Celeste studied it. 'Every hour of the evening has been planned,' she said to Anna with a heavy heart. 'There isn't a time when I can perform my play.'

Anna sat on the bed. 'I'm too tired to think about

it at the moment. What we're going to do is have a nap. Things always seem better after a nap.'

'The king doesn't know about my play,' said Celeste, 'and if he doesn't know...' She yawned. 'I'm not tired,' she added.

'We've got this far,' said Anna. 'We'll just have to hope for some luck.'

Celeste, like Anna, lay down on the bed, which was very comfortable with soft feather pillows.

'I won't sleep,' she said. 'You might be able to but I can't. I'm too worried.'

Before she could say another word they had both fallen fast asleep to the sound of the ship's horn as it bade a long, low, sad farewell to the shore.

They woke to find that the lights in their cabin had been lit and their dresses had been laid out for them.

Celeste stood up and promptly fell over. The ship was on high seas and the weather was stormy. She looked out of the porthole and all she could see were foaming white-tipped waves that tossed the *Empress* about as if she were Neptune's toy. Twice Celeste was thrown from one side of the cabin to the other as she put on the sailor dress with the red pompoms. There was a knock on the door and there was Stephan.

'Can I come in?' he said.

'Is it going to be like this all the time?' asked Celeste.

'There are reports of gales,' said Stephan. 'His Majesty was told that the weather was going to be bad but I don't think he realised quite how bad it would be. I think there will only be ten guests for supper – most of them are suffering from sea-sickness.'

'Which means?' said Celeste.

'It means there's a chance for you to do your play. Anna has told me about it and how important it is, for all of us. You're looking very pale, Anna. Are you ill?'

'No, I feel much better.'

'I'll have the toy theatre set up in the saloon.'

'But the king might not want to see the play.'

'I think he will. He was told this evening about Hildegard, and how close you two were.'

Anna put the shawl Stephan had given her round her shoulders.

'Do you have your sea-legs?' she asked Celeste after Stephan had left.

'Sort of,' said Celeste, grabbing hold of the table. 'Have you yours?'

'Yes,' said Anna. 'Sort of.'

'I hope I have everything in the right order,' said Celeste. 'I'm going to do the play first, then you're going to sing Hildegard's song, and then I'll do the lights. And at the end of it you stand up and say...'

'I can make all this disappear.'

'You must not forget that part.'

'Come here, my little treasure,' she said, and hugged Celeste. She tucked her hair back so that her face could be better seen. 'Do you know,' she said, 'I haven't thought about it until now, but I wonder if those scars are a map that will take us home.' She paused and said, 'Do you think Stephan will be there too?'

'I hope so,' said Celeste.

The interior of the ship was beautiful; the rooms panelled with wood that shone like liquid gold. In the candlelight everything was warm and inviting and completely detached from the outside world.

'We are a small party,' said the king, welcoming them. 'And I am very pleased to see that you two haven't succumbed to sea-sickness. Alas, that can't be said for the rest of the party, or my musicians. Never mind, we will make our own entertainment.'

'I have brought with me my toy theatre, sir,' said Celeste, very seriously. 'I've been rehearsing a play for a long time so I can perform it for you.'

'You have? Well, my little dancer, I would like to see the play. When would you like to perform it?'

'At twelve minutes to midnight,' said Celeste.

'That is precise.'

'It is. I suppose it is a precise play.'

'Then I can think of nothing I would like to see more.' He looked at Anna and said, 'I was informed about the sad death of Madame Sabina Petrova's daughter and was shocked. I feel deeply for your loss and for our loss as a country. The waste of a young life stains all our hands red.'

At dinner Celeste was seated next to a very green-looking lady who only survived the first course before she had to be excused, and two of the other guests also felt the need to retire to their cabins. As dinner finished the sea became still. It was so unexpected that the king asked to see the captain.

'Sir, we are in the waters known in the past as the Devil's Cauldron,' said the captain. 'It often has different weather. I'm afraid I cannot explain it.'

The lady sitting on Celeste's other side overheard and whispered, 'Really, no one wanted to come. But it wouldn't have been proper to refuse.' And she too disappeared to her cabin, not due to sea-sickness, but fear.

In the saloon Stephan had arranged the toy theatre as Celeste wanted. Black cloth surrounded it so that the audience couldn't see her and Anna behind. Backstage, two small tables had been set, either side of the theatre. Celeste carefully laid out the little characters. Anna said she would take the song sheet onto the upper deck where she could practise.

'Don't get washed overboard,' said Celeste.

Now all that was left to do was to wait and waiting was the hard part. It struck Celeste that the clock had decided to go very slowly indeed and drag out every minute of these last hours of the year.

At twenty minutes to twelve, Anna came back from the upper deck. Celeste noticed that her cheeks were rosy and her eyes were shining.

Only four people were well enough to watch the toy theatre production. Whether the other guests had been felled by sea-sickness or by their great anxiety about the danger they might be in was impossible to tell.

The king sat on an upright chair, his legs stretched out before him, and waited for the cardboard curtain to rise. Celeste began the play, and the knowledge that she had performed it before gave her courage. With each scene change the audience clapped.

In the last scene, Anna sang the song that had been written for Hildegard and she sang it with such feeling that tears ran down her cheeks. There was genuine applause and Celeste came out to take a bow with Anna, then stood in front of the theatre and the light from her scars beamed so bright that she became invisible to the audience.

The king stood, and at that moment Anna swept the shawl from her shoulders and said, 'I can make it all disappear.'

Celeste closed her eyes as the beams that came from her shone brighter than ever before. She was certain nothing had happened, certain that if she opened her eyes she would find everything just as it was, certain nothing had changed.

CHAPTER 43

Down she falls and down she falls.

'Twelve o'clock midnight by my reckoning,' says the man in the emerald green suit.

He is seated at the entrance of the cave in the barnacle-encrusted chair and on his desk is the sand clock. All his remaining candles are ablaze. Celeste stands before him. She knows all too well where she is – deep under the sea in the cave of dreamers. Quickly she looks up and is relieved to see they are still there. Some she knows by name now. Their eyes are closed, their heads held high, they are lined up in a neat row, hanging from boat hooks, the passengers, the sailors and the captain of the *Empress*. There among them is her beautiful mother, next to her, her beloved father. She can see the king's son, the prince. But not Maria and it alarms Celeste that among the sleepers it is Maria alone who she cannot see.

'Do you think you have won the Reckoning?' asks the man in the emerald green suit. 'Do you think you have outwitted me?'

'I've given you the three things,' says Celeste, and it is only then she realises that she stands before him with nothing, that all along it has been a trick.

She has been unable to bring him anything except her ability to become invisible in a bright light. There is no stage too small for an actor, there is no Hildegard, no Anna, to sing the song of a bird who can't sing. Why did she never think of this before? In the thousand times she thought about the three things, this had never occurred to her.

'No – wait,' says Celeste. 'That isn't fair. You've not given me a chance.'

Still she looks for Maria. Where is she?

The man in the emerald green suit says, 'I tried to be generous, I tried to help you. Never mind. Here you are with nothing. Oh dear, oh dear. I imagine that you were too busy wondering which order everything went in that you never considered that it would be impossible for you to bring them all to me. Grown-ups make that mistake. They collect so many things and have large bank accounts and forget that they can only take their old bones with them. Whoops-a-daisy. I win again. Don't look so sad. You did your best and, as I said, I tried to be generous.' He rummages for a moment in his barnacle-encrusted desk and takes out the large, leather-bound ledger. 'This is the part I like – a clean page for a New Year, rather joyous when you think about it.' He dips his pen in the ink. 'Maria – now, your name is Maria. Or Maria Celeste, it's all the same.'

'No, it isn't.'

'Isn't what?'

'The same.'

'Are you talking in riddles?'

Celeste is furious. Never has she felt as angry as she does now at the injustice of this game and at this man for what he has done. Lights beam from her scars, they dance across the walls of the cave, illuminating the faces of the sleepers. Now she sees Maria, her beloved Maria, hidden among the empty clothes that once belonged to the nameless lost passengers. At the entrance to the cave, the malicious eye of the great white bird watches.

'Yes, yes,' says the man in the emerald green suit. 'So you can become invisible in your brightness, I know that, but it doesn't mean you've won the game.'

Celeste is filled with molten rage. 'I am not playing your stupid game any more. I don't care if I've won or lost. Your game is meaningless – you are meaningless.'

'That's a little harsh and also a little wrong,' says the man in the emerald green suit.

'I know your name – it doesn't change,' says Celeste. 'There is no mystery to your name: Albatross – Albert Ross.'

To his surprise she strides up to his desk and before he can stop her, she has snatched the sand clock and thrown it down. Celeste isn't expecting it to land, or to break as it does on the coral floor. With the sound of shattering glass comes a scream that for a moment deafens her: it is the cry of lost and drowned sailors. It shakes the cave.

'You shouldn't have done that,' says the man in the emerald green suit. 'That was very wicked.'

'And what about you?' says Celeste. 'What about the grief and misery you have caused? What about the children who lost their parents, due to your selfishness? All the possibilities you stole from them. You, who yourself was once a sailor.'

'Enough,' says the man in the emerald green suit. 'Time is not on your side.'

Celeste ignores his threat and still light pours from her. 'When your ship sank you tried to save a cabin boy – his name was Noah Jepson.'

The cave shudders and she has a feeling that the man in the emerald green suit has become smaller, or that she is bigger. 'But you couldn't save Noah, could you? Both of you had been in the water too long and you were only human after all. Until the great bird took out your eyes and, in return for your life, you believed you had given him your soul. No bird could take your soul. It is an excuse, a miserable excuse for your own cruelty. You call this a game. You, who should have had the wisdom to protect your daughter. I've watched cats with mice. They are very cruel, and they let the mice think they've got away and then they pounce. You are worse than that – you are a monster.'

'Your light is too bright,' says the man in the emerald green suit, shading his face. 'I feel the heat from your scars.'

'This game,' says Celeste, 'means nothing to me. It should mean nothing to you. The great white bird should mean nothing to you. It was Hildegard who should have mattered to you. You should have been at the opera house, watching over her. You should have stopped Sabina Petrova. And now Hildegard is dead.'

The man in the emerald green suit lets out an unearthly wail.

'No, no – my daughter.' He puts his hands over his ears as the cave trembles. 'Enough, enough!' he cries.

'It's never enough for you, is it?' she says. 'You are a cowardly man who uses his power to become a sea monster, a bogeyman to give nightmares to sailors. Do your worst. And, by the way, my name is Celeste. Maria is my twin.'

The light beaming from Celeste is now so strong that the man in the emerald green suit begins to dissolve and she feels herself embraced in the wings of the great white bird. All is feathers, floating feathers. There is the sound of rushing water and still her light shines. She can see the surface of the sea above her. She feels anger leave her, she feels salt water heal her scars, she feels at peace. It is a peace as deep as the ocean itself. Time turns on a wave; the tide changes; the clock resets.

It is over. Celeste closes her eyes and waits.

CHAPTER 44

'Lights, lights,' shouts Father.

Celeste stands in front of the toy theatre with her eyes closed. Even when the lamps are lit, Celeste, the warrior, doesn't open her eyes. She was always smaller than Maria – skinnier, legs like sticks. Maria worried that she wouldn't be strong enough for the game but it is because of Celeste that they are here. Maria moves close to her, puts her hand in her sister's, feels the warmth of her fingers. Still Celeste keeps her eyes shut.

'My darlings, my clever, clever girls!'

Their mother's voice, laughing, her words as warm as her kisses. Only now does Celeste open her eyes, wide with surprise. Before them is their beautiful mother, filled with pride, their father cheering, the prince clapping.

'Bravo! An enchantment. There, Hans,' says the

prince to their father, 'you wanted a new idea for an opera. Massini should see this.'

Celeste turns to Anna who bends down and whispers to her. 'Celeste, we are here. Whatever you did, it worked. You won.'

Finally Celeste is able to trust what she sees and her face lights up with joy. Maria sees straight away that there is not one scar on her smooth skin. Their father lifts up Celeste and she throws her arms round his neck. She breathes in the comforting smell of his dinner jacket, a scent that is her father's alone.

'Who wrote the play?' he asks.

'Maria,' says Celeste.

'No, it was Celeste,' says Maria.

'It was a collaboration,' says Mother. 'And one of the most moving productions I have seen for a long while. Where did you come up with the idea of the cave of dreamers and the man in the emerald green suit? It was quite terrifying.'

'I liked the storm scene best,' says Father, 'with the great white albatross. And the name for the sea – what was it again?'

'The Devil's Cauldron,' says Celeste.

Father puts Celeste down and hugs Maria. 'You two are my little saviours.'

'Why are we your saviours?' asks Celeste.

'Because – between you and me – I have no ideas for the libretto for Massini's next opera. He has written the music, which, he tells me, is about a ghost ship and the sea, and I have yet to come up with a story to fit it.'

'We should have one more drink to celebrate the New Year,' says the prince, 'and perhaps,' he pats Father on the back, 'the beginnings of a new opera.'

'Agreed, sir,' says Father. 'And then you girls must go to bed. You haven't slept at all this year!'

As they move to the other end of the room, the prince says, 'It always seems to me that the period between Christmas and New Year is a strange time. Days float unanchored, adrift, waiting for January to reclaim them.'

When they are out of hearing, Anna puts her arms round the two girls. She checks their faces and pulls up the sleeves of Celeste's dress.

'They're all gone,' she says. 'All the scars. How did you do it? How did you win the game?'

'I told the man in the emerald green suit that he was a coward,' says Celeste, 'and I refused to play his game. Then the albatross swooped down and everything went dark and when I opened my eyes, I was here and so were you.'

'Do you think this will all be here in the morning?' said Celeste to Maria as they went to bed. 'And it's not a dream?'

'You're not dreaming,' said Maria. 'You beat the man in the emerald green suit, Celeste. You shone so bright with the truth, with the ferociousness of love, no monster could face that and live.'

'I wonder if Hildegard is here, in this world,' said Celeste.

'We shouldn't think too much about that,' Maria said. 'I told myself I wouldn't think about Viggo. But I have all my fingers and toes crossed that he is here.'

Anna tucked them in. 'All I hope is that Stephan is waiting for me when the ship arrives at Copenhagen,' she said, adding quietly, 'he asked me to marry him.'

There was a great bustle and busyness on the quay and a crowd was there to welcome the *Empress* back. Celeste looked round to see the other passengers and the sailors who, like her and her parents, were safely returned home, home to their waiting children, their fathers, their mothers, their friends, their relatives, whose lives now would not be marked by tragedy. She smiled to see one passenger, an old lady, waving to her dog who ran along the quayside yapping with excitement at seeing its owner.

Maria said, 'They would all have been lost without you.'

'And you,' said Celeste. 'It was, as Mother said, a collaboration.'

A cheer went up when the prince walked down the gangplank and a brass band played, and he was driven away in the king's carriage accompanied by six soldiers on horseback. Then it was the turn of the Winther family. Ellen and Hans went first, followed by Anna and the girls, the three of them searching the crowd for one face. If Stephan was there, neither Anna nor the girls could see him but there was very little time before the carriage had whisked them away.

'Madame Sabina lived there,' Celeste whispered to Maria as they approached their home opposite the park.

It had started to snow and the city was as enchanting as a fairy tale.

'Poor Madame Sabina,' Mother said, overhearing her.

'Why poor?' asked Maria.

'She lost all her money in an unwise investment,' said Father.

'And then she died in a fire in the old opera house,' said Mother.

'What happened to her daughter?' said Celeste.

'I don't think she had a daughter.'

'I think she did,' said Father. 'If I remember rightly, her name was Heidi. No, Helga. Or Hilda. Something like that.'

'Was it Hildegard?' said Celeste.

'Why, my darling, this sudden interest in Madame Sabina Petrova?' asked Mother. 'You never liked her, and for good reason. She had no patience with children.'

Celeste sat back and looked out of the window.

The house – their house – was completely different from how it was when Madame Sabina had lived there in the city of C—.

'It was cold,' Celeste told Maria. 'There was nothing that made it feel homely. Not like this.'

There is a joy at being back in a place you thought you might not see again. The girls argued as they always did about who was to have which bed. Anna's room was next to theirs and everything was where it should be, including a doll that Celeste swore hadn't been there before but Maria remembered was a present from the king.

'Two worlds,' said Celeste. 'One still overlays the other.'

'And perhaps it will for a time,' said Maria.

'Did you ever come here,' Celeste asked Maria, 'when you were in the city of C—?'

'No, never,' said Maria. 'We lived in the dome of the theatre and before that, an attic. That's all I really remember. I think we once took the tram.'

'I have two shawls,' said Anna who was unpacking. 'Look, they're identical.'

Mother came up to ask the girls how they would feel about performing their play again for the composer, Massini, and the director, Mr Tias.'

'Peter – Mr – Tias?' said Celeste. 'Not Mr Gautier?'

'Mr Gautier is the *intendant* of the opera house,' said Mother. 'He runs it.'

That evening Celeste put on a simple dress with tucks in a soft wool fabric, and Maria wore one of her favourite dresses: velvet, with lace at the cuff and hem. Maria had never worn it before because Celeste hated her dress of the same design. When they went downstairs, their mother was startled.

'This is the first time you two have ever dressed differently,' she said.

Her daughters couldn't tell her that, after what had happened, nothing would ever be the same.

CHAPTER 45

That evening, the first evening they were all back in Copenhagen, they went to Peter's apartment. As they climbed out of the carriage, Celeste saw Anna look up at the windows and knew she was hoping that Stephan was there. She gave Anna's hand a squeeze.

'I'm sure he's waiting for you,' she whispered.

Peter lived in the same apartment as he had in the city of C—, yet to Celeste it seemed bigger than she remembered and definitely tidier.

'Who would have thought that your two girls would have grown so fast,' said Peter to their mother when he saw them. 'But I'm not surprised that they are so pretty. They're like you, Ellen. You must be very proud. Now which of you is

Maria?' Maria stepped forward. 'That leaves you – Celeste.'

Celeste knew what Maria was thinking. *Where is Viggo?*

'Is your nephew here?' asked Celeste.

'Yes – but I don't think you've ever met. Viggo!' he called.

Viggo came out of the room that Celeste had once stayed in. He looked exactly the same as he had in the city of C—.

Straight away, he said to Maria, 'I think I know you.'

This was greeted with laughter by the adults and delight by Maria.

'Perhaps, in a different life,' said Peter.

'I can see that you two are going to be firm friends,' said Father.

Drinks were served while Ellen explained the girls' production to Massini and Peter.

'Massini, don't look like that,' said Father. 'We might be proud parents but there is something here.'

'Girls,' said Mother, 'set up your toy theatre.'

Viggo helped them while the adults chatted.

'I know I've done this before,' he said to Celeste.

'Done what?' said Maria.

'Helped set up this toy theatre. Wait, I have something.' He went into his room.

'It's all right,' said Celeste to Maria.

'But what if he doesn't have it, what will that mean?'

They hardly dared to breathe.

'Here,' said Viggo. He held out the cardboard figure of a little dancer. 'I never knew where this came from. But she looks just like Maria.'

Mr Gautier arrived late. Celeste thought he had changed; he seemed less anxious, his face less crumpled. He was sombrely dressed, but full of plans. He wanted to stage a pantomime next Christmas and thought the clown who played in the Tivoli Gardens would be perfect for the lead role of the Harlequin.

That evening soon felt normal to Celeste and Maria, and it was hard to imagine life had ever been any other way. Massini, who was famous for his operas, was delighted with the idea of the little play they watched. At dinner the talk was about the libretto that Hans would write and how it might be adapted for opera.

It took Celeste longer than Maria to believe they were safe and that the man in the emerald green suit wouldn't call her back. For Maria, her experience took on a dream-like quality and by degrees lost its power. Not so for Celeste. Sometimes, before falling asleep she saw the man in the emerald green suit and she would wake the following morning full of joy to realise she was home where she was meant to be. She thought that it helped Maria that she and Viggo had found each other. But for Anna there was no Stephan. And for all of them, there was no Hildegard.

Anna claimed she couldn't remember very much about the city of C—. But Celeste knew she was fibbing. She had caught her often enough lost in her thoughts. Celeste had heard Mother say to Father that she was worried about Anna.

'If I didn't know her so well,' said Mother, 'I would say she was lovesick. But when can she have met someone to fall in love with?'

The snow melted, spring arrived and to Maria and Celeste the past felt a distant place, and in a week's time it was to be their birthday. Celeste and Anna were out shopping when they found themselves at Mr Holme's hat shop. The bell jangled as they entered. Old Mr Holme was behind the counter. He greeted Anna warmly.

'Do you still have the little black hat that was in your window?' asked Anna.

'No,' said Mr Holme. 'I'm afraid I've just sold it to a fine-looking young gentleman.'

'Oh dear, I've left it too long,' said Anna and started to try on other hats.

Celeste walked away from her and stared out through the window.

She turned to Anna and said, 'I'm just going to have a look at the shop opposite.'

Anna barely noticed she'd gone.

On the corner was a well-dressed young man, a pair of handsome boots on his feet. Why the boots caught Celeste's attention, she couldn't say, but perhaps it was because she feared that if she looked at the face of the owner of the boots, he wouldn't be who she thought he was. She was still staring at the boots when they started to walk with purpose towards her.

'Celeste,' said the owner of the boots. 'Do you remember me?' and she looked up into a face that was Stephan's.

He was holding a hat box.

'Stephan,' said Celeste, 'where have you been?'

'On New Year's Eve, when Anna said she could make everything disappear, I found myself on board the *Mary Bell*, bound for the Americas. I stayed on there to do some business and it turned out better than even I could have imagined. Does Anna remember me?'

Celeste looked round. On the next corner was a café.

'Wait in there,' she said, 'and I'll bring her.'

She went quickly back to the hat shop. Anna came out, pulling on her gloves.

'I'd like a cup of hot chocolate,' said Celeste.

'We really should be getting back,' said Anna, but before she could say another word Celeste had taken her hand and walked her into the café. To her great disappointment Celeste couldn't see Stephan anywhere.

They had sat down at a table and were about to order when the waiter brought a glass of champagne and a hat box.

'For you, Madame,' said the waiter, placing them before Anna. 'With the compliments of the gentleman standing at the counter.'

There is only one piece of the jigsaw left, thought Celeste, as Stephan took Anna in his arms.

FOUR YEARS LATER

Anna married Stephan. Maria went to the ballet school and I studied music, then singing. The piano tuner in the new opera house was a young man and could never – even if the moon shone backwards – have been mistaken for Albert Ross.

Maria and I were sixteen years old when Massini's opera finally opened. I was singing the part of one of the twins and Peter had cast a singer of my age to sing the other. But just before the opening night she became ill with laryngitis. Peter assured me that he had found another girl to sing the role and our voices were a perfect match. She had arrived from Sweden and he asked if I would mind her sharing a dressing-room with me. It had felt very strange to have been given my mother's dressing-room and I said I didn't mind at all.

I don't know why I wasn't there when she arrived. I think I'd gone upstairs to have lunch with Maria. We often sneaked into the dome to look at the chandelier. I was rushing down the corridor, slightly late, when I heard his stick with its unmistakable rhythm, a rhythm I couldn't forget. Tap-tap-tap. My heart turned to ice and I found myself feeling twelve again. The dim light glinted on round, dark goggles and I saw an old man with a stick. Holding his arm was a young girl. In the gloom I caught a shimmer from the emerald ring on her finger.

I flattened myself against the wall.

'Papa,' she said, 'we're in the way,' and gently helped him to the side of the corridor.

'Who is it?' asked Albert Ross.

He put out his hand and I took it and introduced myself, but I wasn't looking at him. I was staring at the face of his daughter.

'I'm Hildegard Ross,' she said, 'and this is my papa, Albert Ross. We heard you sing the other day – you have a beautiful voice.'

Mr Gautier came to greet her.

'... and you've met Celeste Winther? Good. Mr Ross, such a pleasure to see you again. Let me take you to the auditorium.'

338

Albert Ross turned to his daughter. 'Do you have everything you need, Hildegard, my dear?' he said.

'Yes, Papa, don't worry,' and she kissed him on the cheek.

Mr Gautier led Albert Ross through the door that in another life I had passed through and met a king, and I heard him say, 'I have been blessed with a daughter who is not only wonderful but a great singer too.'

'You have indeed,' said Mr Gautier. 'You have much to be proud of...' Their conversation drifted away.

All afternoon we rehearsed so that Hildegard would know where to stand. Only when we were dressed in our costumes and waiting to be called did we have a chance to talk.

She put her head to one side and said, 'I dreamed I knew you. But in my dream, I didn't know you could sing.'

'Neither did I,' I said.

'In my dream,' she continued, 'you try to help me and I keep telling you there's no need.'

It felt too ridiculous to say, 'I thought perhaps you'd died,' so I said nothing.

To my surprise she said, 'The others have forgotten, haven't they?'

I hesitated. 'Forgotten what?'

'Forgotten the city of C—, forgotten what happened to us.' Then she said, 'It's a lonely place to be, where no one else remembers what you remember.'

'You do remember?' I said.

'I don't think if I lived a hundred lives I would forget you, your scars, the way you blinded me with your light.' She took my hand and said, 'Thank you for all you did.'

And for no other reason than that we were there together, we burst out laughing.

Outside the dressing-room, we heard the stage manager calling.

'Act One beginners, please. Act One beginners for *Invisible in a Bright Light*.'

ACKNOWLEDGEMENTS

When I embark on writing a book I am always unprepared for how long it is going to take and how incredibly lost I am about to become. I don't plan, which means I can spend many days on a path that is about to go nowhere. I have to thank Jacky Bateman for pointing out the folly of many a wrong turn. We have worked together for over twelve years and she has ironed my rumpled, misspelled words and turned them into clean manuscripts. I want to thank my agent, Catherine Clark, for her love and support, and Fiona Kennedy, one of the best editors I have ever worked with. It has been a joy to do this book with her. Enormous thanks to Jade Gwilliam in publicity, to Helen Crawford-White for the cover art, to Peter Avery for his inspiration and to all the sales reps who go out to sell a book at a time when book shops and libraries are fast fading away. Finally, I want to thank Anthony

Cheetham for starting an incredible children's list. A book involves so much more than the author to make it a success.

Sally Gardner
Hastings
July 2019